JOEL
AUSTIN

A LONG VIOLENT
HISTORY

VINCI
BOOKS

Vinci Books

vinci-books.com

Published by Vinci Books Ltd in 2026

1

Copyright © Joel Austin 2024

The publisher and the author have made every effort to obtain permissions for any third party material used in this book and to comply with copyright law. Any queries in this respect should be brought to the attention of the publisher and any omissions will be corrected in future editions.

A CIP catalogue record for this book is available from the British Library.

Paperback ISBN: 9781036707804

The EU GPSR authorised representative is Logos Europe, 9 rue Nicolas Poussion, 17000 La Rochelle, France

contact@logoseurope.eu

By Joel Austin

Frank Sherman Thrillers

Happenstance

Reckoning

Perpetua

Nomad

The Last One Out

Regime Change

A Long Violent History

The Old War

To my dad, for all the years of love and support.

Chapter One

Mali, West Africa

The envelope arrived on Captain Frank Sherman's bunk late in the afternoon when the heat pushed everyone inside. A staff sergeant dropped it off with little fanfare, as if getting mail in the badlands of Mali was an ordinary occurrence. Perhaps that was true for most soldiers, but Sherman had no family besides his mother, and she couldn't recall the year let alone write to her son.

Sherman picked up the envelope and turned the rectangle over in his calloused hands. A half-dozen markings decorated the weathered paper—forwarding stamps from one army base to another as the letter followed Sherman around the world.

The original address read Camp Lejeune, where Sherman lived as a teenager decades earlier, back when they followed his father from posting to posting.

He squinted at the return address, which had no street number—Hilt Bay, Oregon.

Where the hell is that? he wondered.

Sherman sat down on the army-issued cot, which was more home than he'd ever known, and slowly opened the envelope.

He removed a single sheet of stiff notecard stock and unfolded the letter. The handwriting slanted across the page in all caps. What began with clean and precise letters took on a hurried edge as if the writer ran out of time.

FRANKY, it began.

No one called Sherman that—at least not in recent memory. Not his mother or teachers, and certainly not anyone in his unit. He hadn't heard the name since childhood, so many years before.

The letter continued:

I'VE BEEN MEANING TO WRITE THIS LETTER SINCE YOUR FATHER DIED, BUT I WAS NEVER MUCH FOR WORDS. THEN AGAIN, NEITHER WAS YOUR FATHER. TWO BRUTES WE WERE. ANYWAY, I'M GETTING OLD, AND THE OLDER I GET, THE MORE I DWELL IN THE PAST, AND THE MORE I DWELL IN THE PAST, THE MORE I... WELL, I'M NOT SURE WHAT. I DO KNOW I NEED TO SPEAK WITH YOU IN PERSON BECAUSE THEY'RE ALWAYS LISTENING. IT'S ABOUT A 'YOU KNOW WHAT' WITH YOUR FATHER.

BEST,
UNCLE HAL

Stunned by the sudden echo of the past, Sherman placed the letter down on his bunk and leaned back against the plywood wall. The air-conditioner crudely attached to the wall buzzed with concerted effort. Voices carried down the hall.

Uncle Hal was Sergeant Hal Cooper, his father's old Marine Corps spotter. A man he hadn't seen since they put his dad in the ground ten years earlier. Sherman recalled a brief handshake and some platitudes, but little else of the exchange at the funeral.

As a child, Sherman hadn't known much about Uncle Hal. The man appeared at family barbeques and drank longnecks with his dad late into the night, but he wasn't a fixture in Sherman's life. He remembered a thin, ramrod straight man with sinewy muscles and thick hands. His brown eyes were so dark, they edged towards black. Scary as most strange adults can seem to small children, but Hal was not unkind. He played catch with Sherman on the front lawn, which was more than his father did.

No one talked openly about what Hal and his father did. They never mentioned specifics. Their missions were, for the most part, state secrets. Sherman only heard scraps here and there. A few boasts by Uncle Hal about how his father was the best sniper, but he'd never be in a record book. *Ten-thousand five-hundred and sixty feet* they'd murmur in hushed voices after one too many beers.

As a child, Sherman didn't understand what that meant. Now, as a Special Forces captain, he knew exactly what Uncle Hal meant about unwritten records. Some stories could not be told, not by anyone, and secrets they would remain.

This thought brought his attention to the last few lines, where the writing started to tilt and lunge across the page. After all those years, what could Uncle Hal possibly have to share about 'you know what', which Sherman assumed meant missions.

He couldn't imagine Uncle Hal breaking his code of silence to tell old ghost stories from Vietnam or the Cold War. The world was a different place back then.

Why bother dredging up the past now?

Even with his security clearance, Sherman wasn't sure he wanted to know about the carnage Hal and his father wrought.

"Captain, a word," said a gravelly voice.

Sherman looked up to find Major Sanders, his commanding officer, hulking in the doorway.

"We just received word that the U.S. Army is *persona non grata* in Mali. Command ordered us to pack up and torch the place on our way out. We don't want to leave anything for the Russians or Chinese."

Sherman glanced around his plywood room and army-issued cot. The base wasn't much to look at, but the CIA had spent millions of tax dollars building a counterterrorism launchpad in the Sahel. Losing the base would set back security in the region for decades to come.

"How long do we have?" asked Sherman.

"Twenty-four hours," answered Sanders. "After that, we're headed stateside. Your men are free for the next two weeks or so until we get our next rotation sorted out."

"Understood, sir."

"Take the essentials, burn the rest," said Sanders.

Sherman nodded and picked up the letter. "Major, one more thing. Have you ever heard of Hilt Bay, Oregon?"

Sanders stopped his exit and stepped into the room. Sherman handed him the letter and the major cast his eyes across the page. He was a decade older than Sherman and much too young to overlap with Uncle Hal, but Sanders was a wise and connected man with many sources inside and outside the government.

The major looked up from the letter and asked, "Who is Uncle Hal?"

"My father's spotter," said Sherman. He didn't need to relate his father's past glory as a sniper. The legend was still alive and well.

Sanders nodded. "Some stories are best left buried."

"Like my father," agreed Sherman. "Do you know the place?"

Sanders handed back the letter. "Not personally, but it's the kind of place you go when you don't want to be found."

Sherman glanced down at the paper. He wanted clarification, but Sanders had already left. Placing the letter in his bag, he focused on the task at hand. But no matter how much he packed away, a question nagged in the back of his mind, stuck like an acacia thorn.

What will I find in Hilt Bay?

Chapter Two

Portland, Oregon

Terrance Wilder hated airports—the traffic, noise, crowds, and, perhaps most importantly, the cameras. They clung to every wall and protruded from every pole, constantly surveilling everyone coming and going. No privacy or anonymity. A perfectly constructed police state rammed down travelers' throats for no reason—at least none he could fathom. Terrorists weren't blowing up planes anymore. No one really needed to take off their shoes. The litany of conspiracies orchestrated by the U.S. Government could fill a book... if Terrance ever got around to writing one. Maybe two volumes with the state of the broken world.

Bah, he thought as he watched people pass his parked car. *You're all sheep walking to the slaughter*.

He'd parked in the passenger pick-up lane of Portland Airport not five minutes before, and the local traffic cop was already giving him the evil glare of authority. Terrance always got the same glare wherever he went as if cops shared photos of those needing intimidation.

Terrance wanted to stare back and give that entitled ass a piece of his mind, but instead, he pulled his hat down and looked away. His was not a joyride. He wasn't picking up family or friends who would understand his animosity to authority.

This pick-up came at the behest of his father, Tom Wilder, during their weekly chat through the plexiglass at Oregon State Penitentiary. Tom caught a bad case of racketeering and was three years in on a ten-year stint. None of the inconveniences of incarceration had stopped Tom from overseeing the family business, but the execution fell to Terrance, and he did not want to disappoint his father. Rage was a family pastime.

The cop's glare burrowed through Terrance's hat, and he felt that all-familiar surge of anger. He was about to circle around to cool off when someone knocked hard on the passenger window.

A rather plain-looking man stood on the other side of the glass. Terrance rolled it down.

"Are you Mr. Wilder?" asked the man.

A wide-brimmed hat that looked almost quaint shaded his face and Terrance couldn't make out his features.

"Who's asking?" Terrance blurted out, forgetting where he was for a moment.

"You're my ride," replied the man. He spoke slowly and evenly, like a schoolteacher explaining the properties of a rectangle to a dense student.

Terrance hated school for his entire life. Book learning never clicked in the way other kids took to it. The only math he excelled at was counting cash.

"Well, then, don't dawdle. Get on in."

The man opened the back door and slid inside, pushing a wave of detritus off the seat. Terrance hadn't cleaned the backseat because he was no taxi and friends sat in the front.

"You can sit up here," said Terrance.

"This is fine," replied the man in his measured tone.

Terrance took an instant dislike to the stranger in his backseat.

"Well… what should I call you?" he asked.

"You can refer to me as Stanton," said the man, who still wore the wide-brimmed hat.

Terrance glanced in the rearview mirror and thought the man a priest or undertaker all dressed in black with that damn Quaker hat.

"Stanton," he muttered to himself. Even the name came out stodgy.

Merging into traffic, Terrance headed back towards home—the only place he felt himself, but even that small joy cooled under the stranger's shadow.

Only when they were well out of Portland and on the coastal highway heading south did Stanton remove his hat. A long glance in the mirror found an early-forties man with hard angular cheeks and blue eyes so pale they seemed to wash away with the overcast light. Where Terrance had an unruly mane of black hair under his baseball cap, Stanton kept his speckled gray hair cropped close.

"It's not polite to stare," said Stanton.

Terrance almost swerved trying to shift his gaze away from the mirror and onto the road. The sudden influx of conversation and the edge to those words sent his pulse rising. He felt like a middle schooler caught daydreaming in class.

"Sorry," he muttered.

"How old are you, Mr. Wilder?"

Terrance hazarded a glance back at those blue eyes. "Twenty-two," he replied.

"Your father assured me you could handle all the details of my visit."

Terrance didn't appreciate the snide remarks about his competence or his age, but his usual rage did not rise, quelled by the quietly imposing figure in the back.

"I can handle anything. I've been handling all the family business for the last three years since Dad got sent to—"

Stanton cut him off. "That's good to know, Mr. Wilder."

"Call me Terrance or Terry. Everyone does. Mr. Wilder is my dad."

Stanton rolled the name around his tongue as if searching for a bad taste. "I prefer to keep things formal, Mr. Wilder," he replied.

Terrance frowned. "Suit yourself, Stanton," he said, drawing out the stranger's name.

They drove south in uneasy silence for another hour as the clouds overhead thickened into a dark gray collage of thunderheads. Wind tore across the road and the air smelled of salt.

Terrance cast another glance at the backseat as they exited the highway where the road cut inland to avoid the undeniable geographic difficulties of the coastline.

The road home crept west through a smattering of roadside businesses that Terrance never visited and homes of families that he considered townies because they were not facing the sea. Finally, they came to a three-way stop and a green roadside sign announcing the possible destinations.

To the left and backward, the sign informed drivers of ways back to the highway. A loop of sorts that skirted sections of the coast, passing through thick strands of ever-greens that only hinted at the churning sea beyond.

Straight ahead was closed according to an orange rectangle affixed to the green sign. Once a temporary affair from a spate of construction, locals had welded the addition years before, and the black letters had faded with time and brine. To further the point, a yellow diamond declared *NO OUTLET*.

Terrance eased the car forward on the narrow strip of asphalt that disappeared into a bank of fog. They rose up a hill into the swirling mass of white. A sense of safety washed over him.

"Welcome to Hilt Bay," Terrance said with a little snigger, hoping to see Stanton's expression change.

The stranger's face remained stoically blank.

Chapter Three

The tea kettle emitted a doleful tune and Hal Cooper shuffled over to turn off the burner. He poured himself a mug of hot water and dabbed a bag of herbal tea into the steaming liquid.

Outside his kitchen window, great walls of fog drifted by like gray ships passing down the street. Unseen in the mist, the ocean roared louder than a freight train.

Hilt Bay was a bit of a misnomer, a geographical joke of history, and Hal's pine bookshelves housed a few thin volumes on the town's disreputable past. The first Europeans arrived via a foundered frigate smashed to smithereens against the nearby point. The sailors washed ashore on a spit of land between two curving rocky outcroppings. Saner souls would have called that stretch of pebbles a beach, but the waterlogged men deemed it a bay, befitting their arrival on foreign shores.

As for the name, Hal found conflicting reports, but his favorite book concluded the sailors saw those curling rocky outcroppings as the embellished ends of a sword's hilt. On a less foggy day, Hal could see the southern point of the hilt from his porch.

The second history book concluded that the bay took its name from one of the sailors. A Russian by the name of Rukoyat, which roughly translated to *hilt*.

Being a visual man, Hal liked the previous story more. He also didn't care much for Russians, even if the town had a fair share of Russian history. The Cold War, for him, had been a very hot and brutal experience.

Hal sat down in his favorite leather chair facing the bay and took a sip of tea. His knees ached a bit from the storm, and he added a splash of whiskey to his mug to ward off the harshness of the day.

A mournful whine came from the floor next to his chair. Hal reached down to stroke his dog—an old hound named Gloria. Her reddish-brown fur felt reassuring against his fingertips, grounding him in the present moment.

Gloria whined again.

"Alright, you booze hound," said Hal, splashing a bit of whiskey on the ancient wood floor of his cottage.

Gloria lapped up the liquid in a few swipes of her big tongue and resumed her station by the foot of Hal's chair.

A car slunk by casting a wall of red brake lights in the fog. Hal raised himself up to get a better look.

"It's that damn Wilder boy," he muttered to Gloria.

Gloria didn't move.

Age had crept up on Hal Cooper like an approaching tunnel. He saw the shaft coming but was unprepared for the sudden constrictions placed upon him. His memory crumbled in the corners, leaving a morass of sticky notes to pave the way through the week. Normally unflappable, his even temperament buckled like asphalt. He saw suspicious figures about town and found a conspiracy on every page of the newspaper. Lately, he'd taken to conversing with Gloria as he withdrew from what little community existed in Hilt Bay.

None of those changes bothered Hal. A loner in high school, he'd spent most of his youth outdoors with fly fishing as his favorite pastime. He appreciated the skills involved–reading the water, the rhythm of casting and patience.

Life, as always, took a turn and Hal's number got called in the draft for Vietnam. Those patient, observant skills honed on the river turned into necessary skills for a sniper-spotter in the United States Marine Corps.

Hal's official postings ended after Vietnam, but to call his professional service over was a very steep lie. Those decades of secrets were seared into his memory and his flesh. The scars bore the truth of those missions, and the more he thought about them, really chewed down to the bone, the more he felt like a pawn moved about for a strategy he never understood.

His once tidy cottage overflowed with newspaper clippings and history books. Papers tumbled off the small dining table, cascading onto chairs and down to the floor.

"There goes that troublemaker again," whooped Hal as Terrance Wilder's rusted sedan stole past in the fog. "Twice in ten minutes! I don't like it, Gloria."

Gloria said nothing. The hound was fast asleep.

Chapter Four

Forty-eight hours elapsed between Frank Sherman getting the letter in West Africa and his boots touching land in Oregon. His team landed in Georgia exhausted and sore from twenty-four undisturbed hours of manual labor packing up the base. Even the turbulent flight back gave no respite. By the time Sherman caught a commercial flight to Portland, he'd been awake for three days straight. Luckily for him, the flight out got stuck on the taxiway. Sherman slept through an hour delay and the angry rants of passengers fed up with airline policies.

Despite the sleep, he stumbled off the jetway, disgorging into the mass of travelers traversing PDX. The sea of humanity overwhelmed him for several minutes as his mind desensitized again to civilian life. Sherman hadn't seen more than two hundred people for the last four months. Summer came and went stateside, and Sherman felt surprised by the fall foliage. All he'd known in the Sahel was dry heat. They'd left before the rainy season.

Bleary-eyed, Sherman made his way through to

baggage claim to grab his army-issued backpack and trudged across to ground transportation. He found a regional bus kiosk hidden in the corner and gazed at the map, digesting the possible routes south.

A gruff woman with more piercings than Sherman could count eyed him from behind the counter.

"Can I help you?" she asked, with a tone bordering on annoyance.

"Hilt Bay," said Sherman.

"Is that supposed to mean something to me?" she retorted.

"Does a bus go there?"

"I don't know. Is it on the map?"

Sherman rubbed his temples and bemoaned the momentous decline of customer service in his lifetime. He pulled out his phone and a map of Oregon. Pinching and swiping south, he found the closest exit off the highway. The off-ramp was not in or near a town or any stop on the printed kiosk map, but a bus did drive by the exit.

Sherman pointed to the spot on the map. "I want to get off here," he said.

"That's not an official stop. Drivers only stop at sanctioned locations."

Sherman's frazzled, sleep-deprived brain almost short-circuited.

"Are there other reasons a driver will stop?"

"Emergencies, of course."

"I'll take a one-way ticket to there," said Sherman, jabbing his finger one city beyond the exit for Hilt Bay.

The woman rolled her eyes but took his cash and held out the ticket.

"Here you go. Bus boards in twenty minutes."

Sherman took the ticket and walked outside to a small

overhang protecting a handful of passengers. Clouds hung low and a drizzle made everything sparkle. The clock outside read a few minutes past noon.

At the very edge of the sidewalk, surreptitiously smoking a vape pen, Sherman spied the bus driver. The guy wore a white polo and dark raincoat emblazoned with the bus line's logo. Judging by his gray hair and jowls, Sherman guessed the man was in his early sixties and not long for retirement, if that still existed.

The driver eyed him cautiously like the woman at the kiosk, and for good reason. Sherman had seen his reflection on the way outside. A thick and grungy beard on top of deeply tan skin and his wild orangish-green eyes. Sherman looked feral, which wasn't far from the truth. He'd seen more combat than most platoons combined. From the moment he'd joined the army after 9/11, Sherman witnessed the complete arc of America's War on Terror, entrance to exit.

"Excuse me, sir. Can I ask you a question?"

The driver gave him a once-over from combat boots to backpack.

"I suppose a question won't hurt."

"The woman inside—" Sherman began.

"Kat, with a K," interjected the driver. He didn't sound impressed.

"Right, Kat said you could only stop at designated locations."

"That is company policy."

"Which I understand," Sherman added. "But I'm visiting an old Marine buddy of mine, and he lives off the beaten path. I'm wondering if you could do me a big favor and let me off here."

Sherman held up his phone with the exit displayed.

"Are you in the Corps?" asked the driver.

"No, army."

The driver said, "My son was a Marine. It turned his life around."

Sherman nodded.

"Alright," said the driver. "I'll drop you off there, but be quick about it when I stop."

"Thanks, I appreciate the help. How long will it take to get there? I haven't slept in days."

The man smiled, friendly like, almost fatherly. "A little more than three hours with stops. I can honk when we get there if you like."

"I'll set an alarm, but thanks for the offer."

"Thanks for your service," said the driver, who then went off to load bags.

Sherman kept his bag close and sat up front, not wanting to make a big scene of his exit. He fell asleep before they left the airport and saw none of the picturesque countryside.

He awoke with a start to his alarm and a soft chuckle from the driver.

"Your exit is a few miles up ahead."

"You made good time," said Sherman, feeling a bit more human after three hours of sleep.

The driver eased off the highway onto a rutted road crowded by looming pines and brambles. The drizzle had grown into a steady rain.

"I hope you brought a jacket," said the driver.

Sherman fished one out and covered his pack. He waved goodbye and jumped off the bus into a small puddle with a squelch. The bus door squeaked closed, and the vehicle disappeared back onto the highway.

Rain pattered on his hood. The air was cold but not wintery.

Walking on the shoulder, Sherman turned west and put boot to pavement. The rain kept coming and mixed with the briny smell of sea water. Wind whipped across the road, stinging his cheeks. Sherman loved every minute—all that water after so many months in the desert.

Saturated down to his toes, he passed a smattering of homes and a few restaurants that looked too kitschy to be good. He trudged on until he reached a three-way stop sign.

The green road sign for Hilt Bay had an orange *CLOSED* sign welded across it. Beyond that was a yellow diamond with *NO OUTLET* written on it. Another nearby square warned of tsunami danger.

The place you go to not be found, thought Sherman.

He took one more glance at the signs and kept going straight as towering pines swayed heavily overhead in the stormy winds. The road continued to narrow as it rose upward towards some unseen apex shrouded in thick fog.

With no more shoulder to walk on, Sherman inhabited the left side of the two-lane road. Just beyond the hilltop, unheard in the roaring storm, a pair of headlights zoomed out of the fog like a two-eyed monster. Sherman managed a quick leap to safety, landing in a scraggly bush as a faded red truck sped by, oblivious to the near miss.

Sherman's mental map of the area indicated only a mile remained, and his descent down the hill petered out into a wider road with fewer trees on either side. He still couldn't see more than fifty feet, but the ocean's wrath grew in volume with each passing minute.

A small wooden sign off to the side of the road announced his arrival in Hilt Bay. The lettering was small and had no welcome message or population total. Only the town name and establishment date of 1812. Space existed for a second sign below the first, but only rusty screws remained.

Two hundred years of history. That's a lot of skeletons to bury, he thought.

As if on cue, ghostly rectangles materialized from the fog, and Sherman knew he'd reached the small business heart of Hilt Bay. A well-worn wooden sidewalk ran in front of the buildings, which looked ancient. The eaves sagged and weathered cedar shake siding covered the exterior walls. A few buildings had fresh coats of trim paint, but most existed outside of time as if the year was 1820 or 1920.

Despite the afternoon hour, nothing appeared open, and Sherman passed Seabrine Hardware, Pushkin's Garage, Berg's Local Market, and a doctor by the name of Calvert who was also a dentist and notary public.

Across the street, a few curtains fluttered closed, and he knew unseen eyes carefully monitored his progress.

The short block ended at a T-junction. Right went north. Left went south. Due west across the street was a long cedar-sided rectangle with dark blue trim and a sign that read *Wellerman's Pub.* A neon sign flickered *BEER* in the window, and it looked open.

Sherman didn't know where Hal lived. There was no return address on the letter... assuming Hal was still alive. A lot could happen to an old man in two months.

With nothing else open, Sherman crossed the road and opened the door to Wellerman's Pub.

From the moment he entered, Sherman knew two things. First, he was not welcome. Second, this was his kind of place. The inside was as worn as the outside. Dirty wood walls weathered by years of smoke and salt wrapped around a bar top made of old ship timbers. Bits of broken masts held up the ceiling, but not in a decorative way. Pictures of shipwrecks adorned the walls. Small round windows looked out towards the ocean beyond. On the back wall, the storage room door was nothing more than a sheet of plywood.

Two tables sat under the windows, with two more on the southern wall. The bar had eight seats, three of which were occupied. Not a single customer smiled as he slung off his pack and stepped up to the bar. Two beer taps rose above the wood, one marked Light, the other Dark.

Sherman liked the simplicity.

The two men at the end of the bar wore thick wool coats and newsboy caps pulled down to their eyes. They glanced at Sherman with a sharp sideways glare. A gnarled old lady with gray hair tucked under a bandana occupied the third stool. She poured herself shots of vodka from a half-empty bottle. The woman sniffed in Sherman's direction as if testing the fumes and went back to drinking.

Sherman took the stool furthest away from the usual clientele and waited for the bartender to approach. Partially hidden in the poor lighting, the guy wore a fisherman's sweater with rolled-up sleeves and tattooed forearms the size of artillery shells.

"You lost?" asked the bartender in a low growl.

Sherman's wet clothes dripped onto the wood floor. "I ain't found, if that's what you mean, but a beer sounds good right now."

The man gave a curious look, as if he'd expected Sherman to run. "Cash only," he said and jerked his thumb towards a cardboard sign behind the bar.

Sherman fished out a soggy twenty-note from his pocket and placed it on the counter. "I'll take a dark."

A thick glass mug with a handle landed in front of him

with a thud and the bartender returned with change. Sherman drank in silence as the men at the end of the bar got back to their quiet conversation and the woman drinking vodka whistled a melancholy tune that Sherman couldn't quite place.

Just after he ordered another dark, two figures entered the bar full of bluster. Sherman caught a glimpse of two younger men, early twenties, with wild beards, wearing waterproof bibs like fishermen. One wore orange, the other red.

They stopped at the bar and ordered a beer before noticing Sherman minding his own business.

"Hey, King, who's the new blood?" one of the men asked the bartender.

King, if that was his name, shrugged and pointed to the army-issued backpack next to Sherman.

"Say, you're a long way from basic training," said the man in orange.

Sherman swiveled on his bar stool and eyed up the guy, who wasn't long out of high school. His friend, in red, stood behind a head taller but not any older.

"I suppose that's true," said Sherman, who'd spent more of his life in the army than out.

"He says I'm right. Did you hear that, King? The soldier speaks."

King crossed his thick arms and said nothing. Sherman swiveled back and raised his finger for another beer. He had no desire to finish the conversation with the two local idiots.

"Hey," said the one in orange. "I'm not done talking to you. Didn't the army teach you respect?"

Sherman swiveled slowly back. "No, they taught me how to kill. There ain't much respect involved with killing. Maybe in death. Maybe."

"Shawn, sit your scrawny ass down and have a damn drink before something bad befalls you," said the old woman with a shot glass dangling from her fingers. Her accent sounded vaguely Slavic.

The man in orange turned to face the woman. "Auntie Zil, take another shot and leave this to me and Vern."

Zil, like the Soviet truck, thought Sherman.

Shawn, in orange, and Vern, in red, stepped closer to Sherman, who still wanted nothing more than another quiet beer but knew there was nothing friendly or quiet about Hilt Bay. A selling point, no doubt, for Hal Cooper.

"Look, guys, I'm tired and wet, and this ain't my town. I get that. Best to let me pass through, visit my friend, and be on my way."

"Who's your friend?" demanded Vern.

"Hal," said Sherman.

Vern snickered. "Old sarge went off the deep end months ago."

What deep end? Sherman wondered.

Shawn shook his head and said, "Friend or not, the only person you're gonna visit today is the doctor."

With that proclamation, Shawn swung his fist at Sherman's seated face. The fisherman, despite his frame, had big, meaty hands and strong arms accustomed to tossing lines and traps—but not punches.

Sherman saw the hook coming and slid off the back of the barstool, under the slicing fist. Clear of the punch, he grabbed the stool with two hands and hoisted it up hard, but not too hard, into Shawn's chin with a tremendous crack. The fisherman's eyes rolled back and he thumped to the wood floor in a pile of orange.

Vern stood transfixed by the sudden violence. His eyes darted from Shawn to Sherman as if deciding the true weight of his friendship and if it tipped the scales towards retribution.

"I told you," said Auntie Zil.

King sighed, walked over to a phone on the wall, and dialed.

Cops, thought Sherman.

The call was short—only a few words—and King returned to the bar where Vern had still not decided his fate. The bartender poured two beers and slid them towards Sherman and Vern.

"Take a drink and sit the hell down," said King.

Sherman placed the stool back down and resumed his perch.

"What about Shawn?" asked Vern, flailing one hand towards his prostrate friend.

"He'll come to in a bit," said the old woman. "Serves him right for being an ass."

"But, Auntie Zil," protested Vern.

"None of that, boy. Sit. Drink. Enjoy your undamaged face."

Vern sat and drank but not with enjoyment.

Sherman did. He figured one more wouldn't hurt before the cops showed up and forced him to explain the circumstances leading to him drunk on a stool and Shawn unconscious on the floor.

"I called Hal," said King, still leaning back with his thick arms crossed. "He'll be here in a few."

Chapter Five

When the phone on his side table rang, Hal Cooper gave it a suspicious glance. He didn't like phones or people. That much hadn't changed with time. Hal hazarded a glance at the Caller ID and, to his surprise, recognized the number.

He picked up the receiver. "Good afternoon, King. Did I forget to pay my tab again?"

"You have a visitor at the bar."

Hal couldn't think of anyone visiting or being invited to visit, then he recalled a letter he'd sent months earlier. An invitation of sorts. The specifics were hazy.

"I'm on my way."

Gloria perked up as Hal grabbed his keys and struggled to her feet, arthritic joints and all.

"Come on, girl," said Hal. "We've got company."

Fog still swirled like long white intertwined ribbons wafting up from the sea. The roar of crashing waves reverberated through the mist. Hal opened the door to his battered old Ford truck and helped Gloria into the cab. Her legs could no longer make the jump.

They drove slowly through the great curtains of white even though Hal knew every inch of road in town. Better to go slow than run over Ms. Bleeker, who loved nothing more than riding her bike in monumental storms. Judging by the speed of his windshield wipers, Hal reasoned it was one of those days.

Parking in front of the bar, Hal left Gloria in the truck with a bone to keep her occupied. Better a little drool splattered about than have her get bored and chew through the seats again.

Wellerman's Pub was not his favorite place for a drink, but it was the only place when the café was closed.

Hal opened the heavy wood door and stepped into the smell of stale beer, brine, and tension. It took him but a moment to see why.

Lying unconscious and unattended on the floor was one Shawn Wilder. A lesser member of the extended Wilder clan that ran roughshod over Hilt Bay ever since their kin chased out the law a century past. Technically, Hilt Bay fell under the jurisdiction of the Oregon State Police, but they mostly left well enough alone. Except for the patriarch, Tom Wilder, who overstepped the bounds of his fiefdom and found himself in prison.

Hal didn't care much for Shawn or what circumstances led to his current state of incapacitation. What interested him was the sopping wet man sitting at the end of the bar drinking a pint of dark. From behind the bar, King tilted his head towards the man, but Hal didn't need the cue. He occupied an adjoining stool and smiled.

"It's good to see you, Franky."

"Been a few years, Uncle Hal," said Sherman.

"Why didn't you say you were kin?" added Vern in protest from two stools over.

"Because it's none of your damn business," said Auntie Zil.

"Did Shawn and Vern give you the Hilt Bay welcome?" asked Hal.

"If that consists of being assholes, then yes, they did that quite effectively."

Just like his father, thought Hal, but he didn't dare voice such an opinion. Frank and his father always had a contentious relationship and Hal doubted six feet of earth had mellowed the sentiment.

"Did he swing first?" asked Hal.

Sherman nodded.

"And you…"

"Lost my patience," said Sherman.

"And knocked him out with a barstool," added King.

"Are you gonna call this in?" Hal asked the bartender, which would have been a grave breach of town etiquette. But Frank was not a local, so custom did not apply.

"I did," answered King. "I called you."

"No cops?" asked Sherman, relief in his voice.

"Town rule," answered Hal. "No cops unless there is a corpse."

"Then I hope he wakes up," said Sherman.

"How hard did you hit him?"

"Not as hard as I could have."

"Just like your mother. How is Sophia?"

"Most days, she can't remember her own name, but occasionally, there's a glimpse of her old self."

Hal nodded with empathy. Losing one's memory if not your mind was a deeply troubling experience, until it wasn't, and you'd gone over the cliff.

Sherman kept looking at Hal, waiting for something.

"Right," said Hal after a moment of arduous concentration. "I invited you."

"And here I am," said Sherman.

"A letter," added Hal, fishing for the exact words he wrote. "Something to do with my father."

The room suddenly felt too quiet, and Hal sensed all eyes on him. Questioning glances. Suspicious looks. He didn't like them. Why did they want to know?

"Not here," he whispered.

Sherman finished his beer and grabbed his backpack without another word about the letter or Hal's sudden mood swing.

"Sorry about all that," Sherman told King and pointed to Shawn.

King shrugged off the apology. "Ain't the first time he slept on that floor."

Hal ushered Sherman out of the bar and into the lashing rain.

"Don't mind the dog, she's harmless."

Sherman glanced inside the cab at Gloria's outstretched frame and tossed his bag in the truck bed.

"Nothing valuable in there, right?" asked Hal, seeing the pools of water forming between bits of old construction materials he'd failed to remove. His truck used to be clean.

When did that stop?

"I don't own anything valuable," answered Sherman. "And whatever is in there needs a wash anyway."

"Then hop in."

"Is there a place to eat around here?" asked Sherman.

"The café, but it's closed today. I've got some clams to fry back at the house if you like seafood."

"Lead on, Uncle Hal."

Sherman did not know Hal well enough to have expectations regarding the state of his house, but he had assumptions—an orderly home befitting an organized Marine who'd spent a lifetime living on the knife's edge of details. A yard or two off and the mission failed.

In the curtains of mist and rain, Sherman couldn't see much of the house, other than it looked like others they'd passed. A single-story building clad in cedar shake siding and west-facing windows. The ocean roared behind them as they walked up to the front door. Quaint was how Sherman viewed the place. A nice, clean, quiet place to disappear, with neighbors far enough away not to be nosey and a gruff town to dissuade unwanted visitors.

Hal opened the door and Sherman followed. The interior glowed with polished wood and brass fixtures. It felt spacious without being big. The small kitchen adjoined a tiny reading nook replete with a cozy chair, but the dining table over-flowing with books and newspaper clippings surprised him.

"Sorry for the mess," said Hal motioning towards the table. "I must've got carried away."

Carried away was not what Sherman saw sprawled about. He saw obsession but said nothing.

"You've got a nice place here, Hal."

"Thanks, I bought it off an old navy captain."

"How long have you lived out here?"

"In Hilt Bay?" asked Hal.

"Yeah," answered Sherman, wondering what else *out here* meant to Hal.

"Oh… a good while, I suppose."

Sherman set down his pack and perused the pine bookshelves stocked with dozens of history volumes ranging from ancient Babylon to Vietnam. Many of the books leaned wildly against others, highlighting the gaps created by those on the table.

"Shucks," said Hal, digging through the fridge. "I thought I had clams. How do you feel about frozen fish sticks?"

"Are they local?" joked Sherman.

"Locally foraged at the market," said Hal with a sheepish grin.

"Beats an MRE."

Hal turned on the oven and tossed the frozen food onto a baking sheet. He grabbed two small glasses and poured a finger of whiskey in each. Sherman accepted the glass and Hal cleared off some chairs, sweeping papers into the corner.

"Cheers," said Sherman.

"*Na Zdorovie*," replied Hal.

"Forgot they taught you Russian."

"You didn't learn?" asked Hal, a smidge of surprise on his face.

"Different war, Uncle Hal. Different war."

"Ah," replied Hal, but his eyes held a faraway gaze. "What did they teach you?"

"Arabic. Persian. Farsi."

Hal chuckled. "Your father always said you were a quick learner. Sharpest knife in the family."

"I don't remember him ever saying that," said Sherman. In fact, he didn't recall much positive feedback leaving his father's lips. The old man was more of a teach-by-example kind of father, which Sherman mostly ignored in his haste to escape.

Hal waved him off. "Your father thought the world of you."

"He had a funny way of showing it."

"I don't imagine he had much of a role model in your grandfather. Probably never heard a kind word from the man."

Sherman laughed at the thought. "Colonel Fire-and-Brimstone? I think not."

"A real strict bastard, your grandfather. From what I heard."

"It's good to see you again, Uncle Hal."

"You too, Franky."

"Now, are you going to tell me why you wrote that letter?"

Hal glanced around the room as if searching for something he'd lost. "Are you in a hurry? Got some place to be?"

Sherman leaned back in his seat and took a sip. "No, not in a hurry."

"Good. Then let an old man reminisce and babble on. I want to hear about your war."

"Have it your way. Most of it is classified."

Hal raised his glass. "To Uncle Sam!"

Chapter Six

Babysitting strangers did not inspire Terrance Wilder, even if the money lined the family coffers. He could have overlooked the chore, chalked it up to necessity had it not been for the peculiarities of his guest. The intervening hours had done nothing to quell his dislike of Stanton.

His father insisted on letting Stanton use the guest cottage normally reserved for visiting family, which, given the sheer size of the Wilder clan, happened often. Tucked away at the edge of town, the house had been in the family for generations. Lore had that Terrance's great-great-grandfather won the deed in a poker game at Wellerman's Pub. Terrance considered the story malarkey. His family were terrible gamblers, but they were decent criminals and stupendous thugs. If anything, his great-great-grandfather shot the owner and took the deed.

Terrance swallowed his nagging pride, knocked on the door, and took a long step back.

A few moments of silence followed, long enough that Terrance thought his guest might be indisposed. Then the door opened, and Stanton's pale blue eyes emerged into the washed-out light.

"Just wanted to stop by and make sure you have everything you need," said Terrance, trying not to spit out any venom with the words.

Stanton still wore his all-black outfit that sent chills up the back of Terrance's neck.

"Mr. Wilder, I appreciate the unannounced check-in, but if I require your services, I will call."

What an asshole, thought Terrance.

"Hilt Bay is not known for its hospitality. I wouldn't want some ill to befall you."

"An ill," said Stanton, looking right through Terrance as if he were nothing more than a wisp of mist drifting in from the sea.

"Or accident," added Terrance. "Stranger things have happened on stormy days. The fog has been known to swallow people up."

"Perhaps they were too drunk or dumb to watch their step," said Stanton, unrelenting in his gaze.

Terrance couldn't bear those eyes any longer and looked away. "How long are you staying? My father didn't say."

"These things take time. A week, perhaps more."

These things, thought Terrance. *What things?*

His father had not fleshed out Stanton's job or why he needed a fixer in Hilt Bay, but Terrance knew better than to ask. If Tom wanted him to know, he would say something, which left Terrance with the burden of helping without knowing and he hated not knowing.

"I guess I'll hear from you later," said Terrance.

"Goodbye, Mr. Wilder," replied Stanton before shutting the door.

Terrance stood on the front porch a minute longer,

trying to piece together what little his father said in their last conversation.

Why the stranger? Why now? What was his job? Why did it take a week or more?

He found no answers in his memory or on the porch and walked slowly to his car. He'd just pulled away when his cell phone rang.

"Vern, what is it?" he asked with a sliver of annoyance.

Vern was not the sharpest crayon, but his cousin, Shawn, worked and lived with the guy, so Terrance gave him a lot of slack.

"Some guy knocked Shawn out."

"Where?" asked Terrance.

"In the head," said Vern, sounding both winded and drunk.

"No, you idiot. Where are you?"

"Wellerman's."

"Not the Hilt Bay welcome act again," said Terrance.

"Got to keep up the traditions," Vern answered unapologetically.

Once upon a time, before Tom's surprise incarceration, Terrance happily intimidated the unlucky stranger who wandered into town unbidden. Responsibility had changed him... or so he hoped. Softness was not a quality encouraged or tolerated in the Wilder clan.

"Does he need the doctor?" asked Terrance.

"I don't know, Wildman, he ain't awake yet."

Terrance bristled a little at the nickname, maybe from that responsibility surge. The nickname had stuck with him since high school when he burned some bridges—both metaphorical and literal.

"Call the doctor. I'll be there in a few."

Terrance sped through the fog and narrowly missed Ms.

Bleeker out riding her bike with no helmet. She never missed a good storm. When he arrived at the pub, Shawn was awake and nursing a pint of dark with a bag of frozen peas glued under his chin between sips. Vern sat next to him with several empty mugs. The doctor was nowhere to be seen.

"Did you call the doc?" Terrance asked Vern.

"He woke up," said Vern as if that negated bodily harm.

Terrance peeked beneath the bag of peas at the nasty bruise already forming under Shawn's chin.

"You look like that time in middle school when you caught a baseball bat to the face."

"Barstool," said Vern.

"I told him not to," said Auntie Zil, who was somehow related to his father, or so he said, but everyone called her Auntie.

"Please... stop... talking. It hurts my head," said Shawn.

Terrance walked over to King. The bartender had a level head and nothing like Vern's room-temperature IQ.

"Care to tell me what happened?"

"Wrong guy," he said.

"I see that," added Terrance. "Who is he?"

"A soldier, I guess. Friend of Hal's."

"Hal Cooper... as in crazy old Hal?" asked Terrance.

"Crazy comes in many shades. He ain't always loopy. There are some clear days in that mind."

"Used to be a lot more. Anyway, tell me about the friend."

King shrugged. "Ain't much to tell. He walked in soaked to the bone and ordered a beer. Those two came in after and started their act. The guy didn't take kindly to it and Shawn kept pushing."

Terrance knew the script well enough to visualize Shawn poking and prodding until he found a sore spot. Once the victim's ire rose, he mercilessly dogged them. Most people left long before it came to blows, and the ones that didn't usually took a beating.

"You said he is a soldier."

"Seemed that way. Had an army backpack and boots but I suppose he could have got them at a surplus store. But he was quick."

"With a barstool?" asked Terrance.

"Shawn went to punch a hole through the guy's face, found only air, and caught the stool on the chin before he could swing again."

Terrance didn't know what to make of the story. Tall tales permeated Hilt Bay like rust on cars. Everyone had some. Big stories, like Auntie Zil and Soviet Russia, or Doc Calvert's escape from the law back east. Terrance took them all with a heavy dose of skepticism, but King usually shot straight with his recounting of events—unless there was a woman involved, and that did not appear as a relevant fact in this case.

"I should probably have a chat with this friend of Hal's."

"To apologize for Shawn," said Auntie Zil.

"To make sure he understands the rules around here," said Terrance a bit too importantly.

"Bad idea," said Auntie Zil between shots of vodka.

"I'm sure Hal explained," said King.

"He knocked my cousin out with a barstool. I can't leave that unanswered. We Wilders have a code. Right, Shawn?"

Shawn didn't answer. He was asleep with his head on the bar.

"Oh, for the love of—Vern, get the damn doc. He probably has a concussion and you ain't supposed to sleep concussed."

"What's concussed?" asked Vern, slurring the words.

Terrance threw up his hands in disgust. "Get the damn doc or you'll find out!"

Vern wobbled out the front door.

"King, can you please make sure Shawn doesn't wander off before Doc Calvert arrives?"

The bartender gave a long, sideways glance at Shawn and nodded. "Don't think that'll be an issue."

"Good. I'm off, then."

"Don't piss him off, Wildman," said King, using that damn nickname.

Terrance glowered back. Rage smoldered just behind his eyes. "Who? Hal or his friend? Because if anyone should be worried, it's them."

Chapter Seven

The meaningless interruption by Terrance Wilder set Stanton back a good hour. Timing was everything in his line of work, but Stanton pushed away the ire. He needed to focus on the tasks at hand. This was the most audacious job in an illustrious career, and the sums of money involved more than compensated for the risks.

Stanton spread out several maps across the dining table and took out his journal and pen. He had a topographical map of the region, a map of the coast, a ship navigation map, and a crudely hand-drawn map provided by Tom Wilder. His job over the next few days involved transforming Tom's chicken scratch into actionable intelligence.

Specifics mattered to Stanton, and he enjoyed the planning phase with every meticulous detail. Where others saw OCD tendencies, he saw precision. The reason for his success and longevity in a profession known for neither.

Using a large piece of trace paper, he neatly outlined Hilt Bay's unique contours. He marked out the points of the hilt and his current residence. In neat, terribly small script, Stanton wrote out distances and tidal measures, ocean depths, and sea currents.

Several hours of intense concentration had passed when his phone rang. Not his everyday phone, but the prepaid burner he bought before boarding his flight to Portland.

He recognized the number and answered.

"This is Stanton," he said.

"Mr. Stanton," replied a voice thick with an unidentifiable accent—maybe Eastern European or maybe fake. The truth didn't matter, only the money. "How are things progressing?"

"I arrived in town today. Everything is on schedule."

"Good. I expect daily updates, Mr. Stanton."

"Of course, sir."

"And you cannot let anything or anyone impede your progress. Is that understood?"

Stanton understood the rules of engagement quite clearly, and while violence was not his preferred action, doing so did not bother him.

"I understand."

"I will call back tomorrow. Good evening, Mr. Stanton."

The call ended and Stanton placed the phone down next to a waterproof black plastic case. He looked at the case for a moment, deciding if such precautions were warranted and decided they were indeed. Too much was at stake for anything less.

He unlocked the case with a small key and opened the latch to a satisfying click. Inside was a custom .45 caliber Glock modified to his specifications. In the event he needed to use the gun, as he had in the past, it would end up in a very deep body of water shortly thereafter and be replaced by another. Everything about it was legit, but the serial number linked a case of weapons misplaced by the factory some years before.

Stanton loaded the gun and placed it in a small holster behind his back. He was a stranger in a strange land and needed to operate as if he was behind enemy lines. At least, that was the image that crossed his mind as he went back to the maps.

———————

Terrance Wilder darkened Hal Cooper's doorstep as he and Sherman finished the last fish sticks and settled into comfy chairs for the evening. Gloria gave a damp bark but didn't get up. Hal parted the curtains for a glance outside into the failing light.

"This day keeps surprising me," said Hal.

"Who is it?" asked Sherman.

"Trouble," answered Hal.

Sherman took a breath and reluctantly stood up from the chair. "Will it go away if we don't answer the door?"

"I doubt it. You knocked out his cousin."

"Oh," said Sherman.

"Best to rip the Band-Aid off and get this over with."

"Get what over with?" asked Sherman. He was ready for bed and didn't care for any more excitement.

"Terrance Wilder puffing out his chest and acting tough," answered Hal.

Sherman stood back and motioned for Hal to open the door.

A wiry young man stood on the other side. Unruly black hair spilled out from underneath a dark-blue wool stocking cap. He wore jeans, boots, and a worn black peacoat.

"Good evening, Terrance," said Hal.

"Hal, I haven't seen you around town lately."

"What brings you to my door?"

"Oh, I think you know why I'm here."

Hal grunted. "Best come inside before the whole damn storm comes with you."

Terrance stepped inside and his eyes fell upon Sherman. The younger man gave his best glare, but Sherman had killed tougher men and didn't budge with pale intimidation.

"Terrance Wilder, meet Frank Sherman, an old family friend."

Terrance didn't offer a hand, nor did Sherman, who didn't see the need for pleasantries.

"Well, this is off to a good start," muttered Hal.

"Now-now, Hal. I wouldn't knock if this wasn't a cordial visit. I just wanted to have a few words with your old family friend."

"I'm right here," said Sherman. "Say your piece and move along."

Terrance chuckled. His lip quivered. "You knocked out my cousin today."

"He swung first," said Sherman.

"Which is why I'm being polite about all this, but that's the last time you'll lay a hand on a Wilder."

Sherman wanted to break his nose but thought better.

"Are there a lot of you?" he asked.

Terrance nodded as if numbers equaled safety.

"Are they as unruly as your cousin?"

The young man's eyes narrowed. "Some more. Some less."

"Seems a tall request in a small town like this. I'm bound to run into your family again."

Hal sighed.

Terrance shook his head in disbelief and said, "Hal, talk some sense into your friend."

Hal shrugged off the comment with a grin. "Frank understands what you're saying. He just doesn't give a damn and neither do I. But it's time you left."

"Both of you should be careful out in that fog. It is awful thick. I wouldn't want anything foul to happen to y'all."

Hal opened the door and ushered Terrance out, who left with an undisguised sneer.

"We probably should have played nice," said Hal after watching Terrance pull away.

"You're making it sound like I insulted the mafia. Should I be worried?"

"With Tom Wilder, yeah, but with Terrance, probably not. He's a little over his head running things on his own and the town has mellowed over the years."

"What are they into?" asked Sherman.

"Smuggling runs in the family, so they are still carrying on the family legacy."

"What kind of smuggling?"

A distant look crossed Hal's face and he turned away. "As long as it ain't people, I don't make it my business to know."

Sherman wanted to learn more but decided sleep was more important than digging for some half-buried truth. The red flags of dementia existed all around him, cluttering up the house with unseen messes and prodigious sticky notes that made the fridge look like a game of Tetris about to end. Taking Hal's word as truth involved crossing a mental minefield.

"I think I'll call it a night," said Sherman. "Where can I crash?"

Hal pointed to the worn but intact couch. "I'll get you a blanket."

"Thanks," said Sherman.

"I'm glad you came, Franky."

"Me too, Uncle Hal."

Chapter Eight

The morning brought little change in the weather. Tumultuous, dark gray clouds swarmed overhead, and rain slanted down at odd angles and with surprising force. Only the fog had changed, shifting to thin, almost viscous ribbons of white that drifted across town.

Sherman awoke early and found enough supplies in the kitchen to make a passable pot of coffee. Sipping on the steaming mug, he gazed out Hal's kitchen window in the pale morning light.

The view had little equal. Across the street and down the hill lay the surging Pacific Ocean, white and frothy from the storm surge. Further out, he saw the southern edge of Hilt Bay curling outward—a thin chocolate-brown line edging against a sea of verdant green trees. The view evoked a sense of rugged beauty that Sherman couldn't pull himself away from. He didn't need to ask Hal why he moved here. The evidence spread out before him.

"That stuff is probably stale," said Hal, emerging from

the back bedroom. "I'm more of a tea drinker these days. Tea and whiskey."

"I'll drink it up if you call it coffee," said Sherman. "Great view, by the way."

Hal joined him at the window and gave a happy sigh. "Now, I have some bacon and eggs in here."

Opening the fridge, Hal found nothing because there was nothing to find but condiments and slices of American cheese. Sherman knew as much. The situation had not changed overnight when they ate the last box of frozen fish sticks.

"Huh," said Hal. "I guess I ate them all. Oh, well. Let's go to the café and get you some real coffee."

Sherman was not about to turn down a hot meal but added, "Maybe we can stop by that market you mentioned too?"

Earthy notes of fresh rain wafted about as Sherman and Hal walked out to the truck. Gloria trundled behind, her fur sparkling in the morning drizzle. Waves thundered against distant rocks and Sherman took in a lungful of salty ocean air.

"I like it here," he said as they got in the truck.

"Me too," said Hal before starting the engine and moving onto the wet road.

"Why here?" asked Sherman.

Hal looked confused.

"Why did you move here?"

"Oh, it just made sense," said Hal before falling silent.

Sherman didn't press because he wasn't sure if Hal remembered and didn't want to say, or if the memory was too faded to grasp.

They bounced down the road in Hal's squeaky truck as the man himself narrated a driving tour of Hilt Bay. That much Hal remembered, and he reveled in telling Sherman how Mr. Kim in the blue two-story house used to sell boot-legged soju from South Korea and Ms. Bleeker grew weed in a greenhouse until legalization and now grew magic mushrooms for higher profit margins. He pointed out the Russian Orthodox church with its patchy onion dome, a holdover from long-forgotten traditions.

Hal parked not far from the T-junction and Wellerman's Pub, in front of a battered yellow building with *Café* painted on the façade in weathered lettering.

"No dogs allowed," Hal told Gloria and she settled down on the bench seat without complaint.

The hour was early, and Sherman didn't expect a crowd, but the small interior had only two seats left at the counter. A waitress with jet black hair tied back in a ponytail bustled between the four tables and six counter seats—two of which Hal and Sherman now occupied.

The woman glanced at Hal and brought out a cup of hot water and a bag of tea. She looked at Sherman for a long moment and poured an extra-large mug of coffee from the pot behind the counter.

"Cream?" she asked, flashing the briefest smile.

"Extra, please," answered Sherman.

She placed a container of cream in front of him and whisked off, trailing scents of bacon and cedar.

"That's Ramona," said Hal. "A real gem in this sea of rough stones."

Ramona had an energetic look and tilting smile that made customers feel seen even in the bustle of a morning crowd. Sherman guessed she was closer to forty than thirty, but time passed differently for each person and the exact number rarely mattered.

"Alright, gentlemen," she said, scooting behind the

counter. "One blue plate special for Hal, and what will you have?"

Sherman hadn't seen a menu, printed or otherwise, but figured if Hal could stomach it, he could too. Besides, the coffee tasted good and if they made good coffee then the rest would follow.

"I'll have the same," he said, and Ramona disappeared into the kitchen.

"Good choice," said Hal. "They only have two options. Red plate or blue plate."

"What's on the red plate?" asked Sherman.

"*Blini* and *kasha*," answered Hal.

"And what did we get?"

"Not that," answered Hal with a grin.

Sherman nodded and sipped his coffee. While the café crowd edged older than the pub, he still felt dozens of eyes flitting in his direction—the new stranger in town. Conversations dipped into whispers, and he caught the occasional thumb jerked in his direction.

Blue plates of biscuits and hash arrived minutes later, and Sherman did not regret his choice or the companionable silence that followed as they ate.

Ramona returned once the plates carried but a speck of food and handed Hal a brown paper lunch bag.

"Bones for Gloria," he explained to Sherman and smiled affectionately at Ramona.

"Are you the mysterious stranger that has got this town buzzing with gossip?" asked Ramona, her head tilting with a curious smile.

"I'm afraid I'll disappoint," said Sherman.

"You did knock out Shawn last night, right?"

"Small-town news travels fast," he said.

"Like wildfire," said Ramona.

"He swung first."

"He usually does," she said.

"Then, I'm guilty," said Sherman.

"He is my cousin."

"I'm sorry."

"For hitting him or for him being my cousin?" she asked with slightly raised eyebrows.

"Certainly not for hitting him," said Sherman.

Ramona nodded thoughtfully for a moment and winked at Sherman. "Breakfast is on me, boys. Enjoy your afternoon. I heard the storm will crash hard this evening."

Hal smiled after her and Sherman placed a twenty-dollar bill under his coffee mug as a tip. Gloria was already drooling when they returned to the truck. Great white spindles spilled out of her jowls, sticking to the towel she lay on.

After some convincing, Sherman got permission from Hal to stock his fridge from Berg's Market, which probably still had canned food from the seventies at the back of the shelves but was otherwise adequate.

They arrived back at Hal's house as the thin wisps of morning fog pulled back out to sea and coalesced into a formidable wall that loomed just beyond the swells.

"Can't remember the last time Ramona gave me a free meal," said Hal as they stocked the fridge.

Sherman doubted the man could remember the last time he bought groceries but saw no need to press the matter. Instead, he asked, "What's her story?"

"Oh," said Hal as if encountering the question for the first time. "She lost her husband a few years ago and decided to move back home."

"She's from here?"

"You met two members of her family last night."

"Terrance did say it was a big family."

"Welcome to Hilt Bay," said Hal with a shrug.

Sherman put the last of the groceries away and lay down on the couch, facing toward the front windows and the now advancing wall of fog.

"Uncle Hal," he began. "Care to tell me what you meant in the letter about needing to talk with me in person?"

"Right… the letter," Hal said hesitantly. "Let me take Gloria for her morning walk and I'll tell you all about it."

"Do you want some company?" asked Sherman.

"No, I like my solitude," said Hal, rushing his words.

Sherman still didn't want to press the issue of Hal's memory or mental faculties.

"No worries. I'll be here," he said.

"I'll be back in an hour or so," said Hal as he gathered up Gloria's leash.

Sherman watched them turn right and head north into the swelling storm. He laid down, closed his eyes, and listened to the waves battle against the rocks.

Chapter Nine

The morning only brought more headaches for Terrance Wilder, and he set about facing them with the same grim determination he had over the last three years. Grabbing a Pop-Tart and energy drink, he started up his rust-worn sedan and headed out.

His first stop was Shawn's trailer, situated on the southern edge of town amid a scraggly patch of stunted pines and a small mosquito-riddled swamp—cheap land for a cheap man.

Vern's car was out front, and Terrance knocked hard on the door until it opened.

"It's early," said Vern, who was Shawn's roommate, in addition to best friend and co-worker.

"Shouldn't you be out fishing?" asked Terrance.

"I called in sick."

"Why? You didn't get knocked out!"

"I drowned my sorrows," Vern answered.

Terrance tamped down his budding rage at Vern's stupidity. "Where's Shawn?"

"In bed, I think."

"Is he still breathing?"

"I don't know," said Vern.

"You were supposed to keep an eye on him. Concussions are no joke."

"I did."

"Did what?" asked Terrance.

"Kept an eye on him. I drove him home."

"You drove home pissing gin," added Terrance.

"It ain't far."

"Move aside, I need to check on my cousin."

"Geez," squeaked Vern as Terrance barged past him.

"Shawn!" yelled Terrance. "Wake up, you stupid asshole."

Black and blue did not fully describe all the shades of Shawn's face, but he was snoring loudly, which meant he was alive enough for Terrance to check off one item from his list of headaches.

"See, he's fine," said Vern as Terrance left Shawn's room.

Terrance said nothing and drove away to deal with a larger problem by the name of Reginald Sows. Reggie was one of the Wilder's distribution experts until he abruptly quit two days before. Tom Wilder, in his prime, would have cut the man to pieces and stuck them in a chest freezer for the winter. Terrance did not share his father's bloodlust for perceived slights against the family—a trait his father found weak and wanting.

Reggie did not live in Hilt Bay but over the hill in an RV parked near the highway. As such, Terrance considered him an outsider and he didn't care for outsiders. They posed additional risks, which meant Reggie was an especially big headache.

When Terrance arrived at the battered old RV parked in a small gash cut from the forest, Reggie sat outside at a plastic picnic table, under an umbrella, sipping on a steaming cup of instant coffee. Next to the cup, still shiny in the dull light, lay a .357 Magnum revolver. The gun was Reggie's pride and joy. He loved waving the revolver around. Terrance guessed the act made Reggie feel important and safe—neither of which were true.

"I told you, I quit," yelled Reggie as Terrance exited his rusty sedan.

"I heard you fine enough on the phone," Terrance replied.

"Then why are you here disturbing my morning ritual?"

"To see if you'll reconsider your position," said Terrance as he approached a respectful distance.

"My position," Reggie scoffed. "My position is that I'm striking out on my own and I ain't working for you no more."

Terrance took a step closer. "You don't just work for me, but Tom Wilder, too. He might be out in a few for good behavior."

Reggie laughed loudly at the idea. "Ain't no way your father leaves anywhere for good behavior and he don't scare people the way he used to."

"Am I not scary?" asked Terrance, taking another step.

"No, boy, you are certainly not."

Terrance stole another step, his blood boiling, rage running hot.

"I'd like you to reconsider. If your issue is money, we can double your ten percent. That would give you twenty percent of the profits."

"Tom would have never given up ten percent without blood being spilled," said Reggie.

"I'm not my father."

"That much is quite clear. If you can afford ten, then you can afford forty."

Terrance saw a ten percent increase as reasonable, the cost of doing business in his father's absence, but a forty percent increase was an insult to the Wilder name.

"That would make us equal partners, fifty-fifty."

"Exactly," said Reggie.

Terrance did not like math, but he understood business well enough to know the deal stank. Reggie was a cog in the distribution machine, not an equal partner in the entire enterprise.

"Twenty percent of the profits is fair," said Terrance, stepping closer.

"Screw what's fair," said Reggie. "You ain't gonna find anyone better to move your product and you know it. Tom knew, which is why he hired me in the first place."

Terrance stood not four paces away from Reggie, having moved forward slowly like a frog boiling in water.

"Look," he said, pulling out a wad of cash from his pocket. "I got two-grand here, take it as an advance on twenty percent."

Reggie scoffed.

Rage bubbled up in Terrance's eyes. His lips twitched. The pressure of keeping the family afloat ate away at his patience from the inside out like cancer, and he didn't have much patience to start with.

"Take the money," he insisted between clenched teeth.

"Fifty-fifty or nothing," said Reggie.

The breaker switch in Terrance's mind tripped. He'd tried nice and tried reasonable. Only one course of action remained.

He tossed the wad of cash in a high, slow arc. Reggie

impulsively grabbed the flying money out of pure greedy human instinct. People love to catch things, and nothing sparks the desire more than money.

While Reggie was distracted by the two-grand, Terrance took four swift paces and grabbed the revolver off the picnic table so quickly that Reggie didn't notice the turn of events until he raised the wad of cash up triumphantly as if catching a foul ball at Wrigley Field.

Terrance pointed the heavy revolver center mass and pulled the trigger.

The gun kicked fiercely, the sharp crack echoing off the RV, but the result was undeniable. Reggie ceased to be a headache—at least a living one. Unfortunately, that left Terrance with clean-up. Being outside of Hilt Bay, that required extra attention to detail to remove any evidence of his involvement.

Terrance grabbed a plastic tarp out of his trunk that he kept for otherwise benign reasons but felt suddenly useful to the task at hand. Rolling Reggie onto the tarp took a good deal of grunting, but Terrance managed even as he kept glancing over his shoulder. Reggie lived by the highway and gunshots, even singular, drew unwanted attention. His father made the mistake of doing business outside of Hilt Bay, and overstepping cost him a ten-year stint in prison.

Lifting the tarp with Reggie inside was a two-part process. Legs first, angled into the trunk, followed by the heavy end. Terrance closed the trunk with a muted thud and took one last look around. Rain had already turned the bloody ground into mud.

What am I forgetting?

He'd already accounted for the body, gun, and wad of cash. That left... the merchandise.

Terrance took another long glance over his shoulder and listened for sirens.

Nothing but rain and the distant buzz of the highway.

The inside of Reggie's RV was not somewhere Terrance wanted to spend time. The place reeked of cigarettes, beer, mold, and sweat. He rifled through cabinets and drawers stuffed with barely edible food. Unsatisfied he'd found everything incriminating, Terrance tossed a book of matches on the yellow plaid couch and headed to his car.

He glanced back only long enough to see flames licking out the open windows before heading back.

A great sigh of relief resounded in Terrance's chest as he crested the hill separating Hilt Bay from the mainland and slipped into the enveloping fog. The grisly tasks of the morning were done, and the disposal of Reggie could take place on home turf.

Skeletons abounded in Hilt Bay if you knew where to search. Two-hundred years of criminal history will do that. Even the occasional body washed up on shore, usually an unlucky fisherman or drunken boater, but the sea gave up her secrets far too often to be useful. Long-term secrets required a different approach, and Tom Wilder showed his son the best spot for such activities when it became clear that he was going to prison. He called it the Smuggler's Well. Terrance knew it as the dark hole. Both names held their own truth—snippets of the past and present.

The exact location was a mystery to no one in town, but few outsiders knew the hole existed, let alone where to find it. From the T-junction, Terrance turned right and headed north until the road turned to dirt and all but disappeared. He circled up the rocks, which overlooked the sea on days when it was not draped in fog and parked by a twisted cedar tree with two trunks.

Terrance stood by his car and listened to the ocean boom. Rain pelted down in long streaks, and he couldn't see more than a dozen feet in any direction—excellent weather for illicit activities and body disposal.

Water trickled down the hill in long rivulets. He struggled getting Reggie's corpse out of the trunk and the tarp slapped against the mud with a squelching sound that turned his stomach.

The dark hole was only a few feet in diameter with jagged rocky edges eroded from the cliffside. Cold air rushed out and up in great briny jets and somewhere below churned the ocean. Terrance hadn't dared to get close enough to look, but the stories held there was only darkness to see. Even the dumbest of his friends never tried to go down there. The morbid lore of the Smuggler's Vault scared those who knew, and those who didn't but stumbled upon it never came out.

Terrance pulled the tarp with Reggie over the edge of the hole and then unceremoniously pushed him in headfirst. There was no splash or sound. Whatever lay below swallowed everything. There and gone.

He stood for another moment wondering just how many bodies met a similar fate over the years. Nothing that went down ever came back out, so the vault kept its secrets.

Two hundred years of skeletons, he thought.

With the deed done, Terrance got back into his car. Removing one headache created others and he considered who would take over distribution and how he would meet his commitments without someone like Reggie. Consumed by the thought, Terrance almost didn't feel his phone vibrating in his pocket.

He knew the number and dreaded answering.

"Mr. Stanton, how can I help you?" he asked.

"I've run into a problem that I need you to take care of," answered Stanton. His voice came across muffled and thin from poor reception.

"What's the problem?" asked Terrance, cringing at the possibility of another interaction with the stranger and his pale blue eyes that cut so deep.

"Not what," said Stanton. "Who."

Chapter Ten

The trail of sticky notes wrapped around Hal's bedroom like a yellow brick road of forgetfulness. Most were benign reminders for appointments and doctor's names or bills to pay, but as Frank Sherman followed the path across the room, the missives grew dark and paranoid—scribbles of rumors and lies about current wars and random conspiracy theories Sherman knew had no truth.

The similarities between Hal and his mother did not escape Sherman. Evidence of cognitive decline, diagnosed or not, filled the house. Like his mother's dementia, Hal's own demons burned bright and obvious.

Feeling guilty for invading Hal's privacy, Sherman moved back to the dining table and sifted through the stacks of books and clippings. Most of the newspapers were old and yellowed at the edges. The dates went further back than Sherman, but a few came from the nineties. One clipping had well-worn folds and scribbles in the margins.

"Local man disappears. Investigation ongoing,"

Sherman read the headline aloud. Something about the article caught his attention.

Was it the man's name? No. It held no water in his memory.

Was it the place? Yes, it was.

Dumfries, Virginia.

"Why do I know that?" he asked himself.

The answer came in a flash of tenth-grade history class. Sherman recalled sitting behind Becky Howard at the local high school and watching her long brown hair brushing across his desk and how he longed to feel it up close. He hated that school. It wasn't close to the base where his father was stationed, but in the town of Dumfries. The drive took time, and he didn't know any of the other kids.

"That's where I know it from," he said, again out loud and into the empty house.

As to why Hal had the clipping, Sherman couldn't say. He and his father were both stationed at the nearby base. Maybe they were friendly with the man. Maybe it was another conspiracy festering in Hal's mind. Maybe there was a corresponding sticky note on the wall. Sherman made a mental note to ask the man.

One hour turned to two as Sherman made himself another cup of coffee and dipped into Hal's curious madness. Somewhere in between two history volumes on the Tet Offensive, Sherman heard a consistent noise at the front door like a tree branch rubbing against wood.

He got up and opened the door.

There was no branch, but Gloria came bounding inside. She had her collar but no leash.

"Hey, girl. Where's Hal?" asked Sherman because it seemed like the reasonable thing to ask.

Gloria did nothing.

Sherman peered into the mist and waited. No one came.

"Hal!" he shouted into the storm.

No reply.

"Hal!" he repeated.

Gloria whined.

"Shit," he muttered and grabbed his jacket.

He walked out with Gloria close behind and turned right into the drifting mist and consistent rain.

Gloria followed by his side as they walked north. Sherman had no idea where Hal went other than the direction of travel and a vague sense of space heading up towards a rocky outcropping behind the house.

Roads and sandy driveways snuck off to his right as the storm churned and the ocean thundered to his left.

"Hal!" he yelled and intermittently repeated the name.

No reply came but the crash of distant waves.

Sherman looked to Gloria for help, but she only whined. *Some bloodhound you are*, he thought.

When the pavement ended and Sherman still couldn't find any trace of Hal, he turned around and headed back. Kernels of worry grew into full-blown concern as the weather made a search nearly impossible. Given everything he'd seen at the house, the possible outcomes felt grim. Hal might have just wandered off and forgot his bearings or the present tense. He might be stuck in the past or his twisted imagination. Worse still, he might have hurt himself, intentionally or not.

Halfway back to Hal's house, an SUV whizzed by in the mist. Red lights sparkled as the vehicle came to a sudden screeching stop and backed up. Sherman watched, hoping to see Hal, but found someone much different.

Ramona Wilder's dark hair fell softly around her face as

she leaned across the seat of the Toyota SUV. "Ah, the mysterious stranger graces my presence twice in one day."

"Not exactly," said Sherman. "Hal took Gloria for a walk but only she came back. I can't find him."

The smile on Ramona's face melted into a frown. "Seriously?" she asked.

"Very," said Sherman. "I walked to the end of the pavement but didn't see any sign of him."

"Get in. I was on my way to take lunch to Ms. Bleeker, but she can wait."

Sherman looked down at Gloria sitting by his side.

"She can get in the back," offered Ramona.

Sherman obliged and gingerly lifted the old and very wet dog into the back while he sat up front. The SUV smelled of lasagna and Ramona, which was some combination of cedar and flowers.

"I don't think we formally met. I'm Ramona Wilder."

"Frank Sherman."

"Well, Frank, nice to meet you."

"Likewise, and thanks for stopping."

"Anything for Hal," she said and stepped off the brake.

"Maybe I missed him in the mist," said Sherman.

"Not that you can see much in this soup. Maybe he sat down for a bit and Gloria wandered off," Ramona offered, but she didn't sound convinced of her argument.

"Does that sound like Gloria?" asked Sherman.

"No," muttered Ramona.

"Where would he go for a walk?"

"Maybe the beach."

"No sand on Gloria's paws," said Sherman.

"You're very observant."

"Part of the job."

Ramona tilted her head but didn't smile like she had at

the café. A question lingered on her lips but never left. "If not the beach, then maybe the cliffs."

"Cliffs?" asked Sherman. He hadn't seen much of anything behind Hal's house. He'd been too busy looking at the ocean when the fog allowed.

Ramona nodded and turned right onto a nondescript dirt road with no sign. They crept by cedar and juniper trees that reached out to grasp at the Toyota. An occasional driveway appeared between the trees, only to disappear into the fog before Sherman could see the address. They drove on with the windows down as a cold damp sunk inside.

"How much further?" asked Sherman.

"Maybe a quarter mile."

"You can let me out here," said Sherman.

"I can drive you all the way."

"Here's good," said Sherman.

She stopped the SUV and slipped it into park as Sherman got out. He walked in front of the car and crouched down to look at the dirt.

"What are you looking for?" asked Ramona.

Sherman pointed at faint paw prints in the damp, sandy soil.

"A lot of people have dogs," she said.

"Only one way to find out," said Sherman.

He walked around and helped Gloria out of the back. She looked up at him expectantly.

"Go on," urged Sherman.

Gloria didn't move.

"She lost her scent years ago," said Ramona. "Hal rescued her from some hunters who didn't want her anymore."

"That explains a lot," said Sherman. "Alright, come on

61

then." He started walking and motioned for Gloria to follow.

"Wait," Ramona called after him. "I'm coming too."

"I don't want to keep you from your day."

"Don't be silly, I volunteer my time in the afternoon. This is as good a cause as any."

"Wouldn't be the first time a man with dementia got lost in the woods," said Sherman.

"You noticed," said Ramona.

"How long has he been like this?" asked Sherman.

Ramona looked up at the trees and thought as they walked.

"He's been slipping for a year or so. Small stuff at first... a wrong name or misplaced event, but it is more pronounced now. Some days are better than others, but the town has noticed. Started calling him crazy old Hal."

"He wrote me a letter two months ago asking me to visit," said Sherman. "But Hal looked more than a little surprised when I showed up holding it."

Ramona nodded as if she had firsthand knowledge of such mental slippage but said nothing.

They walked a couple more minutes in damp silence with only a few feet of road visible in front of them and unseen trees creaking in the wind. The two sets of tracks in the dirt kept going. One human and one canine, along with several different tire imprints.

"Do people come up here often?" asked Sherman. The road looked well used.

"Some like the views. Others like the privacy."

Sherman kept glancing at the ground then back into the mist. His gut started to tighten. He had never known that feeling to be a good one.

"You said that was part of your job," interjected Ramona. "What do you do?"

"I'm a captain in the Army," said Sherman who noticed the footprints getting closer together as if Hal had slowed down.

"That explains Shawn's chin."

"He swung first."

"You mentioned that already," added Ramona.

Sherman didn't respond. The tracks veered right at the top of the hill and he followed them towards a gnarled cedar with two trunks that bent like a hunchback.

"Careful," said Ramona. "There are all sorts of holes up here."

Sherman kept going and pulled up short of a jagged gash in the earth gushing salty air. Gloria laid down and whined.

"That's more than a hole," he said.

"Yes, it is."

Sherman kneeled a respectable distance and examined the ground. He didn't like what he found. Three or four separate sets of footprints cluttered the dirt like a dance hall. Odder still were two drag marks—one large and singular. The other scuffed with two smaller parallel lines, like feet pulled unwillingly across the ground. The single mark was long and pronounced. It started near tire tracks and went straight to the hole. The small marks started closer as if someone was surprised.

Sherman circled the hole, keeping Ramona on the other side, and took a step closer. From deep below, he heard the ocean churn and gush. His gut twisted into knots.

"Where does that go?" he asked.

Ramona, arms crossed, looked pensive. "No one knows. Do you think Hal fell in?"

Sherman shook his head. "No. I think someone pushed him in."

Ramona bit her lip but said nothing.

"You don't look surprised," said Sherman, eying her in a suspicious light.

"I'm surprised anyone would hurt Hal, but it wouldn't be the first time a body went through that hole. They used to call it the Smuggler's Vault. Double crossers and nosey cops ended up at the bottom."

"Did their bodies ever come out?" asked Sherman, wondering if he'd confirm his suspicion.

"They call it a vault for a reason," said Ramona.

No body, no confirmation, thought Sherman.

He dealt in actualities—confirmed kills, not mysteries. Command wanted DNA evidence of dead terrorists, not scuff marks in the dirt and a dim-nosed dog. Despite the uncertainties, the soft edges and vagueness of the whole town, Sherman guessed Hal met an unsavory end. The who and the why were open questions, but he had one starting point.

Terrance Wilder.

The man who threatened Hal with an untimely accident the night before.

Sherman glanced up at Ramona and asked, "Are you on good terms with your brother?"

"That sounds like a *none of your damn business* question," answered Ramona. Her soft eyes curiously narrowed.

"He threatened Hal last night," Sherman added.

"Terrance threatens lots of people. Part of the job. Something you have in common."

Sherman let the unwanted comparison slide. "Does he act on any of those threats?"

"I don't know, and I don't want to know," she retorted.

"Can I buy you a coffee?" asked Sherman.

Throwing out hostile questions was getting him nowhere. He needed to understand the players involved and the local political geography. His unit did something similar in Afghanistan when they wanted to topple a local warlord. Killing him wouldn't suffice. They needed to understand all the interpersonal spiderwebs that bound the area together. Grudges, sex scandals, land disputes, and petty squabbles. Everything mattered because it was all leverage. A little pressure at the right spot created big opportunities.

"I could use a coffee," said Ramona. Then she added, "Or something stronger."

"Maybe out of town," Sherman suggested.

"Definitely out of town. I know a spot."

Chapter Eleven

Dread seeped into the edges of Terrance's mind as he parked in front of the family cottage. The damp shroud of mist didn't help. It sucked the warmth from his chest with every inhale. His brief phone call with Stanton had led to the second unsavory task for the day and he resented taking orders even if they were sanctioned by his father.

He'd done the task begrudgingly. Dealing with locals gave him heartburn.

The door opened as he approached, and Stanton appeared, still dressed in black but without the hat.

"Mr. Wilder, come in."

Terrance frowned and sucked in some cold salty air before stepping into the cottage. The stranger's very presence cast a pall across the house as if he'd sucked out all the colorful history and joy.

A large map lay neatly spread across the table with several sheets of tracing paper stacked in one corner. They reminded Terrance of architectural drawings, rendered with exacting precision.

"Did you take care of the issue I mentioned?" asked Stanton.

"You could have done it yourself," said Terrance.

Stanton's thin smile betrayed his satisfaction. "Perhaps, but that is why you're here."

"To do your dirty work," said Terrance.

"Work is work," said Stanton. "I don't attach judgment to the tasks. You would be wise to follow suit."

"Well, it's done."

Stanton's pale blue eyes flashed dangerously. "Good. Now, I have another task for you."

Terrance said nothing. He wasn't about to happily play along.

"Don't worry, Mr. Wilder. I don't need your adoration, only your cooperation."

At least he didn't say obedience, thought Terrance.

"On the table, you will find a list of supplies that I need procured. They are exactly what I require—nothing more, nothing less. No substitutions or generic knockoffs. No skimping. Am I clear?"

Terrance picked up the list and scanned the contents. Half of the items he didn't know.

"What is this crap?"

"Supplies that I need," said Stanton.

Terrance scowled. "I got that part, but where do you expect me to find an ATC, whatever that is?"

Stanton's face remained stony. "That is your job, Mr. Wilder. Find, acquire, assist. Do what is needed."

"You can't even give me a hint?"

"You're the local."

"And you're an ass."

Stanton's gaze remained fixed on Terrance, chewing through him like lions feasting on a zebra.

"I require the complete list of items tonight," said Stanton.

"Tonight!" exclaimed Terrance. "It's gonna take me hours, and that's for the crap I know."

"Tonight," repeated Stanton.

Rage bubbled up and Terrance clenched his fists, fighting the anger back down.

"I'll call when I have it all," he said.

"Excellent."

Terrance turned and walked away with a rotten taste in his mouth. He viscerally despised the stranger.

Stanton watched the young man leave with a twisted sense of satisfaction. Once the job finished and he got paid, Stanton planned on dumping the diminutive Wilder deep at sea. If the police ever snooped around, they would find a dozen search records on Terrance's phone and no sign of the man himself. Fall guys were as useful a tool as any other.

The burner phone vibrated with an incoming call. Right on schedule.

"This is Stanton," he answered, even though only one person knew the number.

"Mr. Stanton, I want my update."

"Everything is on schedule, sir."

"Good and the local help?"

"Cooperative."

"And your exit strategy?"

"With all due respect, I don't discuss such details with my clients. All I can say is that I don't leave any knot untied."

"Fair enough, Mr. Stanton. The freighter arrives tonight. No mistakes."

The call ended.

Stanton growled to himself and craned his neck from side to side until it cracked. He resented the implication of mistakes, but he had a thick skin when it came to client demands or peculiarities.

Now was no different than the others, except for the paycheck. Retirement was within reach if he ever cared enough to leave the game. In truth, Stanton enjoyed his work more than any view of the beach or game of golf.

Satisfied with his plan, he slipped on his boots and jacket and headed out into the storm again.

Chapter Twelve

The diner Ramona picked had crappy coffee and greasy food, but Sherman understood the choice. Right off the highway, hundreds of people passed through each day—hundreds of faces. They were two in a large pool of randoms, indistinguishable and, therefore, unimportant.

The staff took little notice of them as they took a booth in the rear of the restaurant. Sherman sat with his back to the wall and surveyed the bustling interior. Ramona seemed grateful to have her back to the crowd.

Their waitress, a young woman with purple hair, barely looked up from her notepad as Sherman ordered coffee and a BLT with extra mayo. Ramona skipped the food and ordered a chocolate milkshake.

"Are you afraid of being seen with me or at this establishment?" asked Sherman, who couldn't quite grasp her sudden introversion.

Ramona paused to consider the question. "A bit of both, I suppose. Hilt Bay folk don't venture out often, and this place is not one they patronize."

Sherman understood not wanting to be seen frequenting an outside business. He even understood Ramona not wanting to be spotted conversing with a stranger in Hilt Bay. But they were not in Hilt Bay, and she was still worried about being seen with him. The incongruity piqued his curiosity.

"I get the not wanting to be seen together in Hilt Bay, but who are you worried will see us together here?"

Ramona frowned. "You're very perceptive."

"Part of the job, remember."

"I heard my late husband's brother, my ex-brother-in-law, still lives around here."

"And you're worried because he is somehow jealous?"

Ramona laughed. "No, he's the angry type who collects grudges like I collect tattoos."

"For life?" asked Sherman, wondering where she hid said tattoos because he hadn't seen any yet.

"Exactly."

"Should we go somewhere else?"

"Nothing else around," she said.

"I guess we keep our heads low."

"And fingers crossed."

The waitress appeared with their order and Ramona dumped a small shooter of whiskey into her milkshake. Sherman wasn't one to judge but she caught his amused expression.

"What? This day is going to be hell."

"You're right about that," he replied.

"Do you really think my brother pushed Hal into that hole?"

"The threat was clear, and I don't know anyone else who'd want Hal dead."

"My brother is no saint and he's got serious anger issues,

but that doesn't make any sense. He had no reason to hurt Hal."

"They exchanged words last night," said Sherman. "I got the feeling that Hal crossed a line defending me over the incident at the bar."

"When you knocked out Shawn."

Sherman nodded.

"But he swung first," added Ramona.

"You're catching on," said Sherman between bites of BLT. "In my experience, pride is a good motivator for violence."

"Coming from a man with a long history of violence?" asked Ramona.

Sherman drank his coffee and watched the way she sipped her milkshake with a tilted head and a curious look in her eyes.

"Long enough," he added. "But I'm guessing not as long as your family's."

If Ramona took offense to the comment, it didn't show.

"Do you know the history of Hilt Bay?" she asked.

"Only the broad strokes."

"Den of thieves and smugglers since 1812. Proud of it too. Had that on the town sign until people started getting too curious and my dad ripped it down. No point in attracting attention."

Sherman started on the other half of his BLT.

"Do you know when the Wilders arrived in Hilt Bay?"

Sherman shook his head.

"1812," said Ramona.

"That is a long violent history."

"Yes, it is, and right now, that legacy rests on Terrance's shoulders because my father is doing ten years in Oregon State Penitentiary."

"I think Hal mentioned that fact," said Sherman.

"Which is why Terrance threatened Hal. He's got to preserve the family legacy and keep the business running. But I don't think he'd be so dumb as to kill a local. That goes against the town creed."

"I'd like to talk to him," said Sherman.

Ramona gave him a piercing look. "Talk or *talk*?"

Given the facts at hand, breaking a few bones was within the realm of possibility. Sherman didn't mind the dirty work if he thought the person deserving.

"If you come with me, I'll keep the conversation civil."

"For Hal's sake, I hope you're wrong," said Ramona.

"Why?"

"Because there are a lot of skeletons in that hole."

Two hundred years of skeletons, thought Sherman.

They finished and Sherman paid.

Leaving through the front door, Sherman asked, "Why did you leave Hilt Bay?"

Ramona stopped and gave a long sigh. Her face flushed red against her black hair.

"His brother," she said, pointing at a hulking man in grease-stained overalls and rubber boots.

"Oh," said Sherman.

"Ramona!" yelled the man and advanced with a pointer finger leveled in her direction.

"He looks angry," said Sherman.

"There is some bad blood between us."

The man barreled toward them, arm still extended with accusations and blame. He stood a few inches taller than Sherman's six-foot frame and fifty pounds heavier than his desert-lean frame of one-hundred and eighty pounds of muscle.

"I swore to my mother I'd break that pretty jaw of yours if I ever saw you on this side of the hill."

"Simmer down, Colby. I'm leaving," she replied.

"Nah, I'm done listening to your bullshit."

The gap shrank to two yards before Sherman stepped forward.

"We're leaving," he said.

Colby ignored his words and sent a fist slicing through the air in a quick, precise arc. A surprise attack of sorts. Skip the talk. Straight to the violence.

Sherman just managed to avoid knuckles and countered with a hard—but not too hard—hook to the guy's kidneys.

The punch didn't stop Colby, not even for a second. He whirled on Sherman and sent a flurry of fists his direction. Several missed but two connected with Sherman's ribcage, frazzling his mind with pain.

Should have hit him harder, thought Sherman.

The two men circled each other in the parking lot as Ramona yelled at Colby to stop.

"This isn't worth it," she cried.

"You're next," he barked at Ramona.

Bar fights were one thing, but violence against women or children triggered Sherman's deeply buried anger. The mental shackles of civilian life fell away, and he flipped his internal switch.

Had Colby known what would come next, perhaps he would have picked a different fight, but hindsight was very much a past-tense experience. Sherman, uninhibited and angry, picked apart his opponent, inflicting as much damage as he could until Colby lay broken and bloody on the pavement.

Sherman stood there panting as Ramona and the crowd looked on.

"Frank," she whispered. "We need to go."

Sherman heard sirens in the distance and understood the urgency.

"Lead the way," he said.

They jumped into her Toyota and chirped the tires on the way across the overpass toward Hilt Bay. Ramona drove fast but with practiced ease, leaning into and accelerating out of the corners. Sherman massaged his ribs as pain coursed through his knuckles.

"Probably should have picked a different spot," he said.

"Sorry about that," said Ramona. "I didn't think he'd show up."

Sherman wasn't so sure about that. Something about her look said she enjoyed watching Colby suffer or maybe Sherman was reading too much into the situation.

"You know Colby never lost a fight," she said.

"First time for everything," said Sherman.

Gloria whined in the back as they took another corner at speed.

"Really," she said. "He's undefeated."

"As in professionally?" asked Sherman.

"Underground fight circuit," said Ramona. "That is how I met his brother, Jack. They both fought. We used to host them in Hilt Bay, until Jack died. My dad cut Colby out after that."

"Guessing that didn't sit well."

"I may have also pawned my wedding ring, which might have belonged to Colby's mother and maybe got passed down since the Russian revolution," Ramona admitted.

"Oh," said Sherman.

"Sorry."

"He swung first," said Sherman.

"That he did. Now what?"

"You take me to the doctor so he can tell me my ribs aren't broken."

"Oh," said Ramona. "That bad?"

"No, but I want to ask him a question about Hal, and this seems like a good excuse."

Once they crested the hill separating Hilt Bay from the mainland, Ramona slowed. The restive fog swallowed them up in its gray embrace. Rain began falling, pattering the windshield like a reassuring song.

Ramona slowed further as they entered town, finally parking next to the wooden sidewalk and a sign Sherman recognized: Doctor, Dentist, Notary Public.

She opened the tailgate and helped Gloria out.

"We'll be here," said Ramona and pointed to the doorbell. "Doc Calvert lives upstairs. Ring it and he'll come down."

Sherman rang the bell, and as expected, the door opened a couple minutes later. A thin man with coke-bottle glasses and a thick brown beard stood in the doorway. He glanced from Sherman to Ramona and waved his arm inside.

"Come inside before the fog follows," he said.

Sherman entered a small waiting room and followed the doctor past a tiny room with a dentist chair and into a larger space reserved for doctoring.

"Have a seat," said Doc Calvert, who, in the room's bright light, looked to be in his early fifties with a pale complexion and a receding hairline.

Sherman sat on a ubiquitous medical bed that all doctors have. Calvert pulled a stool closer.

"Well, what brings you in today?"

No names. No paperwork. Sherman liked this version of medicine.

"Took a good punch to the ribs. Want to make sure they aren't broken."

Calvert frowned. "Treatment is the same either way. Rest and relaxation."

"I know, but one diagnosis tells me I can take another punch."

"I don't recommend that," said Doc Calvert.

"No one recommends getting punched, Doc. I just want to know the damage."

Calvert sighed. "Lift up your shirt."

Sherman did and the doctor leaned closer to poke and prod.

"You've got quite the scar collection."

"Occupational hazard," said Sherman.

"Then you already know the ribs aren't broken," said Calvert and slid the stool back a respectable distance.

"Always better to be safe," said Sherman.

"I still recommend rest and relaxation."

Sherman nodded. "Can I ask you one more question?"

"Go ahead."

"I'm an old family friend of Hal Cooper. He's a patient of yours, right?"

The doctor's eyes narrowed. "Yes."

"Is his dementia diagnosed?"

"I can't share personal information like that."

"Understood," said Sherman. "But he's missing. He wandered off today while taking his dog for a walk. Ramona and I are looking for him."

"Oh," said Calvert. "And a tree punched back while you were out looking?"

"No, we ran into Ramona's ex-brother-in-law in the process."

"I see," said Calvert, looking sympathetic.

77

"Hypothetically, would someone with dementia forget even familiar surroundings such as their neighborhood?"

"Hypothetically, someone with a probable CTE diagnosis could forget their own mother when the disease advances far enough. Symptoms include memory loss, erratic behavior, mood swings, and delusions."

Sherman nodded and stood up. "Thanks, Doc. What do I owe you?"

"Nothing," said Calvert. "I hope Hal turns up."

The doctor led Sherman out of the room, past the dentist chair, and to the front door. Ramona and Gloria stood huddled under an awning, and she waved to the doctor as Sherman exited.

"Well?" she asked.

"Not broken," said Sherman.

"That's good."

"He also told me Hal likely has CTE."

"Like football players?"

"Hal took a lot of knocks to the head over the years. Concussive blasts, fights, falls, and who knows what. Life as a Marine is tough."

"What does that mean for Hal?"

"Memory loss, erratic behavior, mood swings, and delusions," said Sherman, repeating what the doctor told him. "Which is similar to my mother's dementia."

Ramona glanced around before asking, "Does that change your theory about Hal?"

"I don't know," said Sherman. "He's gone and there were drag marks into the hole and I don't believe in coincidences. But this could change things."

"Do you still want to talk with Terrance?"

Sherman nodded.

"That's good because I called and told him to meet us here."

Chapter Thirteen

By early afternoon, the trunk of Terrance's sedan was full to bursting and the back seat overflowed with gear from Stanton's list. Some of the items' uses he could only guess at, but Terrance understood the items he got from Marine Salvage —winch, hooks, pulleys, chains, and rope. Basic gear for pulling something big up. Whatever Stanton had planned, it involved serious lifting. But the stranger didn't ask for a boat or scuba gear, which left Terrance wondering where he planned on lifting said item and what it could possibly be. Then, of course, there were the chemicals. He had no clue about those except for the warning labels and they indicated a dire outcome—blindness, birth defects, cancer, and death to name a few.

Terrance was between stops when Ramona texted and asked to meet. He didn't exactly get along with his sister. She was older and, therefore, wiser in her own esteemed opinion. They also had very different personalities. Terrance inherited his father's rage and wild streak while Ramona seemed genuinely interested in other people and wanted to help. A trait Terrance understood on a responsibility level, but intrinsically, he did not like people. People were not to be trusted. A lesson harshly etched in his mind at the age of eight when his mother flung herself off the defunct lighthouse south of Hilt Bay. Terrance didn't care for much of anything or anyone after that.

He parked the sedan by Wellerman's, and the car squeaked from all the extra weight. Clouds swirled overhead in a great dark vortex, churning like waves in the sky.

Gonna get slammed tonight, he thought.

Two blocks later, he spotted Ramona standing under an awning with a dog. Not just any dog, but a hound dog. Hal Cooper's dog. Terrance immediately regretted his decision to meet. Nothing good would come from it.

"Why do you have that dog?" he asked, looking around and wondering if it was some kind of setup.

"Hello to you too, Terrance," said Ramona. "I take it you know Gloria."

Terrance said nothing, judging that silence was the best course of action.

"Do you have a few minutes to chat?"

No, thought Terrance, but couldn't see why she had the dog. Curiosity got the better of him.

"About what?" he asked.

"The dog's owner," said Ramona.

"I'm too busy for this shit," said Terrance and turned to leave.

His path was blocked by Hal's friend. The soldier. Terrance couldn't wrap his mind around how the stranger got behind him... as if he'd materialized from the mist itself.

"Get the hell out of my way," said Terrance, very much regretting his detour.

"Not yet," said the man.

Terrance felt his eyes burn with anger.

"This is Frank Sherman," said Ramona. "I believe you met."

"Briefly," said Sherman.

"Get out of my way or I'm going straight through you," Terrance said. He couldn't believe his sister was helping Hal or his friend. It felt like another in a long string of betrayals. His father wouldn't have stood for such insolence.

Sherman didn't move. Not backward or sideways. Not even a flinch. Terrance did not like his calm exterior. The composure agitated him.

"Move," said Terrance, then took two long strides straight at the soldier who still didn't move.

Terrance went to shove the guy aside with one arm like a running back breaking a tackle.

He made contact center mass of the soldier's chest, not far from where he'd shot Reggie, but then the world spun in a blur and he ended up on his butt back between his sister and the soldier.

Damn, he's quick, thought Terrance, unable to quite comprehend how he ended up on the ground.

"I just want to ask you a few questions," said the soldier, who had resumed his expressionless gaze.

Terrance jumped to his feet and brushed sand off his pants. "I said you'd never lay another hand on a Wilder again and I meant it."

"Shut the hell up, Terrance," said Ramona. "You pushed him."

Who pushed whom and in what order did not matter to Terrance. He'd drawn a line in the sand, and no matter how arbitrary or asinine, he intended to enforce the consequences.

"Is this where a terrible accident befalls me?" asked the man. "Just like what happened to Hal."

"I don't know what nonsense you're spewing, but touch me again and I'll kill you."

The soldier didn't even blink at the threat. The concentration unnerved Terrance like Stanton's pale blue eyes. The two men shared the uncanny ability to look right through him.

"What happened to Hal?" asked the man.

"One too many knocks to the head? I don't know."

"He's missing," said Ramona.

"Why is that my problem?"

"Because Frank thinks you dumped his body down the dark hole."

Terrance froze for the briefest of moments. They thought he killed Hal and dumped his body down the hole. The latter part was true. He had killed and dumped a body, but not Hal. Had they seen him with Reggie? Maybe they did and assumed it was Hal. He had threatened the old man, and it was no boast, but he didn't know anything about Hal's disappearance.

"I did no such thing," replied Terrance. "Seriously. I gave him a hard time last night and maybe I crossed a line there, but I didn't hurt him. I haven't even seen him since then."

The soldier didn't look convinced, and Terrance pinned his hopes on Ramona, who always knew when his truth didn't run straight.

"I believe you," she said, and Terrance let out a silent sigh of relief.

"Why is your car riding so low?" asked the soldier.

Terrance parked further away to avoid his sister seeing

all the stuff in the car because she would inevitably ask questions that he did not want to answer.

"How did you—never mind. I'm running some errands for a friend."

"What kind of friend?" asked Ramona. "The kind Dad told you to help?"

Terrance grunted a quiet expletive in her direction that no one heard. Then he took a deep breath and tried to occupy the higher ground in their unequal relationship.

"Someone must keep the family afloat. Without the business, who'd pay for the mortgage on your house or Cousin Darren's medicine or Auntie Zil's medical bills? I stepped up. Not you or Shawn. Me!"

"You're a self-important ass," said Ramona. "I hope you know what you're doing. Otherwise, you'll join Dad in prison, and the precious family business will rot along with you."

Terrance threw up his hands in disgust. She always got deep under his skin, burrowing like a chigger, with no way to remove those barbed words. He turned to the soldier still blocking his path.

"Can I leave now?"

The man took a step closer and leaned forward. He beckoned Terrance to do the same, which he reluctantly did.

The soldier leaned even further and whispered, "I want to be clear with you, just so there aren't any mix-ups or assumptions as we're strangers to each other. If you hurt Hal or know who did and withhold that information from me, I will find you in your moment of greatest safety, when all in the world feels right, and I will cut you to pieces with the dullest blade I can find, and when I'm done with you, I'll find Shawn and Vern and burn them alive. I'll keep going down your family tree until it is nothing but bloody sawdust. Am I clear? Do you understand me?"

He's a psychopath, thought Terrance.

"Good thing I don't know shit about crazy old Hal disap—"

Pain rippled up his stomach and Terrance couldn't complete his sentence. The soldier had hit him in the stomach so hard and fast that Terrance never even saw his fist. Terrance bent forward and the soldier grabbed him by the shoulder with a crushing grip.

"Consider that a down payment."

"For what?" asked Terrance, struggling to regain his breath.

"For being an asshole," said the soldier, who then shoved him down the street towards his car.

Rage mixed with bile as Terrance did all he could to fight the urge to get his shotgun from the house and shoot the soldier then and there. Hate was too kind a word for the emotion coursing through his veins, but Terrance had a deadline and more gear to gather, and with no distribution channel, he needed Stanton's money to keep things afloat.

He kept walking and swallowed his pride.

Sherman watched Terrance wobble down the street towards his rusted sedan weighted down with so much gear the leaf springs might warp. He didn't like Terrance, but the feeling was obviously mutual. Guys like that, with a chip on their shoulder and something to prove, always bothered Sherman. They were arrogant and he didn't abide arrogance.

"And you believe him?" he asked Ramona.

"I do, and you didn't have to punch him like that. Terrance is a hot-headed idiot, but he's still my brother."

"Sorry," said Sherman.

"You don't look sorry."

"Fine, I'm not sorry. Your brother is a—"

"A jerk, I know," said Ramona. "What did you tell him?"

"I politely explained that I will not tolerate lies about Hal and that should he come across any information regarding Hal's whereabouts, to contact me immediately."

Ramona tilted her head and gazed hard at Sherman. "I'm guessing you didn't use those exact words."

"More or less."

"You're a bad liar."

"Not part of the job," he said.

"And what does a captain do in the army?"

"Depends on the captain," said Sherman. "This one is standing in the rain in a strange Oregon town."

Ramona motioned towards the SUV and opened the back to help Gloria up. Sherman did the lifting, wet fur and all. With the engine on, windows up, and heat blasting, they moved off into the storm.

"Where to?" she asked.

"Hal's house," said Sherman. "On the off chance he really did just get lost."

Ramona frowned but she clearly had not given up hope. She had an expression that said *hope to the bitter end*.

"You didn't answer my question about what you do in the army."

"Have you heard of Seal Team Six?"

"Yeah, they killed Bin Laden."

"Like that but without all the swimming."

"Oh," said Ramona as if suddenly connecting all the dots.

Chapter Fourteen

By the time Sherman, Ramona, and Gloria arrived at Hal's cottage, they had all warmed up but not dried out. The humidity prevented that even with the heat on full blast. Slicing off the water, the chilling wind picked up pace, swaying the tall pines and shrubby junipers. If not for Hal's sudden disappearance, Sherman could not have been happier. He loved a good storm.

They parked in the driveway and Sherman lifted Gloria to the ground. She snorted happily and headed towards the front door.

"You really shouldn't leave the door open like that," said Ramona. "Things will warp with all the moisture."

Sherman looked at the front door, slightly ajar, and searched his memory for when they'd left. He concluded that he had closed it.

"I didn't leave it open," he announced.

"Hal?" yelled Ramona, sounding hopeful.

Sherman pushed the door open with the toe of his boot.

"Hal!" he called out as the door swung open.

Not Hal, he thought.

The inside of the cottage was an absolute mess. Stuff cluttered the floor, covering every inch that Sherman could see from the doorway. The contents of drawers, cabinets, and bookshelves lay on the polished wood. Not a random break-in but a thorough search. A professional job, no doubt about it.

"What the hell," said Ramona over Sherman's shoulder.

"Stay here," he said.

She didn't protest and Sherman stepped into the chaos. He checked the living and dining areas with a single glance and cleared the kitchen with one step to his right. The cottage layout allowed for few places to hide. All that remained was the bathroom and Hal's bedroom.

Sherman stepped gingerly over books and papers, pictures and knickknacks. All the warning bells and deeply buried instincts clanged and thrummed.

"Frank, be careful," Ramona called from the doorway.

Sherman waved her off without looking back. His eyes soaked in everything. The books on the ground. The over-turned drawers and slashed paintings. They settled upon a series of faint outlines on the polished wood floor.

Footprints. Mostly dry, but still visible, as if having dried for some time but not completely.

Sherman scanned the bathroom and into the bedroom. The mess continued but whoever had made it had left. Sherman was certain.

"All clear," he shouted out of habit.

Ramona appeared with Gloria moments later.

"What the hell is going on?" she asked.

"I'm not sure," answered Sherman. "But I don't like anything about it."

They stood in Hal's bedroom in a methodically

created chaos created by professional hands bent on finding a very specific item. Whoever searched the house knew what they were looking for and took the time to do the job properly. Everything but the sticky notes cluttered the floor.

"This is messed up," said Ramona as Gloria whined.

Sherman nodded in agreement, but his attention gravitated towards a gap in the sticky note line of forgetfulness. The missing square came from a group of Hal's thoughts somewhere between coherence and insanity. The notes around it suggested a man consumed by the past and the unseen machinations of foreign governments and agencies called by their acronyms.

Leaning in, Sherman examined the area around the gap. Some of the notes had dates and places. Events that Sherman knew to be true. Others had questions or names.

Ramona leaned in too and asked, "Is he crazy?"

"Maybe," said Sherman and pointed to the empty square. "But someone thought this one was worth taking."

"Do you know what it said?"

"Not a clue, but this section is not too far from the truth —a bit far-flung but bordering on reasonable. Hal was working something out here, something he couldn't remember."

"Is that good or bad?" she asked.

"I'd say bad. Whoever tossed this place were professionals. They searched everything and everywhere."

"Great," said Ramona sarcastically, then tapped her chin in thought. "Could this be the FBI or something? Maybe they arrested Hal and came back to search the house."

Sherman looked around the house. The search was thorough enough to be the FBI. They even slashed the couch cushions, but there was no police tape or agent out front to ward off nosey neighbors.

"No, they would have sealed off the place," Sherman answered. "Whoever did this isn't building a criminal case against Hal. Maybe the CIA."

"Wait a sec… why would anyone, let alone the CIA, ransack Hal Cooper's house?"

"Hal and my father did some heavy hitting for them back in the day," answered Sherman, which was more than he should have said and about all that he knew.

A spark of concern kindled in Ramona's eyes as she watched Sherman. Her head tilted to one side, and she asked, "Is that the sort of thing a captain in the army might do?"

Sherman said nothing, which was a *yes* to Ramona.

"I knew it."

"Knew what?" he asked.

Ramona looked ready to burst with information, but she stopped when she saw Sherman's expression. He hadn't said anything, but it was already more than she should know. His identity was not a state secret, but his military history was carefully crafted and highly classified.

"That you… like coffee."

Sherman took out his phone and took pictures of all the sticky notes in the area for future reference.

"When do we call the cops?" he asked.

"We don't. No corpse—"

"No cops," said Sherman, finishing the phrase he'd already heard.

"Exactly. Some customs don't go away."

"Which makes that dark hole convenient for keeping the authorities out of town. Is that a well-known spot?"

Ramona nodded. "Not a secret."

"And you don't get many outsiders?"

"Not many that stay."

"It's not much of a leap to say—"

"Someone local did this," she interjected.

"Yeah, or someone with local help. Insider knowledge or a fixer of sorts."

Ramona said nothing but she had a faraway look of concentration.

"Any suspects spring to mind?" asked Sherman.

"No," she said, but the way she said it made Sherman think no did not mean no.

"But?"

"But we had a few new arrivals in the last year or so, which is about when Hal started losing his marbles. Otherwise, it is someone who's known him for the last fifteen years since he bought this place."

Sherman liked her reasoning. The sticky notes on the wall had dates from before Hal moved to Hilt Bay and locations ranging from Burma to Budapest. He doubted someone living in town for so long would suddenly kill Hal and search his house.

"Okay, who moved here recently?"

"Doc Calvert, some guy with the last name Mendoza, and Karl Scholtz."

"I'm guessing not the doctor," said Sherman. "He had ample opportunity with Hal and all his medical appointments."

"I agree. He's running from some serious trouble back east. Not like he moved out here for Hal."

"Tell me about Scholtz."

"Ah," said Ramona. "Scholtz—" she began but stopped when Gloria barked loudly.

Sherman whirled around and glanced out of the

bedroom towards the open front door. For the briefest of moments, he saw a silhouette slide by in the mist. A fuzzy fringe of black there and gone in an instant.

"Shit," he muttered and went to check the kitchen window to no avail.

"What is it?" asked Ramona, tension in her voice.

"I saw someone," said Sherman.

"Who?"

"Don't know. Someone in black, I think. It happened too quick to get a good look. They disappeared into this damn fog."

"I hate to admit this, but I don't think Hal is coming back. Maybe we should leave too," said Ramona.

"You're right, but I need to check one more thing. Does Hal have a storage shed out back?"

"A little tool shed."

"Come on," said Sherman more to Gloria than Ramona, who was too spooked to stay inside alone.

Dense curtains of gray hung over the town and Sherman could see a dozen feet but no more, which meant the stranger could be anywhere around and he wouldn't know until they bumped into each other. Sherman's head swiveled rapidly as they walked around Hal's house to a small shed with identical cedar siding. The structure leaned a bit to one side and looked older than the house. There was no lock on the wood doors and Sherman opened them quickly.

The shed, like the house, edged towards clutter. None of the tools hung on the pegs so carefully laid out for them, but it remained unsearched.

"What are you looking for?" Ramona hissed.

"I'll let you know when I find it. Keep an eye out for trouble."

"Frank, I don't like this."

Neither did Sherman. Nothing about Hilt Bay or Hal's disappearance made sense to him. He wasn't a detective by training or inclination. He was a soldier. A follower of orders. But he was observant enough to know when things were not as they seemed, and Hilt Bay set off all his internal alarm bells.

"Just watch from the door, I'm almost done," he said, sorting through toolboxes.

His search ended with a large, scuffed steel toolbox with hints of rust older than him. He opened, confirmed, then closed the top and grabbed the heavy item.

"Got it. We can go."

"Got what?"

"A memento," said Sherman, motioning towards the SUV.

Ramona frowned but followed with Gloria at her heels.

"Is there a motel in town?" asked Sherman. "I need a new place to stay."

"No, you're staying with me," said Ramona, then started up the Toyota.

Chapter Fifteen

Ramona Wilder's house was also small with cedar siding and white trim, but further from the sea. She lived in town, if such a thing existed. In practicality, she lived adjacent to the T-junction, up a small dirt drive that forked off in several directions to other similar looking homes.

Shrubby evergreens served as a fence along the driveway, and she swerved around gnarled branches destined to scratch any vehicle wider than the SUV.

"I apologize in advance," she said as they parked. "The place is messy. I'd like to think I would clean for guests, but even if I knew someone was coming, I'd find some excuse not to."

Sherman had slept in foxholes that smelled of piss and shit. A dirty house did not bother him.

"Consider yourself forgiven in advance," he said.

They helped Gloria down and Sherman carried his pack and newly acquired toolbox up the front steps lined with potted plants that he could not name and through the front door.

Messiness was relative and Ramona's version did not rise very high in Sherman's book. Modestly messy, at best. A few random articles of clothing lay on the dark wood floors and a few dishes covered the small kitchen counter, but the place felt warm and lived in. The floors and fixtures didn't have as much polish or brass as Hal's, but they shone, nonetheless. More plants dangled from the ceiling like clouds of green below a white sky.

Pale light filtered through the fog and Sherman knew sunset would soon follow. He set his things down in the corner alcove of the dining area while Ramona found an old blanket for Gloria to lay on. The hound circled three times and settled down with a heavy sigh.

"She misses him," said Ramona.

Sherman nodded and took a seat on a high-back dining chair.

"And you've known Hal since childhood?" she asked.

"Sort of," said Sherman.

Ramona sat down across from him and tilted her head, waiting for more information.

"He and my father were close. As close as you can get. Hal was the spotter. My father was the sniper. He spent more time with my dad than my mom ever did."

"That sounds like a tight bond."

"For them, yes. My mom and I never cracked that code. Uncle Hal, I called him growing up, but I never knew the man. Not really."

"I imagine there were lots of things he couldn't tell you."

Sherman nodded. "Secrets galore and all the gory details they kept buried down deep. The truly terrible and atrocious stuff they did for the greater good."

"And what family do you hide your secrets from?" she asked, then frowned as if she'd overstepped.

Sherman gave her a smile. "It's fine. I don't have any family, except for my mom, and her dementia is so bad that she doesn't know my name."

"Sorry," said Ramona and it felt like she meant it.

"She's living a decent life, so I wouldn't feel too bad for her. Every morning, she finds out there is an ocean view from her house for the first time. Gushes how amazing it is whenever I visit and the day after and the day after."

"Got it," answered Ramona, who was deceptively easy to talk to. A trait Sherman reminded himself to be careful around.

"What about you?" he asked.

"What about me… well, I left town, got married, built a life, lost my husband, and moved back home. That covers most of it."

"Why come home?"

"Jack died and I had a choice. Stay with his truly awful family or come back home. It was not an easy choice, let me tell you. Which says something about this place."

"Fair enough," said Sherman, who couldn't leave home fast enough when he was a teenager and didn't have a home to go back to anymore.

In many regards, Sherman was stateless. He owned no home, had no permanent address, and went wherever the army sent him. A well-armed vagabond.

"Are you going to tell me what's in the box?" asked Ramona, clearly glad to change the subject.

The dull steel toolbox sat in the corner next to Sherman's bag.

"You might not like the contents," said Sherman.

"Then why did you bring it?"

"You might want the contents."

"Frank, please open the box. A girl can only handle so much mystery in one day."

Sherman placed the toolbox on the dining table and opened it. The top swung completely open, revealing a small tray designed for drill bits and such, but filled with military medals, ribbons, and commendations.

"Wow," exclaimed Ramona. "I had no idea Hal was a damn war hero."

"I don't think he wanted anyone to know. That's why he moved here."

"And it worked," she added.

"Until today," said Sherman.

"What else?"

Sherman picked up the tray of personal history and set it down on the table. Underneath was something bulky wrapped in layers of oil cloth. He took the item out and placed it next to the tray with a metallic thump.

"That's a gun," said Ramona, staring at the bulky oil cloth.

"Not just any gun," said Sherman, unfolding the cloth to reveal a black Colt 1911 pistol. "They gave my father a matching one when Hal retired."

"What did they give your dad when he retired?"

"He never did. Died of a heart attack behind a desk. The man couldn't handle sitting still."

"Oh," said Ramona. "Were you worried about me and the gun?"

Sherman nodded and Ramona laughed.

"It's obvious Hal did not tell you about my father."

"Tom, right?"

"The original Wildman," she said.

Sherman raised an eyebrow in confusion.

"Terrance got the nickname *Wildman* in high school for all the stupid crap he and his friends did. But the real wild one is my father. Now he is an intimidating guy."

"So… the gun doesn't bother you?"

"Do you know how to use it?"

Sherman nodded.

Ten-thousand times over, he thought.

"Then I'm better off than my childhood with shotguns in closets and pistols taped under dining tables."

Sherman raised both eyebrows. He wanted to hear more but Ramona frowned at her own admission.

"I should tell you about Mendoza and Scholtz," said Ramona.

"You're evading, but go on," he added and began to disassemble and clean the Colt.

Ramona hesitated then plowed on. "Mendoza moved into Ms. Bleeker's guest house about three months ago. She says that he mostly keeps to himself. Helps her out with the magic mushrooms and odd construction jobs like fixing fences or installing new shingles."

"How old is he?" asked Sherman, already reassembling the pistol. It didn't need much cleaning.

"Late twenties or early thirties, I guess."

"Not him."

"Why not?" asked Ramona.

"Too young and wrong continent. Hal retired before that guy could drive, plus I never knew my father to speak a lick of Spanish and he learned something wherever he went. Unless I don't know."

"What about what you don't know?"

"There are two kinds," explained Sherman. "The unknown I know about and the unknown unknown. Mendoza is the former. I know I don't know his story, which, in a way, I do. Fleeing violence, looking for a better life, maybe a smatter of drugs, maybe not. The details matter less."

"Are we skipping him?"

"For now. Tell me about Scholtz."

"Tall, elderly, pale, and German are the words that come to mind. I only met him once when he came into the café."

"What did he order?" asked Sherman, thinking back to his breakfast with Hal.

"A red plate."

"That says something about the guy."

"A lot of locals order the red plate special," said Ramona. "Hilt Bay has a long Russian heritage."

"Is he German or East German?"

"Is there a difference anymore?" she asked.

"There was when Hal was an active Marine."

"The wall came down in 1989. That is a long time to hold a grudge."

Sherman finished assembling the Colt and examined the ammunition, which was not old. The gun hadn't been dirty either, but Sherman wasn't a man to leave things to chance. He also wasn't the kind of soldier to use another's gun, but circumstances were unavoidable, and Hal used to keep things in working order.

"The dates on the sticky notes were all in the early nineties. Assuming the missing note relates to those dates, then whatever is going on happened a long time ago. Which makes sense because Hal and my father were active back then."

"Actively what?"

"Creating grudges that last a lifetime," said Sherman.

"I see."

"Where does Scholtz live?"

"The southern edge of town. He bought one of the fringe cabins on the rocks facing the ocean."

"We should visit," said Sherman.

"In weather like this, you'll have to stand on the porch to see the place and it doesn't have a porch."

"I just want a few words with the man."

"Polite words?" asked Ramona.

"Naturally."

"Because your conversation with Terrance failed to meet the threshold of civility."

Sherman considered his interaction with Terrance Wilder to have been an illustration of restraint. He only hit the guy once.

"You punched him in the gut, remember?"

"I recall," said Sherman.

"I can't have you walking around hitting every jerk in town. Your knuckles would bleed, and people would notice, and I'd be looking for your body in the dark hole."

"Understood," said Sherman.

Ramona eyed him cautiously. "What are you going to politely ask him?"

"Did he kill Hal Cooper and push him into the hole."

"Frank—"

"I'm kidding," said Sherman. "I'm going to extend an invitation to dinner from Hal and judge his reaction."

"Odd choice."

"You told me to be polite."

"Don't you want to know where he lived in Germany?" asked Ramona.

"Yes, but he won't just tell me that. This way, I can judge if he knows Hal and thinks he's still around."

"Fine," said Ramona. "We should go before it gets any darker."

They left Gloria sleeping on the floor and got in Ramona's SUV, slipping past the gnarled driveway branches, down the lane, and across the top of the T-junction. Hilt Bay had no grid of formal layout, but Sherman felt confident he could navigate the northern half of town. The south was brand new to him.

Great white sprays lifted from the ocean to their right as the fog thinned and receded. More business appeared on the left east side of the road. An old tin building called Marine Salvage that looked more like a junk yard than a store. Next door were machine shops and a lumber mill piled high with freshly cut trees.

"Less homes over here," Sherman observed.

"This is the working heart of Hilt Bay. Most of it is not strictly legal, but a lot of the town used to work down here."

"Doing what?"

"Stealing and smuggling," answered Ramona, and Sherman detected a hint of pride in her answer.

They traced an arc towards the southern end of the hilt and the land grew soggier and less desirable.

"Shawn lives over there," said Ramona, pointing across a mosquito laden marsh.

"Looks wet," said Sherman.

"No one else wanted it."

Finally, the road buckled upward over a large cliff of dark brown rock. Trees all but disappeared from the horizon. The few houses dotting the landscape were small and exposed. Sea winds buffeted the Toyota and Sherman got a feeling as if this was the end of the earth.

"We call this the fringe," said Ramona. "The people out

here enjoy their solitude and no one else in town wants to be out here."

"Views aren't bad," said Sherman.

Straight west was the Pacific Ocean and Sherman could imagine on a clear day it would appear endless and all encompassing. Right then, the ocean looked ferocious and threatening as the storm built in fury.

"Yeah, we should hurry," said Ramona. "All that is coming ashore soon."

She parked off the main dirt road next to a short driveway leading to a squat house. A few tenacious shrubs and grasses clung to the windswept soil around the house, but otherwise, it was exposed to the elements. The house itself was a smaller version of Hal's, streamlined to assure no overhanging edges existed for the wind to catch.

Only the faintest amount of pale natural light remained, and the interior was bathed in a soft orange glow. Sherman saw movement between the curtains as they walked up the driveway. The silhouette of a man weaved between the fabric heading towards the door, which opened seconds later.

A slender man in his mid-sixties with closely cropped gray hair and a black wool sweater appeared in the door-way. He had one hand on the doorknob and the other behind his back.

"What do you want?" shouted Scholtz, his German accent still thick and resonate.

"Mr. Scholtz, I'm Ramona Wilder and this is Frank Sherman. We are hoping to have a quick word."

"About what?" he yelled.

"We'd like to extend an invitation to dinner from Hal Cooper," said Sherman.

Chapter Sixteen

The headlights of Terrance's rusted sedan perforated the gloam but did not raise his spirits. Having spent all day gathering supplies for Stanton and running up a mighty tab, he now had to deliver those supplies to the man and his pale blue eyes. Between the stranger and the soldier, Terrance didn't know who he despised or feared more. Both men made his jaws clench and his teeth hurt.

Stanton was already outside when Terrance arrived at the cottage and the headlights seemed to falter as they tried to illuminate his black clothes.

"You're late," said the stranger after Terrance parked and exited.

"You said by tonight and it ain't fully night yet," replied Terrance, already chaffing under the man's gaze.

"Did you secure everything on the list?"

"Yeah, no help from you."

"You did not need my help, Mr. Wilder. That much is clear."

Terrance couldn't tell if that was a compliment or not, but his tone said not.

"Where do you want it?" he asked.

"Not here," said Stanton, who stepped over and got in the passenger seat.

What now, thought Terrance.

"Come along, Mr. Wilder. We are running short on time."

Terrance got in and started the car.

"What now?" he asked.

"I have a list of locations and supplies we need to deposit," said Stanton. He held a long list in his hand.

Terrance sighed. He'd hoped for a pint at Wellerman's before it closed but the list foretold a long, wet night in the storm.

"Alright," he said. "Let's get this done."

———

Sherman felt the weight of the Colt tucked into his pants behind his back like a two-bit street thug. The pistol pulled on his waistline, but Scholtz hadn't moved or said a word, and Sherman was pretty sure the German had his own gun hidden behind his back. Except that weapon was in his hand and didn't need to be withdrawn from a pair of jeans.

"Did you hear me?" asked Sherman, struggling to project over the wind.

"I heard you just fine," said Scholtz. "Now, answer me two things. Who the hell is Hal Cooper and why are you two here inviting me to dinner at his house?"

Not good, thought Sherman.

———

Terrance had a similar thought run through his mind at the northern most point of Hilt Bay, near the rocky outcropping that formed one corner of the eponymous hilt. Wind tore across the rocks and the rain lashed sideways, stinging his face. The storm surge crashed against the beach and rushed inland. This was pint time, not dropping off supplies on distant shores time. Supplies that he didn't understand or care to understand.

"This is a fool's errand," he yelled to Stanton as they covered a large box of ropes and chains with a black plastic tarp.

"It is what I pay you to do," said Stanton.

"I haven't seen any cash," replied Terrance.

"Everything was arranged through your father."

The idea of his father arranging for payment from prison did not instill confidence in Terrance. In fact, the transaction brought up the opposite feeling. A sense of foreboding that perhaps this was not the financial lifeline he imagined. Perhaps there was no money at all.

"How much did you give my father?" he asked.

Stanton placed another large rock on top of the tarp and looked up at him.

"Didn't your father tell you the details of our arrangement?"

Tom had not informed Terrance and his face flushed red with anger and embarrassment.

"He said this was a great boon to the family."

Stanton nodded and went back to lifting rocks as if that answered everything, which only filled Terrance with more doubts and questions. What had his father agreed to? And if there was no money, how would he cover the distribution gap? Without Reggie, none of their product moved, orders went unfulfilled, and the income stream turned to piss.

"We're done here," Stanton yelled.

"We should go back," Terrance yelled back and gestured towards town.

"One more stop," replied Stanton while holding up a finger.

I'll show you a finger, thought Terrance, but he trundled back to the car instead.

Stanton sat down inside and checked his watch.

"We need to meet some acquaintances at the edge of town," he announced.

"Who and why?" asked Terrance. "This storm is about to crash down on us. We should have a pint and wait it out."

"Don't worry, Mr. Wilder. This is the last stop."

Night had completely fallen by the time they reached the edge of town just beyond the wooden Hilt Bay sign. They pulled off on the narrow shoulder as the headlights battled against the rain to illuminate the base of the hill.

"This is the only road in or out, correct?" asked Stanton.

"Yeah," answered Terrance. "Are you worried your acquaintances got lost?"

"No. They'll be here in a few minutes."

Terrance opened his mouth to speak, to ask why that mattered, but closed his lips because he knew Stanton would not give him any truth.

They waited in mutual silence as the rain lashed and the wind howled. Punctually, a pair of headlights twinkled in the distance as the vehicle descended the hill into town.

A large black truck pulled up level on the other side of the road and Stanton got out. The driver rolled down his window a crack and Terrance strained to get a good look but couldn't. Between the tinted windows, the rain, and the dark, he could barely see Stanton.

The strangers spoke for several minutes as Stanton stood in the rain, gesturing and pointing up the road. Terrance couldn't decide what they might be interested in. The only thing along the road were trees.

Finally, the conversation ended, Stanton returned to the car and the truck made a wide U-turn and pulled ahead of them by a hundred feet and stopped at the base of the hill.

"What's going on?" asked Terrance. He didn't like strangers in his town, especially ones behind tinted windows.

"An insurance policy," said Stanton with steam rising off his wet jacket.

"To hell with your riddles," yelled Terrance. "What are they doing here?"

Stanton—stony faced as usual—studied him for a moment before replying.

"My apologies, I shouldn't keep you in the dark," said Stanton in a softer voice. "This is your town, after all. Come on, I'll show you."

Damn right, thought Terrance as they exited his sedan.

Stanton walked a few feet in front of the car, casting their shadows down the road. He pointed to the forest on either side of them. The towering trees loomed over the road like sentinels guarding a precious path.

"Do you see it now?" asked Stanton.

Terrance saw pines and cedars and rain, but not answers. Only more questions. He took a step and tried to imagine what the hell Stanton was going on about.

"No. I don't see shit," he said and turned back to the stranger.

Stanton stood facing him, arm outstretched, and in that briefest of moments, Terrance realized he held a pistol—black and angular.

Instinctively, Terrance swung his left hand toward the gun. There was a flash and a crack that split open the world before his hand connected with cold polymer.

Searing pain consumed his shoulder.

The gun flew sideways in a wide arc. Terrance saw it in slow motion, tumbling through the air, as his brain dumped every resource into survival mode.

He saw the look of surprise and rage on Stanton's face. Only one hope remained.

Run.

Terrance bolted into the forest, thrashing through bushes, legs pumping and shoulders burning bright with pain. Twigs and branches tore at his flesh, but he didn't stop. He couldn't stop.

From the darkness behind, he heard shouts and the thrashing sound of someone chasing. A terrible fear descended upon him, pressing down on his chest and making it hard to breathe. He pushed forward blindly through the bushes until he found the soft bark of a redwood.

Terrance turned for a moment.

A single burst of light split apart the night.

The sound never arrived. Just the impact, pain, and darkness.

Nothing but darkness.

Chapter Seventeen

Stanton saw the bullet hit center mass, saw Terrance crumple and fall backward, but could not find the body. Somehow, the idiot had bungled dying itself and rolled down into a gully thick with undergrowth.

Disgruntled over the untimely demise of his fall guy, Stanton stood for another minute listening for moaning or rustling. All he heard was the rain patter and the wind howl.

"Worthless," he said over Terrance's unseen grave and walked back to the car.

The two men, trusted accomplices from another state, had already unloaded the chainsaws from the truck. They looked to him for the word.

"Leave a chainsaw in the car trunk," he shouted and stuck a thumbs-up in the air, illuminated by the sedan's headlights.

Hilt Bay lay dormant behind them. The locals bunkered down for the night. The storm swallowed most of the noise as the two men, braving the strong winds, started cutting trees to block the road.

One way in. One way out.

Stanton turned to leave as the chainsaws growled with the wind. The walk back would do him good. Blocking the road was only step three in a long plan of action.

Killing Terrance had been further down the list, closer to number nine, but he happily moved it up. Stanton's only lament, more of a minor disappointment, was that he had not seen the look on that stupid Wilder's face when he pulled the trigger for a second time. That, and he wanted to dump his body at sea, but an overgrown ravine would do for now.

Walking out of Scholtz's modest cottage, Sherman didn't know if the man was a Nazi sympathizer or just a dealer in Nazi memorabilia. After they'd established that he had no knowledge of Hal Cooper or desire to accept the fictitious invitation, Scholtz invited them inside. The sheer volume of antiquities surprised Sherman, who had only seen that caliber of World War Two artifacts in a museum. The German even offered them tea served in cups belonging to an SS general. Sherman politely refused.

As they reached Ramona's SUV, she turned to face Sherman and broke out laughing, giddy as a kid watching milk squirt out of a friend's nose.

"That was not what I expected," she said, a little out of breath.

"No, I admit the collection of Field Marshal Göring's jackets took me by surprise."

"I feel a bit icky," said Ramona. "Like you saw your parents having sex."

"I know the feeling," said Sherman.

"What do you make of someone like him?"

"A German selling Nazi stuff," said Sherman.

"As a person," she added.

"A bit off kilter, but stuff doesn't have any inherent power, only what we breathe into it. Besides, I've seen way worse than a dead man's jacket."

"Like what?" asked Ramona, a little absentmindedly as she started the SUV.

"The dead guy," said Sherman.

"Oh, I walked into that one."

"Let's check out Mendoza just to be safe," said Sherman.

"Can it wait?" asked Ramona, pointing to the storm. "We should get back to my place before it gets bad."

Thick drops of rain already slapped against the windshield with percussive force and Sherman wondered what she meant by bad, but he nodded in agreement. The young guy staying with Ms. Bleeker was unlikely to be involved with Hal, but with Scholtz a dead-end, any theory was better than no theory. Otherwise, the whole town was a suspect. Sherman hoped it was an old grudge that caught up to Hal. Something from his past, but maybe it was something from his present. A neighborly slight of sorts, but that didn't explain the professional search of his house.

The SUV stole forward, rocking with the wind, wipers swinging full tilt and failing to keep up with the rain. Sherman was still lost in thought as they rumbled down the road off the rocky heights and past Shawn's swampy trailer.

They were passing the top of the T-junction, almost back to Ramona's house, when an incongruity caught Sherman's attention. Nothing major or significant, but an object out of place like a fork in the bathroom.

"Stop," he said.

Ramona stopped just after the junction. "Did you forget something?"

"Go back to the junction. I saw something."

Ramona made a U-turn and went back. They both peered east down the sole road in and out of town. Ahead of them, just beyond the edge of town, they saw brake lights glittering in the darkness. A car idled on the side of the road. The headlights were on, and illuminated in that distant cone of yellow were long horizontal objects lying across the road.

Ramona squinted through the rain. "Are those trees?" she asked.

"Is that your brother's car?" added Sherman, noticing the one broken taillight he'd seen earlier when Terrance met them in town.

"Probably," she answered. "But what the hell is he up to?"

"Only one way to find out," said Sherman.

Ramona turned left and headed east past the two blocks of downtown Hilt Bay and the wooden town sign before pulling up behind a rusted sedan. Ramona turned off the engine, leaving the car in front as the sole source of light.

"That is his car," she said.

"Those are definitely trees," added Sherman.

Six or seven trees were clearly visible now. They lay across the road in one thick pile of timber. A complete blockage of the road. No one in and no one out.

"That is a lot of fallen trees," said Ramona. "But the storm is just starting."

Neat and purposeful, thought Sherman.

Nature didn't do neat and purposeful. Nature did wild and majestic, not one thick pile. The alarm bells in Sherman's mind tolled loudly.

"They didn't fall down," said Sherman. "They were cut down."

"Why would anyone cut them down?"

"Maybe your brother knows," said Sherman, trying to stitch together the facts at hand.

One way in and one way out, he thought. *Which direction are they blocking? The escape or the rescue?*

"I think I see him," said Ramona, pointing at a shadowy figure approaching through the trees.

Sherman opened the SUV door with the Colt already in his hand. The figure kept coming, sliding between pine trees, hand raised high against the glare of headlights.

"Terrance!" shouted Ramona in a stern older sister tone.

The figure stopped, dropped a chainsaw from one hand, and pulled a shiny pistol out from under their jacket.

"Get down," ordered Sherman.

The guy, who was visibly not Terrance, fired in their direction. Blinded and probably confused, the shooter hit the rusted sedan. The rain accentuated a thick stream of pops and sparks. Glass crunched and metal screeched.

Sherman fired back over the SUV door. Two shots from thirty feet away. Both hit center mass. Nothing fancy. No frills.

The guy toppled backward, tilting and twisting on the way down.

A stream of expletives erupted from Ramona.

"Stay down," Sherman ordered.

The road had been clear of trees when they went to Scholtz's house, which meant all the work was recent and too much for one person with a chainsaw.

Two or more, thought Sherman as he advanced the thirty feet to the contorted body.

Sherman took a good look at the guy on the ground. Late twenties, square jaw, close cropped hair, and calloused hands worn hard by work. A spiderweb tattoo crept up his neck. A stereotype for a certain type of American male.

Without another thought, Sherman put a bullet in the stranger's temple. No remorse or hesitation. No half-measures. Sherman did not take chances with unseen vests or still breathing targets. He played to survive no matter the cost.

He swapped the half-empty magazine for a fresh one in his jacket pocket and moved forward. The light was at his back, which helped to spot targets but made a silhouette out of him and almost all target shooting was at silhouettes.

Edging right into the trees helped break up his outline and Sherman slowed his pace. He didn't want to miss anything or anyone. Illuminated by the headlights, the rain came down so hard, it created a solid visual wall.

Sherman moved from tree to tree in short, practiced steps with his pistol up and ready to engage. Tree to tree until there were only stumps left and the shooting began.

He saw the shadows shift and stepped back moments before a staccato burst of gunfire competed with the storm for the loudest noise in the forest.

Snaps and pops filled the rain air. Peeking out from behind a pine, Sherman spotted the second shooter further down the road next to a truck he hadn't noticed earlier.

The second shooter fired again and again, moving back towards the truck with each burst of what Sherman's mind knew was a rifle caliber. He couldn't be sure in the storm, but it sounded like a .223 variant and his ears were usually right. They'd heard enough gunfire over the years to pick out the different calibers used by warring parties across the globe.

He leaned out between bursts and returned fire. Three quick trigger pulls at a distant smudge. A howl of pain came back as at least one bullet found flesh.

A moment later, the truck started up and raced forward. Sherman fired the rest of the magazine at the quickly disappearing vehicle and managed to hit metal and glass but not the driver.

The taillights disappeared up the hill and Sherman swapped back to his half-empty magazine, hoping there were only two guys cutting down trees.

By the time he got back near the SUV, Ramona already stood over the mess he'd made. Her slim figure stood out in relief against the lights and rain slipped off her jacket in tiny rivers. Sherman expected a look of disgust or horror or pity. Instead, she appeared angry and worried.

"Who is… was that?" she said.

Sherman stuck the Colt back in his pants and bent down to search the body. He found a wallet, a broken cell phone, pocket litter, two extra magazines and the shiny pistol.

He flipped open the wallet. It was thick and well-worn with creases from too much stuff.

"Steve Howard. Idaho license and address," said Sherman.

The phone had a bullet-sized hunk missing. Sherman found it in the breast pocket of Steve's jacket and whatever information it once contained was now embedded in his body. Sherman tossed the phone aside.

"Where is Terrance?" asked Ramona.

Sherman glanced around as water trickled into his hood. The question explained Ramona's look of worry and anger. Either Terrance was involved with gun totting, tree cutting, thugs from Idaho or he'd run into them as well.

He took the shiny pistol—a cheap 9mm Beretta clone—and inserted a fresh magazine. He offered it up to Ramona first.

"I'm guessing you know how to use it."

Ramona looked for a moment then took the gun and checked the chamber.

Well, enough, thought Sherman.

"Let's check Terrance's car," said Sherman, who decided the Colt was better off in his hand.

The rusted sedan was off and the engine cooling but still warm. Sherman looked inside and found two wet seats but saw none of the gear he'd seen earlier. Opening the trunk revealed a spare tire and random bits of trash.

"What the hell is going on?" said Ramona, her voice rising in frustration and maybe fear.

"They're not long gone," said Sherman.

"As in plural?"

"Both front seats are soaked. They were probably in and out of the storm. Maybe from unloading all the crap he had packed in here."

"Maybe Vern or Shawn," she added.

Not Shawn, thought Sherman, remembering the previous day's encounter that left the man out cold on the barroom floor.

"This is all sorts of wrong," said Ramona.

Sherman turned his attention away from the car and toward the surrounding forest. If Terrance was involved, he couldn't be too far away, and Sherman hoped he wasn't involved. He had just armed Terrance's sister and did not want to make that kind of choice if Terrance emerged from a bush armed and angry. She may have not liked her brother, but surely family bonds would call for retribution if Sherman shot him.

The mud in front of the sedan had numerous footprints, some of which were Sherman's. Understanding what happened was all but impossible and Sherman switched to looking for outliers.

He quickly spotted two sets of imprints leading into the forest. They weren't much more than oblong puddles now with all the rain, but the other tracks went east and west along the road. These were the only ones that went south.

"Do you have a flashlight in your SUV?" asked Sherman.

Ramona left and returned with a long, thick, heavy Maglite from the nineties. It weighed more than two Colts and Sherman raised an eyebrow in surprise.

"For personal protection," she said and shrugged.

"Or baseball," he added and turned back to the muddy tracks.

Following the imprints into the surrounding forest did not require much skill or effort for the first few yards. The large gouges were easy enough to see and Sherman flicked the flashlight between the tracks and the trees. Soon enough, the path obscured. Scraggy bushes blocked the way, and the mud gave way to a thick floor of pine needles that didn't register footprints so vividly.

"Where now?" asked Ramona. Her shoulders were hunched against the cold, and she grimaced.

Left was the obvious choice with less bushes and a clearer path, but Sherman wasn't sure. The steps thus far went straight with no deviation or meandering, as if someone ran hard in one direction and only one direction. Sherman was no expert, but his gut said straight.

He pushed through the bushes, which scratched against his jacket, followed by Ramona who cursed at the undergrowth. On the other side, they were rewarded with slim imprints in the soil. Sherman pointed his flashlight up and found another wall of undergrowth and young trees. The tracks kept going straight.

"Again?" asked Ramona.

"Afraid so," said Sherman and plowed on.

They wormed through thickets of prickly scrub. First one, then two. Each time, Sherman felt sure the tracks went straight on like an injured animal running hard with no other thought but survival.

Finally, they broke into an opening under a towering redwood swaying in the wind like a metronome. Sherman swung the beam of light in front of them only to find it disappeared downward. He stuck out an arm and made sure Ramona stopped.

"Whoa," she said.

The ravine below sloped steeply down fifteen feet into a tangle of green bushes and fallen trees. Dead branches stuck up at odd angles like a collection of pre-historic bones.

Sherman scanned the bushes, but the rain ate up the light. He pointed the beam closer and found deep divots in the soft dirt on the ravine slope as if a boulder had tumbled down. Or maybe a person.

"We're going down," said Sherman.

Ramona looked down and bit her lip anxiously. "Not my favorite idea, but okay."

Sherman wasted no time and jumped down onto the bare dirt slope, which promptly disintegrated under his boots as he slid all the way to the bottom. Not only had the rain soaked through every layer of clothing, but now he was also covered in mud along his backside. At least he'd kept the pistol out of the muck.

Seconds later, Ramona arrived at the bottom of the

ravine in a similar state of disorder, but with a childlike grin on her face.

"We used to do that as kids," she said with a little laugh that quickly faded in the cold and wet night. "Now what?"

Sherman hadn't thought that far ahead. The tracks dipped down and he began looking for the next clue. Little time passed before his boot found it.

A soft something underfoot. Soft, yet solid.

Sherman shone the flashlight down and saw what his gut already knew.

He was standing on a body.

Chapter Eighteen

The flashlight beam revealed Terrance Wilder belly-down in mud and covered by thick layers of gooseberry leaves.

Dead, thought Sherman.

Ramona let out a muffled wail of anger or despair.

Sherman handed the flashlight to her, bent down, and rolled Terrance over. His hand came back bloody, and Sherman felt for a pulse.

"Is he—"

"He's still breathing," said Sherman, pulling open Terrance's coat.

Two entry wounds on his front still oozed blood. One was just under his scapula near the left shoulder. The second was above and to the right of his heart. Statistically, Terrance should have died long before they found him, but Sherman knew the human body could take a good deal of trauma and, with luck, survive. Terrance, it seemed, had a significant amount of luck—most of it bad, but some good.

"We need to get him out of here," said Sherman, looking around for an easier way back up.

"Over there," said Ramona, pointing the flashlight at a less steep edge of the gulley partially hidden by undergrowth.

Terrance maybe weighed one-hundred and sixty pounds dry, but soaking wet and limp, Sherman thought it double. With Ramona's help, he got the younger Wilder over his shoulder in a fireman's carry and struggled over to the easier way out, which was not easy. Sherman kept slipping as his boots cleaved off sections of dirt, leaving deep muddy gouges.

"No way," said Sherman, panting from the effort.

He set Terrance down on the slope to catch his breath.

"Take one arm, I'll take the other and maybe we can pull him up as we go," said Sherman.

Ramona's expression said she would try anything, so they climbed and pulled Terrance up behind them like a wet sack of rice. They crested the lip of the ravine onto flat ground and fell backward from the effort.

After another minute to catch their breath, they repeated the fireman's carry back to the SUV with Ramona on point with the flashlight in one hand and a dead man's shiny pistol in the other. Sherman slid Terrance into the back of the Toyota as Ramona rushed to start the engine. Great sprays of mud flew up from the tires as she turned around and raced the short distance to Doc Calvert's office. The drive took less than thirty seconds.

The SUV came to a sudden, juddering halt and Ramona jumped out, running over to the building to ring the bell. The lights above the office were still on and the hour not so late.

Sherman took his time sliding Terrance out and onto his shoulder for the third and, hopefully, final time. The guy was heavy and bleeding all over Sherman.

The office door opened, and Doc Calvert took one long look at them.

"Oh," he said and ushered them through the waiting area, past the dentist chair, and into the room with the ubiquitous bed.

Calvert tossed a sterile sheet over the surface and had Sherman set Terrance down on top. In the bright lights, Terrance looked even worse than Sherman initially thought.

Doc Calvert worked quickly and precisely to cut away his patient's coat, shirt, and pants, leaving the dirty clothes in a heap on the floor. He checked for exit wounds and frowned, finding none.

"This is going to get messy, and I need an extra set of hands," said Calvert, looking at Sherman. "I'm guessing you've seen this before."

"I have."

"Good. The sink is over there, and gloves are on the counter."

Sherman peeled off his rain jacket and long sleeve layer, rinsed his arms, and donned a pair of surgical gloves. Unable to sit still, Ramona picked up all her brother's dirty clothes and placed them in a trash bag. Then she stood nearby and watched as Doc Calvert did his best to save Terrance.

Judging by his skill and unflappability, Sherman guessed Calvert had a good deal of trauma experience. He didn't strike Sherman as a military man, but maybe someone from a big city hospital.

It took over an hour for Calvert to extract the bullets, or most of them, and stop what internal bleeding he could find. The tedious work wore on Sherman, memories of similarly unpleasant days surfaced. He'd seen the insides of too many friends to count. Some lived, many died, and those images never left him.

One incident bobbed to the top and wouldn't leave—a terribly long night spent on the Syrian border. Sherman's team dropped in behind an ISIS outpost with some Air Force special ops guys. The mission was straightforward. Watch the outpost and call in the bombs. Like all good plans, it went to hell almost as soon as their boots hit dirt. One of the Air Force guys fell down a latrine hole and came out with a twisted ankle, smelling like a pig. They set up an overwatch and dropped some awfully large ordnance on unsuspecting jihadists, but the bombs didn't kill everyone. At exfil time, one of Sherman's guys took a round through the gut. They holed up at the hut while hellfire rained down from every available airborne asset. The guy who fell and smelled like a pig was a PJ and a damn fine battlefield medic. He and Sherman spent the night keeping his man alive long enough for the Blackhawks to land. The guy lived, but Sherman's combined memory of blood and shit never left.

Ramona brought out a large pot of coffee as Calvert and Sherman sat down in the waiting area, already exhausted.

"He needs a real hospital. Can I call for an ambulance?" asked the doctor.

"You can but the road is blocked by a small forest of downed trees," Sherman answered.

"Helicopter," suggested Calvert.

"Not in this storm," said Ramona. "Ain't nothing landing for another twenty-four hours."

Calvert ran his hands through his thinning hair and gazed down at the floor.

"You did good, Doc," said Sherman. "Far better than most, and I've seen a lot of carnage."

"Thanks, I guess, but Terrance needs more than I have."

"Do what you can," said Sherman.

Calvert sipped a cup of coffee and gave an uncertain frown. "I make it my business not to ask... but what happened?"

"We're not sure," said Ramona.

Sherman was blunter. "He got shot."

"In town?" asked Calvert.

"Not five hundred yards up the road," said Sherman. "Either right before or right after two guys with chainsaws cut down a small forest to block the road."

"Why would they block the road?" asked Calvert.

Sherman noted the doctor didn't ask why Terrance got shot as if that was an occupational hazard and needed no explanation.

"Good question," said Ramona.

"Only one reason to block the road," said Sherman. "To stop our rescue or block our exit. Maybe both."

"That's two reasons," said Calvert.

"Interrelated reasons," said Sherman.

"We're stuck then."

"For the time being."

"And how is Terrance involved?"

"No idea," said Ramona.

Sherman shrugged but assumed Terrance was the type of guy who might get shot for any number of reasons. "Between Terrance and Hal, something foul is in the air."

Calvert nodded. "When you said Hal disappeared, I thought you meant he wandered off."

"Down a deep, dark hole in the cliff. At least, I think so.

It might have stayed just a hunch until someone trashed Hal's house searching for something while I was out."

"That's terrible," said Calvert.

"I think Hal is the least of our worries at the moment," Sherman replied.

"You mean the guys shooting at us," said Ramona with a sour tone.

"Yeah, them."

Ramona eyed Sherman. "You seem remarkably calm after shooting—"

Calvert held up his hand for her not to say any more details. Details required answers from cops when they came knocking, and Calvert did not seem the type to want to answer questions from the police.

"After what happened out there," Ramona finished.

"Part of the job," said Sherman.

Ramona gave him a suspicious look but took a sip of coffee and didn't reply.

"Look, I realize I'm the newcomer in town and you don't know me, but I have a history in matters such as this."

"A long, violent history," Ramona added.

Sherman was not ashamed of his past and saw the comment as a restatement of fact.

"Don't we all," said Calvert quietly, but not to himself.

Sherman continued, "And during that time, I've developed a certain skillset that will be useful."

Ramona and Calvert nodded at the obvious.

"Glad we agree. Here is the real problem. The guys cutting the trees down are not the primary threat. They parked on the far side. Their job was to block the road and had no problem leaving when things got real. Which means the threat—"

"Is still in town," Ramona interjected.

"That is my assessment," said Sherman.

Calvert, who looked like he knew a thing or two about such situations, spoke up. "If the threat is in town, shouldn't we warn people?"

"Of what?" asked Ramona. "Wild speculation and hearsay. We don't know why those men shot Terrance."

"Which leads to my final point," said Sherman. "They didn't shoot Terrance."

"How do you know?" asked Ramona.

"The gun I gave you, the one I took off the thug from Idaho, is a 9mm. The slugs our doctor here dug out of Terrance were bigger than that but still not the rifle rounds the other shooter used. Neither of them shot Terrance. The threat is still in town, which opens the door on another issue."

"Another issue?" Ramona asked, rankled by the number of problems.

"Your brother might be a witness and a loose end."

Ramona sipped her coffee, processing the point. Such a theory might bring people to the breaking point of hopelessness or fear, but not Ramona Wilder. A fact that Sherman admired more and more. She was flexible and not easily spooked despite all that she'd experienced.

"I'll call Vern, see if he can come over and watch the place, assuming you're still alright with keeping Terrance here, Doc."

Doc Calvert looked up from his coffee a bit surprised by the question. "Of course he can stay. It would go against my oath to kick him out."

"I'm more worried about your life," said Sherman.

"I have a solid security system that should give us fair warning if anyone comes looking for young Terrance."

"Are you okay if Vern stays too?"

"Whatever you think is best," said Calvert.

Ramona looked to Sherman. He didn't see Vern as anything more than a bullet sponge, but help was help and he didn't object.

She picked up her phone and dialed.

"Vern, it's Ramona. … No, I don't want to join you for a pint. Where are you? … Of course. How drunk are you?"

Ramona sighed and shook her head.

"What about Shawn? … Okay, forget I called."

She hung up.

"Vern is six pints deep at Wellerman's as we speak. I'm gonna try Shawn. He is still at home."

"Sleeping off a concussion," Sherman added.

"Better than Vern after six pints. It must be karaoke night."

"They have a karaoke machine?" asked Sherman. The pub did not seem the place to encourage singing.

"No, they just declare it after five or so pints and start singing."

"Ah."

Ramona picked up her phone again and called Shawn.

"Hey, are you awake? … Yeah, I bet. About that, I need your help. Grab a shotgun and head over to Doc Calvert's place. Terrance got shot."

She put the phone down.

"He's on his way but let me talk with him first. He's still pissed at you, and now, thanks to me, he's armed."

"Oh," said Sherman.

"I'm going to check on the patient," said Doc Calvert.

"Doctor, what's your professional opinion on moving him to a different location?" asked Sherman.

"Personally, that seems like a good idea. Professionally, I don't recommend it. I can't help if he's not here."

"Understood," said Sherman.

Doc Calvert left Sherman and Ramona in the waiting area.

"I'm sorry I got a little testy earlier. This day…" she said and trailed off.

"I didn't take it personally," said Sherman. "Not exactly how I wanted to spend my vacation either."

"Hilt Bay has always been a rough town, but we stuck together when the bad tide rolled in. This feels so different —frightening, if I am honest. It's about the only time I wish my dad were still here. He'd know what to do."

"What do you think he'd do?"

"Scour the town with pitchforks and torches," said Ramona with a faint smile.

"Solid strategy," said Sherman and smiled back.

"Why did you never visit Hal before?" asked Ramona, switching the conversation away from herself. A fact that Sherman noted.

"He never invited me before. I didn't even know he lived here."

"Would you have come if he had?" asked Ramona, looking like her earlier self with her head tilting quizzically to one side.

"Maybe," said Sherman, which felt like the closest thing to the truth. "I wasn't the biggest fan of my father and Hal got tainted by association."

Ramona raised her coffee mug in mock celebration. "To the shitty dad club."

"Cheers," said Sherman, raising his own mug.

The rumble of a large motor mixed with the storm and Sherman reflexively stood up.

"That's Shawn and his obnoxiously loud truck."

"While you sort things out with him, I'm going to walk

back to your place. I need a few supplies from Hal's toolbox."

"Hurry back and don't forget to feed Gloria," she said and handed him a housekey. "Oh, there's a shortcut—"

"Just past the market," said Sherman.

"How did you know?"

"Part of the job," he answered.

"Check the closet by the front door. My dad keeps some things there."

Sherman nodded at the cryptic suggestion and slipped out the back door.

What things? he thought.

Chapter Nineteen

Stanton stepped inside the vacation house just in time to answer a call without the storm drowning out the sound. He hurriedly slipped off his jacket and boots and made for the table covered in maps.

"This is Stanton," he answered.

"Mr. Stanton, an update, if you will," said the slippery, Eastern European voice.

"The supplies are in place at the specified locations, and any chance of escape is blocked for the night."

"Very well. My men will depart the freighter as it passes your location."

"And they know the sea is very rough?" asked Stanton but regretted it. Never question the client was a basic tenet of his business.

"They are professionals like yourself. Do not forget that."

"Of course. My apologies."

"My men will provide updates once they land. You will be paid upon retrieval of the items."

Stanton expected nothing less. Payment for service rendered always happened after, although he often took a deposit as an assurance of intent.

"And the target?" he asked.

"Their extraction is discretionary," said the man.

"Of course," said Stanton.

"Thank you for your efforts, Mr. Stanton. Goodbye."

The call ended and Stanton stretched his arms and back until they cracked. He took out the Glock and loaded two more .45 caliber bullets into the magazine, replacing those he used on Terrance Wilder.

Pulling off his wet clothes, Stanton turned on the shower. He planned on using this hour to warm up before venturing out again. He set his phone down and jumped under the hot water, letting it run until his skin turned bright red and the storm's chill disappeared.

After toweling off, Stanton saw his phone blink rapidly. Not the burner on reserved for clients, but his normal business phone. He picked it up and typed in his nine-digit password. An encrypted messaging app showed three new messages. He clicked on the icon to read them.

Job is done.

Steve's dead and I'm shot.

Don't contact me again.

Stanton stared for a moment, gathering his thoughts, analyzing the facts and preparing a logical response. His first reaction wasn't logical, it was pure anger and he yelled out loud, cursing the two accomplices from Idaho.

Quieting down, he looked at the texts again.

The first one—the important one—arrived ten minutes before the second. *Job is done.* Stanton expected nothing less. The men were reliable, and the road was blocked. He hadn't lied to his client about that important fact.

The second text had nuance and ambivalence. *Steve's dead and I'm shot.* Stanton assumed certain facts as he read it. Steve must have been shot and killed. His brother wouldn't text such a thing if Steve got smashed by a tree.

The big question was... who shot them? A local perhaps. The town had a rough reputation. Maybe they came along and didn't appreciate ancient timbers downed across the road. The unfortunate outcome of the shooting was not Steve's death—Stanton cared nothing for the man or his brother—but that someone knew the road was blocked. He'd hoped everyone would hunker down in the storm and the blockage would go unnoticed until morning. Still, the brothers cut down a lot of trees. It would take the locals all night to clear the road.

The third and final text arrived four minutes after the second. An emotional but not unreasonable response and Stanton had no interest in contacting him again.

He deleted the texts and the contact, purging them from his electronic record. His earlier anger cooled as he thought through the ramifications of Steve's death. An unfortunate event, yes, but he saw no reason to abort the operation. Not now. Not after so much effort and planning. One more body didn't matter. There'd be more by the end of the night—of that, he was sure.

The porch light twinkled like a crystal chandelier as Sherman approached Ramona's house. He took the shortcut and emerged onto her dirt road with the other similar homes and skirted the gnarled branches guarding the driveway.

Sherman waited in the shadows and watched. If they shot one Wilder, going after another was not a stretch, although he didn't see much overlap between their worlds. One was a café waitress escaping her husband's death and the other a smuggler trying to fill his daddy's shoes, but blood binds and Hilt Bay was a small town. So, Sherman waited and went in the back door.

The key worked and the door opened after a gentle shove. Gloria appeared moments later, tail wagging. Either she knew it was him or she was happy for any human company. Sherman hoped it was the former but couldn't be sure. The only dogs he'd known in recent history wore muzzles and bullet-resistant vests and loved nothing more than jumping through windows and biting jihadists.

He didn't bother changing into dry clothes but grabbed his pack and set it next to the kitchen table with Hal's toolbox on top. Sherman reloaded both magazines from the relatively new box of ammunition, leaving a handful of bullets left. Not enough to reload again but better than throwing rocks. He tossed the box into his pack and looked around.

Gloria sat expectantly in the kitchen.

"Are you hungry?" he asked.

Her tail wagged enthusiastically in response.

"That looks like a yes. Let's see what I can find."

The kitchen cabinets seemed a reasonable starting place and Sherman searched them in quick succession. He found the usual suspects of plates, bowls, glasses, cups, and spices but nothing a dog would eat. The fridge was mostly bare, and he suspected that Ramona ate most of her meals at the café.

A tall, slim cabinet next to the fridge held more options and Sherman realized he should have started there. The canned food selection was not extensive and edged towards green beans and corn, but he found two cans of tuna that looked good enough to feed a dog. Finding a can opener took longer and required the opening of all the drawers.

Gloria whined as he placed a bowl with the tuna in front of her but ate with messy gusto.

Water, he thought and placed a large metal mixing bowl next to the food.

Sherman stood in the kitchen, with all the cabinets and drawers open like a stranger in a new land, overwhelmed by the volume of options. If he ever got a place of his own, the kitchen would be much smaller, like Hal's. Although even the thought of home ownership gave Sherman heartburn. Life after the army was not a topic he cared to dwell on for any amount of time.

The couch held a pile of unfolded but presumably clean clothes and Sherman grabbed a few warmer items for Ramona and added them to his pack.

Remembering her suggestion, Sherman opened the closet by the front door and flipped on the light. A dozen jackets and coats dangled from wire hangers. The floor was equally cluttered with footwear for all seasons and activities. Sherman, by contrast, owned boots, running shoes, and flip-flops—nothing else.

Rummaging through the bottom yielded nothing of interest and he turned towards the top shelf above his head. Sherman couldn't see, but with one touch, he knew what he'd found. A soft-sided gun case slid off the shelf and Sherman placed it on the ground. Judging by the size of the case, he guessed a hunting rifle. Unzipping revealed an unexpected piece of history. A rifle, yes, but not one designed for hunting deer. The wood body of the Russian-made Mosin-Nagant rifle shone warmly in the light. The gun was old and scratched and marred from use, but well-cared for over the years.

Sherman checked the bolt, barrel, and firing pin. Everything appeared oiled and in working order even though the rifle was almost one hundred years old.

He zipped up the bag and found a box of ammunition from the Vietnam War era sitting at the back of the shelf. The casings and seals looked intact, so they went in the pack as well. Two weapons were better than one and good designs never go bad.

Gloria was already back on her bed of blankets and showed no interest in going outside for a potty break. Sherman gave her some affectionate scratches and left out the back door with his backpack on and rifle case in hand.

The rain still came down in thick splotches driven by a hard eastern wind that whipped through the trees. Leaves and twigs zipped down the dirt road with a life of their own and the air smelled briny. On any other night, Sherman would have happily stood in the storm, soaking up the moisture and making amends for all those years in the desert. But not that night.

Sherman cut down the slim path carved by countless feet and emerged next to Berg's Market. He stood in the shadows just beyond the swaying cones of yellow light cast by the streetlights and watched.

To his right, at the end of the T-junction, Wellerman's Pub appeared full and lively. The occasional lyric or line floated on the wind, and he imagined the locals singing away their blues over a pint of dark. It was a nice thought, comforting in its simplicity and camaraderie.

To his left was the doctor's office with Terrance clinging to life, and beyond that, the corpse of Steve Howard, growing colder by the minute. How a few blocks could make such a difference continually baffled Sherman, but such was life. He instinctively understood the twists of fate and luck. He'd seen so much of the good and bad over the years.

He remembered the corporal who crossed the street to kick a soccer ball back to the kids and then vaporized in a cloud of pink and gray from an IED. The sergeant who stopped to tie his boot and dodged a sniper's bullet. Even the time he kicked a rock downhill and set off an anti-personnel mine concealed on the path. There was no rhyme or reason to such occurrences. They existed outside of any rational explanation and that was enough for him.

Satisfied that no one was lurking nearby, Sherman turned left and walked back to Calvert's office. Arriving at the front door, he took a breath and knocked, hoping Ramona had tempered Shawn's anger and he wouldn't catch a stomach full of buckshot on the other side.

Chapter Twenty

Ramona's relieved smile met Sherman at the door, not the business end of Shawn's scattergun. For that, Sherman felt some relief. Although, deep down, he wondered if he should have swung the barstool a little harder. Surely, the world would not miss Shawn Wilder.

"Did you find it okay?" asked Ramona.

"The house or the rifle?" asked Sherman, holding up the case.

Ramona stepped aside to let him in the waiting room.

"I was thinking the house, but I can see my doubt in your abilities was very much misplaced."

"You don't live very far from here."

"Most people still get lost," she said.

I'm not most people, thought Sherman.

"You!" growled Shawn from across the room. Bruises covered most of his face and his chin had doubled in size. "You owe me an apology."

"Shawn—" Ramona began but Sherman cut her off.

"It's okay. I'm sorry, Shawn."

Shawn looked a bit stunned and wobbled on his feet, searching for solid ground. He eyed Sherman warily as if looking for a trap or alternative motive.

"Alright," he finally replied. "I'll give you a pass this time."

I'll hit you harder next time, thought Sherman.

"Stop pissing in the wind, Shawn," said Ramona. "Frank here cleaned the floor with Jack this afternoon."

Shawn's gaze narrowed. "As in your ex-brother-in-law?"

Ramona nodded.

Still unconvinced, Shawn added, "Jack, the undefeated king of the ring?"

Ramona nodded again.

Shawn fell silent for a moment, his head bobbing in thought, then asked, "What the hell were you doing on the other side of the hill?"

"We needed a place to chat without everyone staring at us. Hal Cooper disappeared this morning and Frank thought Terrance dumped him down the Smuggler's Vault."

Shawn started laughing but winced from the bruises. "Why would you ever think Terrance would do such a thing?" he asked Sherman, who had grabbed another cup of coffee.

"They had words. Threats were made," he answered.

Shawn waved this off. "Terrance has words with everyone. Half the town would be down that hole if Terrance acted on impulse. Threats is just Wildman being Wildman."

Sherman felt reasonably sure that was true but reserved the right to change his mind.

"Besides," Shawn continued, "looks like we got bigger fish to fry than crazy old Hal wandering off again. What happened—"

"Wait," said Sherman, cutting him off. "What do you mean *again*?"

"Vern and I found him wandering the far side of the north point one day. We was out fishing and spotted him on this little hidden beach. Hard to get to that beach. Only can at low tide. When we saw him, the tide was up and he was stuck. We gave him a ride back and the man is a verified loon. Talked nonsense the whole way back. Nukes in the desert and two-mile sniper shots. Who says shit like that?"

"Oh," said Sherman. Those were real stories—about the only one of his father's missions he knew to be true. Hal had inadvertently spilled state secrets. "That does sound crazy."

Ramona tilted her head in that curious way but said nothing. The information cast a new light on Hal's condition and his disappearance, but Sherman kept that to himself.

"What's crazy is Terrance getting shot," said Shawn.

Apples and oranges, thought Sherman. They were not comparable facts, but again, he remained quiet. Not his town. Not his people. He just happened to be stuck there too.

"Do you know who did it?" asked Shawn.

Sherman glanced up at Ramona. She had not told Shawn of the night's events or maybe only a sliver while he was gone. Perhaps she had used his absence to smooth things out with Shawn. She nodded for him to answer.

"No, but do you know a Steve Howard? Idaho license and address," said Sherman.

"Never met no Steve Howard from Idaho or otherwise," said Shawn. "But did you just say he didn't shoot Terrance?"

"He did not," said Sherman.

"Who is he then?" asked Shawn.

"Dead," said Sherman.

"What?" asked Shawn.

"He shot first," said Ramona.

"Wait, my head is swimming," Shawn replied. "Start from the beginning, Ramona."

Ramona obliged and explained the circumstances and events that led them to park behind Terrance's car next to a road blocked by felled trees. She walked Shawn through the shooting, although she omitted who pulled the trigger and killed Steve, and the subsequent discovery of Terrance at the bottom of the ravine.

Shawn stood there, shotgun in hand, jaw drooping with wonder like a kid discovering candy stores for the first time.

"Holy mother of the sea," he exclaimed. "If the dead guy didn't shoot Terrance, who did?"

"That's why you're here," she said. "We don't know who they are and if they're still in town, but they might come back and try to finish the job."

Shawn shook his head vehemently. "That ain't happening. No one comes into our town and hurts our family."

The statement was forceful, naive, and utterly useless. Sherman could have killed them all a dozen times over without being seen, but at least Shawn looked motivated and awake. How long that would last was unclear, but Sherman took the good news in stride with the bad.

Doc Calvert emerged from the back room and refilled his cup of coffee.

"How is he?" asked Ramona.

"Critical but stable."

"Any chance of him talking soon?" asked Sherman.

"I've got him doped to the moon right now, even if he woke up, I doubt you'd get anything coherent."

"Do you have the security camera feeds?" asked Sherman. If he couldn't talk with Terrance, at least he could keep an eye on the perimeter.

Calvert nodded and retrieved a tablet with live video streaming. "Two in the front and two in the back," he said.

Sherman eyed the feed. The cameras overlapped and gave a full visual of the front door and street, plus the back yard and adjoining woods. Knowing wouldn't save them from a determined assault but would give him a fighting chance.

"Thanks, we'll rotate every thirty minutes. Any longer and you'll lose focus. Shawn, you take first watch of the cameras."

Shawn took the tablet and found a seat, resting the shotgun across his lap. Ramona paced, while Doc Calvert went back to check on Terrance. Sherman took the opportunity to nap in the dentist chair, which he found surprisingly comfortable when unthreatened by loud drills and shiny steel hooks.

He awoke from a dreamless sleep forty minutes later with Ramona urgently tugging his arm.

"Am I up?" he asked.

"No, something else is going on."

Sherman sat up, sensing the alarm in her voice. "What is it?" he asked.

"Vern called Shawn. He spotted a boat nearby."

"I assume that's not normal."

"Not in this weather. He's going to *investigate*. His words."

"Six pints deep?" asked Sherman.

"Probably more," answered Ramona.

"What kind of boat?"

"He didn't say."

"Like an oil tanker off course?" asked Sherman.

"I think that would be bigger news if they could see an oil tanker in this weather."

"Smaller then," said Sherman. An idea percolated through his mind, and he did not like the implications.

"I suppose, why does that matter?" asked Ramona.

"They blocked the one way in or out by vehicle. It stands to reason whoever is still here has an alternative means of transportation."

"A boat," said Ramona.

"That would be one option," said Sherman.

"They'd be crazy to anchor in these seas."

"The SEALs have boats you drive right up onto the beach."

"You think they are soldiers?" asked Ramona, looking extra worried.

"No, I'm just pointing out there are options for them to get ashore that don't involve foundering on the rocks."

"That doesn't assuage my anxiety."

"Is Vern calling back?" asked Sherman.

"In a few minutes."

"Let's have Shawn put it on speaker."

They found Shawn on the waiting room couch, shotgun leaning against the wall. He did not look concerned. His phone rang soon after and he put the call on speaker, which began with Vern's slurred but excited voice.

"Holy crap, Shawn. This dude is coming in on the surge. What a total badass."

"What kind of boat?" asked Sherman.

"Who's that?" asked Vern.

"Vern, it's Ramona. What kind of boat?"

"Uh, small and black, I think. This rain is crazy thick right now."

"How many people?" asked Sherman.

"Who is that?" asked Vern again.

"How many people, Vern?" Ramona asked.

"Can't tell, maybe—oh, wait, they just went straight up on the beach. Crazy. Who does that?"

"How many?" repeated Ramona.

"Five," answered Vern. "I'm gonna go talk to them."

"No, turn around and get out of there," said Sherman.

Ramona didn't wait for Vern's question and repeated, "Run, Vern!"

Vern was not listening, and they heard muffled shouts of congratulations on such a crazy, stupid stunt, then two muffled gunshots.

"Vern!" shouted Shawn, suddenly at the edge of his seat. "Vern!"

The call ended shortly after, but Sherman thought he heard a word over the ocean and rain and Shawn's expletive laced rant.

"Did you hear that?" he asked.

"The gunshots?" asked Ramona, rising off her seat and pacing. "Those were gunshots, right?"

"Yes," said Sherman. That much he didn't need to guess about.

"They shot him!" yelled Shawn. Tears trickled down his cheeks and he flailed his arms in frustration. "They shot Vern!"

Sherman remained focused on the word. "At the end of the call, did you hear another voice?"

Ramona took a deep breath and focused on his face. She seemed intent on regaining emotional control.

"A voice. Yes, I did."

"A word?" asked Sherman, not wanting to influence her recollection with his own.

"Yes, um, something Russian sounding. Oh, what was it? Auntie Zil says it all the time. *Svoloch*."

"*Svoloch*," Sherman repeated. "What does it mean?"

"Bastard," said Ramona, her expression souring.

Sherman hadn't known the translation, not his war after all, but he guessed it was Russian. He'd heard enough over the years to get an ear for the language. He knew a few words here and there, but *svoloch* was not one of them.

Shawn bolted for the door, shotgun in hand.

"Sit down," said Sherman.

"Not a damn chance. I'm going for Vern and you ain't gonna stop me."

"Sit down," ordered Ramona. "Or you'll end up shot too."

Shawn stopped. His face flushed and lips curled.

"I need you to stay here and guard Terrance," said Sherman. "I'll go and check on Vern."

"Are you sure?" asked Ramona.

"Better to know who we are dealing with."

"And Vern?" asked Shawn, looking relieved that the adults in the room stopped him from a reckless decision.

Sherman had already dismissed Vern and his chance of survival but nodded as if he cared. He handed his phone over to Ramona and said, "Call your number so I have it."

She did and he took the phone back and opened his pack. Sherman found his darkest colored clothes and put them on—a pair of dark blue pants and a black fleece he'd bought en route to Portland. Coming from northwest Africa, he had nothing but fatigues and running shorts. His rain jacket was black and wet, but everyone else wore brightly colored ones and that wouldn't do.

He tucked the pistol with reloaded magazines into his pants like a gangster and slung the bolt action rifle over his shoulder like his great-grandfather did during the Meuse-Argonne Offensive in World War One. The extra bullets jangled in his pockets. It was an odd juxtaposition, but beggars should not complain, and Sherman worked with what was available.

"I'll call when I know more," he told Ramona. "No one comes in here but me. Am I clear?"

"No one but you," she repeated.

"Even if you know them," he added.

"I got it," she replied. "No one is to be trusted."

"Sounds like a good mantra," he said and slipped out the front door.

The rain stung Sherman's face and he kept his gaze down, keeping to the shadows on the main street. A few windows above the shops glowed warmly like beacons of safety and comfort, but he didn't see anyone else. Only when he hit the T-junction and turned left did he hear human voices. A mournful tune, sung loudly and proudly, drifted out from Wellerman's Pub—an ancient song of love and loss.

Chapter Twenty-One

The roar of waves crashing down blunted the noise of Stanton's phone and he almost missed the call. With one finger in his ear, he pressed the device to the other and yelled into the receiver, fighting the howling wind to be heard.

"This is Stanton," he yelled.

"Mr. St—delay—off course—land—south—now."

Stanton only heard every fourth word or so, but he got the gist.

"South Beach?" he asked.

"Yes," came the reply.

Stanton turned away from the northern point where he'd stationed all the gear and faced south. His client's men were certainly not as professional as they sounded, and they'd let the storm push them into town.

He walked on, cursing himself for not taking Terrance's car as a mode of transit and cursing his client's men for their incompetence. Even with his rubberized jacket, rain slipped into his hood and trickled down his neck. He forced the storm and cold from his mind, pushing them to the recesses of consciousness. Only the job mattered. This job. The last job ever if he so chose.

Down on the paved road, off the rocks, Stanton watched as a woman whizzed in his direction on a bicycle. She was in her sixties with a wild mane of gray hair and a look of pure joy on her face. She turned around where the pavement ended and circled back.

Stanton stuck out an arm as she passed.

The force knocked her and the bike to the pavement, and she skidded to a stop, contorted and dazed. The woman moaned in pain as Stanton picked up the bike and set off south towards the incompetent crew.

The crosswind nearly pushed him over multiple times, and he felt oddly incompetent and angry at the retiree who rode so freely and with such skill. Despite the odds, he made it to the southern edge of Hilt Bay and dropped the bike with a look of disdain as if it had personally insulted him.

In the pale and frazzled light, Stanton saw men on the beach near a long black silhouette he assumed to be a boat. He approached cautiously. Two of the figures pulled gear from the boat as the other three stood around a dark shape on the rocky beach. Stanton kept his hands high and walked slower when he realized the shape was a body.

"I'm Stanton," he shouted across the wind-torn shore.

The men glanced at each other and holstered guns, which Stanton had not even seen.

"You're late," said the closest man. He had a square face and a large flat nose that reminded Stanton of a pig.

"You're at the wrong spot."

The man shrugged. "I am Serge."

Serge wore a dry suit identical to the other men. The thick black material rippled in the wind.

"Who is that?" asked Stanton, pointing to the body on the ground.

Serge did not look down when he answered, "A no one."

Stanton thought he looked local. Perhaps a fisherman, perhaps a no one out for a stormy walk. The details didn't matter. He was a dead someone and Stanton didn't care. The body count could rise to a hundred and, if he got paid, it would not bother Stanton in the least.

"Where is the gear?" asked Serge.

"To the north where we agreed to meet."

Serge looked north and sniffed the salty air. "The storm is bad, lots of waves pushing the boat."

Do better, thought Stanton, but said, "Come on. We walk."

Serge did not look pleased and eyed Stanton with disdain.

"I expected you north," said Stanton. "Is this a problem?"

"No problem," said Serge and turned to one of the other men who he called Demetri.

They spoke in a language Stanton assumed was Russian.

"He stays," said Serge. "We follow you."

Stanton nodded. "Okay, we need to leave now."

"Now is good."

"And the target?" asked Stanton. "On the way there or the way back?"

"We are here for the items. The target is secondary."

"The way back then," said Stanton and they set off north across the rocky beach.

Between the lashing rain, the turbulent wind, and his circuitous route to stay in the shadows, Frank Sherman made poor time to the beach. He walked down the main road past the lumber mill until cutting across onto the beach. Intermittent streetlights provided little visibility against the storm. The sea roared to his right, pounding and churning against the rocks.

Sherman moved slowly across the beach, cautious with the storm. He didn't want to run into five Russians with only an eight-shot pistol and bolt-action rifle he could only hope worked.

Further south, a border of spindly grass grew between the road and the ocean. Sherman used it to break apart any silhouette he made. As the road turned west towards the point and the fringe houses on the cliffs, Sherman knew he was close. There wasn't much beach left.

Venturing out of the grass, he scanned the night horizon hoping to see something. To his left, the road disappeared after a final streetlight. Under the wavering rain-streaked glow, he saw a bicycle lying on the shoulder with no owner in sight. His eyes moved right onto the beach and in the pale-yellow light cast from that lone source, he spied shapes near the water.

One figure moved around what Sherman guessed was a boat pulled up and out of the ocean. He looked everywhere around him but did not see the other four men, which meant they were off doing whatever cruel tasks brought them to Hilt Bay as the straggler guarded their exit.

Sherman considered taking a shot with the rifle. Maybe on a clear day after seeing if the thing worked, he would have tried, but two hundred yards at night in the rain with an untested gun and who knew how old ammunition was not worth the risk.

He dropped the heavy gun in the grass and headed west towards the surging ocean crashing down on the rocky beach. Sherman hugged the edge of the surf, letting his pants and boots get soaked. The sound and motion of the waves masked his own movement.

Two-hundred yards became one hundred, then fifty, then twenty.

Sherman turned east, following the path of the boat they had pulled up on the beach. The guard sat on the rubber bow and smoked a cigarette. His broad shoulders were outlined against the streetlight, and he wore what Sherman thought to be a dry suit like arctic divers. An assault rifle hung over his shoulder casually like he didn't think there were any threats.

Cocky, thought Sherman.

He picked up a rock, a heavy one, the size of a softball and held it in his right hand. The left held the Colt. Either hand was good enough to shoot the guy from twenty yards.

Even distracted guards hear people sneaking up on them. A byproduct of millions of years of evolution and life in a world where we were not always at the top of the food chain. The mind processes those sounds separately as if in their own audio channel. The *I'm about to get eaten* core of the brain.

Unfortunately for the guard, his brain didn't register any noise over the storm. He didn't hear Sherman's careful footsteps. He didn't react or turn around. Sherman hit him hard—but not too hard—with the rock and the man crumpled on the beach like Shawn at the pub. Lights out.

Sherman kicked away the rifle and flipped the guy over on his back. He wore a modern tactical vest with extra magazines, flashlights, zip-ties, field dressings, and a tourniquet. The same type of rig Sherman wore in the field. Not as fancy, but similar enough to set some more alarm bells ringing.

The guy was still breathing. Bloody and unconscious but breathing, and Sherman borrowed a zip-tie from his vest. After binding the man's hands and feet, Sherman took his vest off and slipped it over his own head. It was a little too big, but he cinched it down hard.

The rifle lay a few feet away and Sherman took it as well. The gun was newer than he'd initially thought—an AK-100 model with polymer grip and stock.

Nice setup, thought Sherman, turning over the gun.

It had a suppressor, holographic sight, flashlight, and laser. A professional's weapon. A room-clearing, take-no-prisoners type of rifle. The alarm bells tolled louder.

After Sherman propped the unconscious guard up against the boat, which was an inflatable Zodiac with an outboard motor like the SEALs used, he took a longer look around. That's when he spotted a figure lying face up on the rocks with arms splayed wildly. Sherman stepped over to take a closer look.

Vern had one hole in his chest and one in his head just above the eyebrow. The result of no-nonsense shooting. One for the kill and one to make sure he stayed dead. Professional actions from men with a military-grade boat, guns, and gear.

Sherman didn't know Vern and their one interaction left a sour residue, but he didn't deserve that ending. Sherman heard the call. Vern was excited and drunk, not threatening, but he got in their way, which meant these men took no prisoners and gave no quarter. A policy of which Sherman took note.

The guy propped up against the boat moaned and Sherman walked over and took a knee. His captive's head still lolled about to one side and a thin stream of blood slipped out from under his dry suit hood before quickly washing away in the rain.

Sherman slapped him on the cheeks a few times to bring the man into the present and he arrived with surprise and anger. He tried to lunge at Sherman but fell flat on the rocky beach.

"I wouldn't do that," said Sherman.

The man spat at him in reply and wriggled about, trying to get free of the industrial zip-ties.

"That won't help either."

Rolling onto his side to look at Sherman, the man seethed with rage and contempt like a bull locked in a cage.

"Why are you here?" asked Sherman.

No reply. Not even a look of disdained understanding.

"Do you speak English?"

No reply or spark of understanding followed.

"*Svoloch,*" said Sherman, remembering the word he heard before Vern died.

The man spat again, vehemently, passionately.

"Great, Russian," said Sherman. "Not my war."

He dug the phone out of his pocket and called Ramona. When she answered, Sherman could barely hear her above the storm and surf.

"Did you find Vern?" she yelled.

The phrasing was implicitly pessimistic as if she'd prepared for bad news.

"He didn't make it," said Sherman, softening the edges of his normal bluntness.

"Oh," she said and took a deep breath.

"Who do you know that speaks Russian?"

"Auntie Zil. Did you hear more words?"

"More than just words," said Sherman. "I found one of

the men from the boat and I need a translator. The only word he understood was *Svoloch*."

"He's alive?" asked Ramona with a tinge of surprise in her voice.

"And angry. I need a ride. Can you meet me on the road just before the fringe?" asked Sherman, describing the rocky outcropping on which Scholtz lived.

"Is it safe?"

"His friends aren't here, so safe enough for a short drive."

"What if they're coming here?" asked Ramona.

"I would have bumped into them, and we probably wouldn't be having this conversation."

"What does that mean?"

"On the road, by the fringe," Sherman repeated, ignoring her question.

"I'll be there," said Ramona.

Sherman hung up and turned his attention to the boat and it was a nice boat. The Zodiac had all the bells and whistles. A professional's boat. The kind you got through official channels or maybe from a procurement officer open to a fat bribe.

He found a well-honed knife attached to his newly acquired vest and used it to cut down the length of the inflatable boat. A great whoosh of air expelled from the rubber raft and Sherman fired two rounds from his newly acquired rifle into the motor to be sure no one could use the thing and that the rifle worked. The suppressed gunshots disappeared into the storm, sounding no louder than cracked knuckles.

Sherman pulled the man to his feet and fished around for a makeshift hood for his prisoner. He settled on a scrap of fabric he found on the boat floor, which he wrapped around the guy's eyes. Sherman didn't want the mercenary to see Ramona or Auntie Zil just in case he held a grudge, which he would. Guys like that were hardwired for action.

Sherman pushed him towards the road.

"Walk," he said.

The man understood enough English to walk forward as instructed.

Chapter Twenty-Two

Ramona jumped a little when Sherman stepped out of the shadows wearing a military-grade vest and holding a Russian army rifle, but not the one he'd left with. The rain came down unabated in long streaks caught by her headlights.

He opened the back door like he had for Gloria and pushed the prisoner in face-down, then zipped the two restraints together hog-tie style. The guy groaned and spat and yelled what Sherman assumed were very bad words in Russian before he stuffed a rag in the man's mouth.

"He really hates you," said Ramona.

"You understood what he said?"

"Just the juicy bits. Do you know who he is?"

"The enemy," said Sherman. "That is all I need to know."

Ramona glanced in the rearview mirror and frowned with concern.

"I don't like being away from Terrance," she said.

"Take me to Zil," said Sherman. "Then you can head back to the doctor's office."

"She lives nearby but is usually at the pub right about now."

"Your town, your call," said Sherman.

"Pub first," said Ramona and made a U-turn on the wet street, spraying water in high arcs through the air.

They passed the salvage yard and the lumber mill, both dark save for a few security lights illuminating the slicing rain.

"What happened to Vern?" she asked, letting out a sigh as if the question had swelled inside her.

"They shot him," said Sherman.

"Like Terrance," Ramona replied and looked in the rearview mirror. "Did he shoot Terrance?"

"No, he just got here and doesn't have a pistol."

"The shooter is still out there," she said.

"Afraid so."

She glanced over at Sherman who held the rifle barrel down and stock up like he did on any other mission.

"That looks like serious gear," she said.

"Professionals."

"That's... bad."

"Depends," said Sherman. "They could be in and out. Get what they came for and leave. That's usually how I operate. It's best if no one knows I'm there."

"What if they were after people? Say, the Wilder clan for instance."

"Have you made that many enemies?"

"We have a long violent history in this place."

"Doesn't track," said Sherman. "If someone wanted you all dead, there are easier ways than a Russian wet team."

"Do I want to know?"

"Probably not," said Sherman.

Ramona made another U-turn at the junction and parked in front of Wellerman's. The cheap Casio watch on Sherman's wrist read 11:00 p.m. Raucous music still poured out of the place.

"She might be drunk," said Ramona.

"Is she from Russia?"

"Legend says she left when they were still communists."

"Then she'll be fine," said Sherman.

Ramona took a steadying breath and burst through the front door. Sherman kept his eyes on the street. The widely spaced streetlights created many shadowy pockets. Plenty of hiding spots for an ambush. Assuming the new arrivals left behind the weakest link to guard the boat, Sherman did not like the odds. At least four heavily armed mercenaries plus the fifth man who shot Terrance, against him, a half-functional Shawn, and Ramona.

Not great, he thought.

Two minutes turned to three as the guy in the back flopped around with muffled grunts.

The front door opened, and Ramona exited followed by the old woman Sherman met the day before when he arrived soaking wet and unannounced. In the colored neon glow of the pub signs, she looked about Hal's age. Early seventies or late sixties. Her gray hair twinkled with drops of rain, and she wore a red sweater—the handmade kind.

She didn't look drunk but walked with small, stiff steps as if she had bad hips or knees. Ramona held open a car door and the woman climbed in the back seat. Ramona got behind the wheel.

"Auntie Zil, this is Frank Sherman."

"We've met," said the woman with a slight accent. "For

what it is worth, I told them to leave you alone, but no one listens to old women anymore."

"I appreciate your attempt," said Sherman.

"Young Ramona here tells me you need a translator, although her explanation of why lacked specificity."

Sherman immediately liked Auntie Zil. She had an edge or sharpness that he recognized and appreciated.

"I need help with an interview of sorts. Question and answer stuff."

"Who?" asked Auntie Zil.

Sherman jerked his thumb backward and she looked into the back of the SUV. "Oh," she said. "Where I come from, we call that an interrogation."

"We do too," said Sherman.

"Let's use the proper word then. No point in dancing around delicate edges that do not exist."

"Sounds good," said Sherman. "I need to find out what this man knows or what he will tell me."

"Is he a violent man?" she asked, looking at the restrained captive.

"Yes."

Auntie Zil turned back to Sherman. "Are you a violent man?"

"Yes."

"Do you plan on directing that toward him?"

"Not at present," said Sherman. He wasn't a believer in torture or enhanced interrogation techniques but understood their role in the great game of national security.

"Very well, do I translate now? He doesn't seem very talkative."

"Not here," said Sherman and turned to Ramona. "Drive us back to the fringe. No one will bother us there."

158

Ramona glanced back at the doctor's office down the street and furrowed her brow.

"Maybe it is best I drive," said Sherman. "You can check on Terrance."

"No, you don't know where you're going."

Sherman could navigate to Scholtz's house but didn't like to drive. Offering, however, felt like the right thing to do.

"Fair point."

"Can we go?" asked Auntie Zil. "I don't normally leave a bottle of vodka once opened."

"Thanks for making an exception," said Ramona.

They pulled away and slipped past the salvage yard and lumber mill again. Sherman could just make out the deflated boat on the beach. Ramona kept going up onto the barren cliffs fronting the open ocean. They parked off the road, not a hundred feet from the edge, which fell away into a roaring and foamy morass of churning water.

Sherman jumped out and opened the back door of the SUV. He pulled out the rag and got into the seat next to Auntie Zil.

A stream of obscenities flowed forth from the prisoner like a swollen river. Auntie Zil said something, and the guy's covered eyes faced in his direction.

"Ask him why he's here," said Sherman.

Auntie Zil translated into Russian, and the man replied with a sharp tone.

"He says to sleep with your sister," said Auntie Zil.

"I'm an only child, so he's out of luck," said Sherman.

Auntie Zil turned back and spoke again in a dangerously quiet voice, the kind Sherman's mother used when a world of trouble came his way.

The man gave a two-word answer.

"What did you say?" asked Sherman.

"I told him we would throw him off the cliff if he didn't say something truthful."

"And what did he say?"

"He is here for the money."

"What are they paying him to do?" asked Sherman.

Auntie Zil faced the prisoner once more and spoke again. The man replied with brevity.

"Recovery of an item and... this one does not translate so easily. Snatch and take," she said hesitantly.

"Snatch and grab," said Sherman.

"They are here to take someone back with them," said Auntie Zil.

"Hal?" asked Ramona.

Auntie Zil remained very still but her eyes danced around like a pinball machine. She turned around and pulled off the cloth around his eyes and stared at the man as she spoke. Her words came out rapidly.

As they spoke, Sherman sensed fear rising in Auntie Zil's voice. Not the fear of a stranger, but the fear of someone she knew.

"They're here for me," she said.

"What?" asked Ramona.

"I took something with me when I left. I thought I got out clean, but they're here now."

"What did you take?" asked Ramona.

"The only thing of any real value in Soviet Russia," said Auntie Zil. "I took secrets."

Sherman did not like secrets or the people who gathered them—spooks or spies or intelligence agents, whatever they called themselves. He was a man of action, the tip of the spear, and often, the spear was guided by people with no name who existed in the shadows. Often, their secrets were no better than rumors. Bloody rumors that cost people their lives. Sherman lost good friends during ops based on bad intelligence sourced from shadowy figures who traded information like currency, but he understood one thing very clearly. Secrets had immense power over those involved, be it warlords in the wilds of Afghanistan or post-Soviet Russia.

"Do you know who sent them?" asked Sherman.

"He does not know, and it does not matter. There are many names on those lists."

"Why now?" asked Ramona. "You've been here my entire life."

Auntie Zil nodded. "I've been here longer than anywhere else, but I arrived with nothing except what I took. Your father helped turn those names into money. He would whisper them into the correct ear, and it would go up the chain until someone in your government took action. The money then trickled back down to me. Not much, mind you, but enough."

"My dad knew?" asked Ramona, more statement of fact than question.

"I could not have stayed without his help. It was a... mutually beneficial relationship. We both profited off those names and now they've come for me. Life is a great circle. You cannot escape what you've done."

"Do you know Hal Cooper? Was he involved with all this?"

Auntie Zil's eyes narrowed ever so slightly, and she asked, "Why?"

"He disappeared this morning."

She said nothing for a few long moments as if processing the details and sorting them into levels of importance. "Hal was a kindred spirit running from the past, but we rarely spoke."

"Unconnected," said Sherman, relieved to hear Hal was not tied up with the current mess but even more perplexed as to what happened to him.

"I wonder how they found you?" asked Ramona.

"Nothing stays hidden forever," said Auntie Zil. "I suppose I always knew a day like this would come, but I hoped I'd be dead by then. Perhaps that is today." She looked over at Sherman, still holding the newly acquired rifle. "Or perhaps not."

"He mentioned recovery was their goal," said Sherman. "You talk of these secrets as physical items. Where did you hide them?"

"I never told anyone. It was an insurance policy, but your father always asked."

"That sounds like my dad," said Ramona. "Always wanting more. He called you the golden goose."

Sherman said nothing. He didn't care about the secrets or what power they held. He wanted a direction to go. A place to point the spear.

Auntie Zil's eyes narrowed in a strange recognition of facts. She paused for a moment before repeating, "I never told anyone."

"Yet they're here," said Sherman. "And recovery was the first order of business, not you."

"What do you mean?" asked Ramona.

"They know where I hid it," said Auntie Zil.

"Or they have good intelligence suggesting a location," said Sherman. "I never saddle up for anything under eighty-percent certainty. Sending five guys halfway across the world sounds like more than that."

Auntie Zil must have agreed because she turned back to the man and asked several more rapid-fire questions. The guy answered in clipped sentences, more yes and no than any detailed response.

"He says there is a man in town helping the operation."

The sixth man, thought Sherman.

"A local?" asked Ramona.

"No, an outsider," answered Auntie Zil.

"Terrance was running errands for someone," said Ramona.

"With lots of interesting gear in his car," said Sherman.

"Ropes and chains and such?" asked Auntie Zil.

"Along those lines," said Sherman.

"Then they know and only one person could have told them."

"The same person who tells Terrance what to do," added Ramona, rubbing her temples.

"Your father cut a deal with the devil," said Auntie Zil.

"Not the first time," said Ramona.

"Your father is in prison, right?" asked Sherman.

"And very resentful of his circumstances, but he only talks to Terrance."

"We could try to wake your brother up," said Sherman.

"What happened to Terrance?" asked Auntie Zil, connecting the dots.

"He got shot and left for dead," said Ramona.

"You should have led with that."

"And Vern is dead."

"That boy… God rest his soul," said Auntie Zil.

"What should we do with him?" asked Ramona, gesturing towards the back of the SUV.

Auntie Zil glanced back and then peered up the road. "Drive a little further and we'll leave him there."

Ramona didn't argue and pulled forward until told to

stop on the far side of the fringe where the great barren expanse sloped down toward a precipitous drop.

Auntie Zil got out and opened the back door. When Sherman arrived to help, she had already pulled the nearly two-hundred-pound man out of the SUV and onto the ground. Together, they moved him off to the side of the road and Auntie Zil leaned close to ask one more question. The man said something that sounded like a name, *Nadia*.

Nodding at the answer, Auntie Zil shoved the man hard off the shoulder of the road and down a steep rocky slope. Sherman clicked on the rifle's flashlight and watched him tumble uncontrollably towards the edge. The man desperately tried to stop his descent, to grab anything of substance, but his hands and feet were bound behind him and there was nothing to grab. With a muted scream swallowed by the wind, the man went over the edge and into the sea.

Sherman clicked off the light and turned to Auntie Zil. "We could have just shot him."

"I like you," she said and got back in the car.

Chapter Twenty-Three

The men made good time, but Stanton still resented their miscalculated arrival. Walking from one end of Hilt Bay to the other ate up valuable time designated for the recovery efforts. They arrived at the first cache of supplies a full ninety minutes behind his mental schedule.

Serge pointed to the covered pile of gear and spoke a few words in Russian that Stanton didn't know but understood.

The men moved to uncover the supplies and the tarp flew away in the night sky, blown by the storm's easterly gale. They worked quickly to stash everything in bags or over shoulders.

"Which way?" asked Serge once his men were ready.

Stanton pointed up towards the forested northern edge of Hilt Bay. He'd memorized the route but still carried his refined copy of Tom Wilder's map in a waterproof case.

"We can cut through there and then head up to the cliff."

Serge waved for his men to follow, and they trudged into

the swaying trees. Despite the overhead cover, rain cut through, slapping off the men's dry suits. Stanton wished he had the same. Even with expensive rain gear, he felt the water seep through.

They reached the edge of the cliff a full two hours behind schedule. Serge's men, in all their tactical gear, moved slowly with the addition of Stanton's supplies. The men said nothing, but Stanton could see their displeasure.

"We rappel down from here," yelled Stanton as the wind ate up his words.

Pointing over the cliff, he motioned for the men to get ready. Two ex-soldiers pounded pitons into thin cracks above the edge. The exposed, rocky lip left no trees of any size to anchor around, and Stanton didn't have time to buy a drill and bolts.

They drove four pitons into the rock and attached lengths of chain to the circular holes at the top of the pitons, locking them into place with carabiners.

Stanton ran a rope through the chain ends, creating a redundancy if a piton should fail. The rope felt thicker than he'd listed, but it was too late to yell at Terrance. The man was dead.

He pulled the rope through until he saw the pattern change and knew he'd reached the halfway point. Stanton carefully reached down and tied a figure-eight knot below the chains and tossed both ends off the cliff into the void below.

One of Serge's men strapped a harness around his waist and connected a rappelling device, looping both halves of the rope through the device and locking them into a carabineer. Slowly, he inched closer to the cliff edge until he could lean back over the void and lower himself down towards the sea.

Serge called the man Ivan and spoke to him in Russian. Ever the soldier, former or current, Ivan refused to give up his rifle and slung it over his back. Stanton wanted to tell Ivan to leave it, but the man didn't understand English and began his descent.

Stanton and Serge dropped to their bellies and leaned forward over the cliff edge as far as they dared.

Ivan slipped on the wet rock with one leg swinging outward. The momentum caused Ivan to collide with the cliff on his hip. For a second, the soldier loosened his grip on the two ropes and dropped a few feet in frightening succession.

"Hold on tight," yelled Stanton.

Serge added something in Russian that Stanton hoped translated to his suggestion.

Ivan steadied himself and continued his descent. He'd almost rappelled out of view when a tremendous gust of wind caught his rifle and pushed it off his shoulder. Ivan did as most soldiers would and reached for the weapon. In doing so, he let go of the rope. Gravity took over and Ivan plummeted unseen into the darkness.

They yelled down into the storm but received no reply.

Ivan was gone. Swallowed by the churning sea.

Serge glanced at Stanton twitching with anger. "You go next," he growled.

Stanton did not want to go next, but if he didn't, Serge would likely shoot him on the spot and be done with the local fixer, so he grabbed the second harness and strapped in. He followed the same routine as Ivan with the rappel device and shuffling back to the edge of the cliff. The headlamp he wore looked feeble compared to the rain, but Stanton focused on his feet. He kept them far apart and way down in his harness, making an L with his feet against the rocks. Slowly, painfully, he descended into the darkness.

The world opened into a great bright space filled with shapes, each one blurry and slipping across Terrance Wilder's vision. The moment made him nauseous and he hated the feeling. It reminded him of hearing the news that his mother, the only good thing in his life, jumped off the lighthouse south of Hilt Bay. Ever since then, nausea always reminded him of her and doubled into nausea and terrible sadness.

His mind ran slowly, grasping for thoughts and words, but questions surfaced. *Where? What? How?* Terrance struggled to understand and remember.

The memory, jumbled and distorted, suddenly rushed back in a moment of fear and despair. He remembered Stanton, the gun, searing pain, and stumbling through the forest. Then came the flash of light, more pain and darkness.

Terrance tried to sit up, to run away again, but his body didn't follow.

"Relax, Terrance," said a voice. "You're safe."

Terrance struggled to focus on the voice and the blurry shape that made it. Slowly, the shape turned into a face. A face he knew.

"Doc," he whispered.

"Take it easy and please don't move," said Doc Calvert.

Moving caused his whole body to explode in cataclysmic pain and he felt himself slipping into a yawning abyss of darkness.

"Breathe," said the doctor.

Terrance did and the moment passed.

"What… how…"

Terrance struggled to speak. The words fell awkwardly from his tongue as if not his own.

"It's not my story to tell," said Doc Calvert and motioned towards the door.

Another figure slipped across Terrance's peripheral vision, emerging into focus moments later.

"Hey," said Ramona.

"Hey," replied Terrance, suddenly overjoyed to see his older sister.

"I'm sorry to ask, but we have some questions. The doc says you can only handle a few minutes without the meds."

"We?" asked Terrance.

Ramona waved her hand and Terrance experienced the strange, blurred vision until a third face emerged.

The soldier, he thought and tried to scowl but couldn't control the necessary facial muscles.

"Him… I don't like him," said Terrance.

"Frank saved your life," said Ramona. "He found and carried you out of a damn ravine."

"Oh," said Terrance. He recalled a sensation of falling after the bright flash in the forest, but didn't remember a ravine, just pain and darkness.

Ramona took his hand. Her touch reassured him.

"Just a few questions," she said.

He nodded with his eyes.

"You mentioned a job for Dad. Did you bring someone into town?"

"Stanton," said Terrance, spitting out the name.

"Did he shoot you?"

"Yes," said Terrance.

Ramona nodded quietly but he saw the Wilder rage burn in her eyes.

"Why is he here?" she asked.

"Don't know," said Terrance, upset for not pressing his father for more details. He should have asked more questions. Demanded details. He'd bent too much for his father and his acquiescence nearly cost him everything.

"But Dad sent him?"

"Yes. Wait," Terrance croaked. A memory floated just out of reach. Something about Stanton. At the vacation house on the… table. "He had maps."

"Maps of what?" asked the soldier, who stood just behind Ramona. Not hiding, but at a respectful distance.

"The north point," said Terrance. "Handmade."

"You did good, Terrance," said Ramona. "Get some rest."

"Be careful, Stanton is dangerous."

Doc Calvert came over and injected something into the IV that Terrance couldn't see. The edges of his vision dimmed like a tunnel, and he felt buoyant as if floating on air.

***

As the painkillers washed over Terrance, pulling him back into the dark pool of unconsciousness, Sherman retreated to the waiting room with Ramona. Auntie Zil sat on the couch, waiting with an intense gaze. Shawn dozed in the corner.

"Well?" asked the old woman.

"They have a map of the north point. Handmade," said Ramona.

"Tom figured it out," said Auntie Zil. "After these many years, he figured out where I hid everything and cashed in."

The details of betrayal mattered less to Sherman than their current tactical situation. Five heavily armed men were moving through the town. The question bouncing around his mind was simple. A matter of odds. Would those men come for Auntie Zil? If the odds leaned that way, which seemed likely, he couldn't leave her at Wellerman's to await a cruel fate.

"Best to head them off now," said Sherman.

"Wait, before you go, I have a confession to make," said Auntie Zil. "I'm sorry I didn't say it earlier, but life is hard without friends, and good friends are worth protecting."

Ramona and Sherman said nothing but shared a quick glance.

"Hal Cooper was more than a kindred spirit. He helped me with the list. Before Tom Wilder went to prison, when his noose grew taut, I cut ties with him. There was too much risk for me. I see that was shortsighted now, but I didn't want him to have leverage over me."

"I don't blame you," said Ramona. "My father is a hard man to stay connected with."

"Your father has a strong will and a quick temper, and I underestimated his resolve."

"And Hal?" asked Sherman.

"He found me out years ago. Hal had a nose for trouble and that was me. At first, he said nothing, then one night at Wellerman's, he took a stool and told me my life's story. How he knew, I can't say, but he wasn't wrong about much."

"Probably called in a favor to learn more," said Sherman.

"I figured that. He knew me and I instinctively knew

him. The same way I knew you ten minutes after you walked into the pub."

"I'm an open book," said Sherman.

"If the book was redacted," added Ramona.

"After our initial conversation, we talked more and a sense of mutual respect formed," Auntie Zil continued. "When Tom went away, I needed help and Hal did just that. He knew the right ear to bend, and I saw more money than ever."

"Do you know what happened to Hal?"

"No, I went to check on him earlier, but I saw… you, I think."

"The figure in the fog. Why didn't you say something earlier?"

"I was trying to protect Hal."

"From what?" asked Sherman, sensing something larger at play.

"I didn't want the pointy end of those names to come back at him. We swore each other to secrecy. He and I used to be on opposite sides of our war. I suppose I didn't want to sully his name or reputation."

"They searched his house. A professional job. Do you know who might do that?"

Auntie Zil shook her head.

"Did you know about his mental decline?"

"Yes, but I tried to ignore his missteps and forgetfulness. He was happy to help, almost excited."

Sherman didn't think Hal had excitement in his life anymore. The endless rows of sticky notes pointed to obsession, but perhaps that was a form of excitement.

"Did you know about the sticky notes in his bedroom?"

"No," Auntie Zil said again.

"He was working something out. An old question with no answer. Did he mention anything?"

"Hal was a driven man with a past filled by demons and ghosts, but you know that. I suspect you are the same in many ways."

Sherman wasn't sure about the comparison, but he'd made plenty of ghosts.

Auntie Zil continued, "But he didn't tell me specifics, the same way I didn't ask. I did not care about his past and he chose to forget mine."

A missing piece to the puzzle fluttered in front of Sherman but he couldn't catch the answer. He was missing something about Hal and his past or present.

"Last question," said Sherman. "Where are these guys headed?"

"A little hidden beach just past the north point. You can only get there twice a month at neap tide and then you need to climb a bit to reach the spot. In this weather, they'd need to rappel down from the cliff."

Sherman said nothing regarding Shawn's story about Hal stuck on the beach and Ramona looked too distracted to connect the dots.

"Stay inside. Watch the cameras. Shoot anyone not me," said Sherman.

"Be safe," said Ramona.

Auntie Zil shook her head. "No, good hunting."

Chapter Twenty-Four

All of Stanton's energy and focus converged on the belay device clipped to his harness. Water rolled down the ropes and pooled against his tightly gripped hands. Strong gusts threatened to twist and slam him against the rocks. Stanton concentrated on letting the rope slide slowly through his hands a few inches at a time. In the darkness below, he heard waves crash against the cliff face.

The cliff stood a good ninety feet above the water, less so in the storm. Tom's map indicated a spot on the face about ten feet above the beach on the right side. The specifics were vague, and Stanton assumed Tom didn't fully know. Whoever had stashed the item or items had wisely not let Tom Wilder in on the secret. Stanton considered that a smart move. Tom was a snake. He couldn't help but bite, it was in his DNA.

At about ten feet above the surging water, Stanton walked his feet across the cliff face to his right and started scanning with the headlamp. The beam of light scattered in the rain and Stanton cursed the storm.

For the next several feet of descent, he only found wet rock. The ocean leaped up at him like a blue-black tongue emerging from an unseen monster.

When Stanton thought he could go no lower without being swallowed up by the waves, something metal glinted in the light. A box wedged into the cliff poked out just enough for him to see one end. He swung himself closer and stretched out an arm, reaching for the metal handle at one end. He caught it on the second try and pulled.

The box didn't budge.

Stanton focused on his breathing and the task at hand but felt his heart pounding in his chest. All this way for a stuck box was not part of his plan.

He pulled again, desperately holding the rope in a brake position down by his thigh with the other hand. The box moved an inch, then two, then in one quick pop, it slipped out of the rock and over the ocean.

The momentum spun Stanton to his right over the ocean, and for a brief second, he felt his fingers slip on the metal handle. He squeezed with every muscle he knew and some he didn't and managed to hold onto the box and the rope but couldn't stop his crash with the cliff. His shoulder hit first with a dull thump of pain, followed by his ribs, which yelled in sharp streaks of agony.

It took a minute for Stanton to compose himself and slow his heart. He clipped the box to his harness, which felt lighter than he expected. Most things of value weighed more, like gold but perhaps not diamonds. However, such questions didn't matter to him. The contents were not his concern.

Stanton attached ascenders to the ropes and began the arduous climb back to the top. One arm up, then step, then repeat. His muscles ached, but Stanton kept his focus. This was the easy part. He'd found the item. All that remained was the target.

Serge helped pull Stanton over the ledge and he unclipped the box. Serge took the metal container and flipped a tarp over it to protect the contents from the rain. Stanton saw his illuminated face peering intently at the metal surface. He cut the small lock with bolt cutters and opened the box.

It was empty.

"Nothing," bellowed Serge, flinging off the tarp and looking accusingly at Stanton.

"No," said Stanton, equally confused. "It has to be in there."

"There is nothing!" Serge yelled as a vein bulged across his temple, fueled by rage.

"*Kontakt zadniy*," shouted one of the men.

Stanton and Serge swiveled away from their silent accusations as the man raised his rifle. The words meant nothing to Stanton, but they intoned urgency.

He affixed his gaze to the soldier just in time to see the man's head splatter apart in the rain.

Even with the raging storm, Sherman clearly heard the unsuppressed gunshot. The crack echoed through the trees before dying on the wind. He'd nearly reached the area Auntie Zil described, and he pushed forward toward the shot.

He wondered, *Who's shooting who?*

The heavy crack indicated a large caliber and the rifle he'd acquired had a suppressor. He assumed the others would have similar attachments.

The answer came seconds later with the muted pops of suppressed weapons. Dozens of shots. Return fire. Designed to keep your enemy's head down. The Russians were fighting back.

Another crack rumbled in front and Sherman knew he'd reached the edge of a firefight. The unsuppressed shooter was off to his right, deeper in the forest, while the other Russians were in front of him near the cliff edge.

Sherman slipped forward with the thrum of more return fire. Tree to tree he went, keeping a slim profile should the Russians focus further to their right.

Three silhouettes were still moving above the cliff edge. Two looked unhurt, a third limped badly on one leg. They kept firing to Sherman's right, deep into the swaying pines. One man fired his rifle while the third limped. The second guy did not match the others. He had on different clothes and held a pistol that he didn't use. He seemed content to stay in hard cover behind some rocks.

As the Russian fired the last of his magazine into the forest, a howl of pain echoed back. A visceral sound like a wounded animal.

The soldiers heard it too. They turned at the noise like hunters to wounded prey, sensing blood. The limping man barked an order that Sherman didn't understand and the man still standing advanced towards the shooter in the forest. The other two men turned in retreat and Sherman lost them in the trees.

Not knowing what he'd walked into, Sherman stayed hidden. The Russians were a known quantity, plus the sixth man. The Stanton character that Terrance mentioned. The extra shooter added an unexpected element. A local perhaps, or another interested party. If the list was so valuable, reason dictated others might try to take it too. Maybe Tom Wilder cut a deal with multiple devils.

Curious and not wanting to be caught in the crossfire, Sherman tacked right, paralleling the Russian as he moved into the forest.

The soldier clearly had a good idea of the shooter's location and moved with purpose, pressing deeper into the forest. Every few yards, he fired several more shots into the trees, keeping the unseen head down.

"Godless Commies!" yelled a voice that cut through the wind.

A voice that Sherman knew.

Hal, he thought.

The shout gave away Hal's position and the Russian advanced with assured steps. He clicked on his rifle-mounted flashlight. From Sherman's angle, he saw Hal outlined behind a tree. He was on his butt, back against the trunk of a pine and holding his side with a crimson-covered hand.

Sherman took several quick steps forward, looking for a clear line of sight to the Russian, who stood twenty paces away. When he found the shooting lane, Sherman didn't hesitate. He put two rounds into the guy's head in the blink of an eye.

The Russian crumpled in an uncontrollable heap of muscle, bone and flesh. No sooner had the guy hit the pine needle-covered ground than the big rifle cracked again, nearly taking Sherman's head off. Chunks of bark ricocheted off his hood and one sliced across his nose.

"Hal," yelled Sherman. "Hold your fire."

"Sherman? Is that you?"

"Yes, I'm coming out. Don't shoot me!"

"Heard," said Hal.

Sherman moved up, checking his left to see if the two remaining men decided to push the fight. He slid around Hal's tree and kept an eye towards the danger. He didn't bother checking the Russian. The chunks of exposed bone and brain confirmed everything he needed to know.

"Where are you hit?" asked Sherman.

Hal moved his hand off his abdomen. In the weak light, the hole looked like a small pool spilling out oil. Sherman reached around to his back and found a larger exit wound leaking an equal amount of blood.

He searched through the pockets of his newly acquired vest and found one field dressing. Sherman leaned Hal forward off the tree, slapped the bandage over the wound, and wrapped it all the way around him.

"It's bad," said Hal.

"It ain't good," said Sherman before adding, "I'll be right back."

Hal nodded and Sherman went to search through the dead Russian's vest. He came back with one more field dressing and repeated the process with the exit wound. The lack of first-aid supplies seemed shortsighted or cocky—maybe both.

Thirty years earlier, Hal might have hiked out on his own, but a seventy-year-old body could only take so much trauma. Sherman wasn't sure if he could get Hal off the hill, let alone if he would survive.

"Thanks for showing up, Major," said Hal.

"What?" said Sherman. He was a captain and happy with his rank.

"What's our exfil plan? Is the bird in the air?"

Shit, thought Sherman.

The only major they both knew was his father and this was no warzone.

"What's my full name and rank?" asked Sherman.

"Major Sherman. Best damn shooter to walk this green earth."

"Oh," groaned Sherman.

Chapter Twenty-Five

Blood ran out of Serge's dry suit like a river, and Stanton watched him cut one leg of the fabric open with a knife.

"Watch the ridge," Serge instructed as Stanton considered his options.

Several thoughts flashed through Stanton's mind. The first involved shooting the Russian in the back of the head and rinsing his hands of the whole affair. Doing so would take little effort—a single trigger pull—and a hike out of Hilt Bay. The long-term consequences, however, were significant. First, he would lose out on the payday. Second, he would be blackballed from any future business opportunities. Lastly, without a doubt, someone like Serge would put a bullet in the back of his head just when he felt safe.

Helping Serge felt like the better choice, so Stanton covered the Russian while he slipped a tourniquet over his leg, cranked up the pressure, and started a timer on his fancy diving watch.

Serge pulled out a radio and tried his man on the beach and the shooter he ordered into the woods. Neither responded to his calls. A look of quiet desperation filled his face, which appeared extra pale in the dim light.

"Let's go," said Serge.

"With you," said Stanton, but the words meant nothing more than a statement of present tense.

Sensing the unspoken qualifier, Serge added, "You get nothing if I die."

Stanton guessed Serge's life had nothing to do with his getting paid, but he went along with the façade. Besides, a bigger question loomed in his mind. Where were the contents of the box? Terrance Wilder was too dumb to connect the dots, unless his father told him, but telling a fool only begets idiocy, so Stanton doubted that occurred. Maybe another local or friend of the target.

"We go to Plan B," said Serge and took out his phone. He dialed and someone, somewhere, answered.

"*Otpravit' vsekh*," he said in Russian.

"What did you tell them?" asked Stanton.

"How do you Americans say it? Send in the cavalry."

Based on Serge's grin, Stanton worried about the outcome ahead, but if that got him paid, it mattered not.

"How many?" asked Stanton.

"Many," answered Serge.

"How long until they arrive?"

"Soon."

Stanton cared nothing for the town of Hilt Bay or the inhabitants, but he worried about the potential repercussions of a full-scale Russian invasion on a small Oregon town.

"I need a dry place to deal with my leg," said Serge. "My men will meet us there and we can find the woman."

Stanton assumed he meant the target. "Do you think she'll give up the contents of the box?"

"Those are my concerns."

No concern if I get paid, thought Stanton, and then added, "We're not far from Wilder's vacation house."

Serge stopped and leaned against a pine tree. "I will say this only once, Mr. Stanton. This deal rests on the contents of that box. My money and your money. If I must go house to house searching for it, I will. You understand this, yes?"

"I do," said Stanton.

"Good," said Serge, limping forward again. "Do you still have the local contact?"

"No, I had to sever that connection," answered Stanton, relishing the memory of Terrance tumbling backward into the ravine.

Serge grunted in understanding.

"But Tom Wilder gave me two names."

"Oh," said Serge.

"My local connection has a sister. We can leverage her."

The combined weight of two rifles and Hal was almost too much for Sherman to carry, but he continued down the hill. He had no other choice. No second option. No help or reinforcements.

Step-over-step they went, one at a time down the slick pine needles and soggy dirt with Sherman carrying Hal over his shoulder, as he did with Terrance, down from the cliff until they reached Hal's house.

Blood soaked through Hal's bandages and ran down Sherman's jacket. The old man struggled to breathe, and his chest heaved with effort and pain.

The effort of carrying Hal down had drained Sherman of all his energy and then some. He'd dug deep and tapped a familial source of energy hidden in his soul. His muscles burned and ached. His heart pounded loudly in his chest like a deep bass drum.

Upon reaching the front door, Sherman heaved it open and deposited Hal on the couch with slashed-open cushions. Blood dripped down onto the white stuffing soaking into the material and saturating it with crimson.

Sherman called Ramona on his phone.

"Are you okay?" she asked.

"I'm fine but you need to drive over to Hal's house now and tell Doc Calvert to prep another bed."

"Frank, what's going on?" she asked with panic creeping into the question.

"Just drive, now," he said, then hung up.

"You look like hell, Major," said Hal.

Sherman knew enough about dementia to roll with the current reality. He'd tried to force the truth on his mother too many times with poor results. The truth only confused and frightened her more.

"Well, Sergeant," he began, using Hal's old rank. "What was the nature of your mission?"

"Trying to cull the herd," said Hal.

"What herd?" asked Sherman.

"Them Russian bastards. Not sure how they got here, but pre-emptive action was needed."

"Why up there on the cliffs?"

"I figured they were going for the box. I caught one of them scouting the area. He had cold eyes, and I knew. I knew he was after it."

"What box?"

"She hid it up there years ago and they were looking for it."

Sherman assumed he meant Auntie Zil. "Okay, you

spotted the scout and then waited for the rest to show up. Good plan. Caught them off-guard."

Hal smiled.

"Did they get the box?" asked Sherman, wanting to know if that meant the men might leave.

"Yes, but no," said Hal.

"Clarify."

"I emptied out the box before they got here. After I spotted that guy snooping, I went down and got the list."

"Where is it now?"

Hal blanched and his lips shook, spluttering meaningless sounds.

"Sergeant," said Sherman. "Where is the list?"

"I-I don't know," said Hal, and his shoulders slumped.

"Don't know or don't remember?"

"Both," said Hal and groaned. "I tore this place apart looking for it, but I just can't remember what I did with it."

Not professionals after all, thought Sherman. Just a determined owner, lost in his own mind.

"Understood," said Sherman, although he couldn't fully understand what Hal was experiencing.

"We've got company," said Hal and pointed out the window.

Headlights blinked through the windows before turning off.

"It's Ramona," said Sherman.

"Who?" asked Hal, and Sherman knew he existed in another time and place.

"A friend," said Sherman and walked to the front door to meet her.

Ramona paused on the porch when Sherman stepped outside. She had that tilted look of curiosity.

"Well?" she asked. "I drove like you said."

"Listen, just follow along. If you call him out, it will just make him more confused."

"Who the hell are we talking about?"

Sherman pointed inside and Ramona leaned forward to look.

"Holy mother of… Hal."

"Yeah, I need your help moving him into the SUV."

"And you're gonna explain what the hell is going on soon, right?"

Sherman walked to the bedroom and stripped off a blanket and folded it in half.

"Well?" Ramona asked, following him inside.

"Yes, now help me get Hal onto the blanket. We can carry him out using it."

Ramona obliged but had a look of muted exasperation that disappeared when she saw Hal's wounds. Together, they lifted him onto the blanket and into the back of the SUV. Blood soaked through the fabric in wet, red splotches.

The storm whipped angrily around them as they drove back to Doc Calvert's office. Bits of branches and debris flicked by in the wind, momentarily frozen by the headlights.

Sherman took a moment to recap what he knew. The speed of events felt like a whirlwind, and he barely had enough energy to keep his eyes open, let alone digest the information.

What struck him as the true wildcard was Hal. Untethered from the present, Hal's actions might provoke a much harsher response from the Russians. Sherman recalled a story about the Soviet army retold to him by an Afghan elder one night over mint tea.

The elder was a young man when the Soviets arrived in his valley. They were after his uncle—an outspoken critic of the invasion. When the villagers refused to hand him over to the Soviets, they burned the valley down. Few escaped the slaughter.

Sherman didn't know how far the mercenaries would go in pursuit of their goal, but the precedents were not far in the past.

When they arrived at Doc Calvert's, Ramona didn't bother with a U-turn. She parked in front of the office facing the wrong way. They lifted Hal out of the SUV as Calvert opened the front door.

"Oh," he said as they rushed by Shawn and Auntie Zil in the waiting room, past the dentist chair and into the makeshift surgery.

An extra bed stood clean and ready in the middle of the room. The doctor had even mopped up Terrance's blood from the floor.

Sherman scrubbed and slipped on a pair of gloves without being asked. The doctor motioned him over and Sherman had the distinct displeasure of digging through the innards of two different humans in a single day. The doctor cut and stitched things Sherman didn't know existed and quite a few he'd seen before spilled out on faraway battlefields, like the corporal in Fallujah who had his stomach torn apart by an RPG, or the major in Syria who left his guts on the Humvee dashboard after an IED blast.

Hal was still breathing when they were done but Doc Calvert wore a worried, bedraggled look on his face like he'd done a lot of work for little hope. Sherman didn't want to place bets either way and knew Hal to be a tough bastard, but even steel breaks under enough force.

"Thanks again, Doc," he said, stripping off bloody gloves.

"Don't thank me yet. Hal isn't a spring chicken anymore

and he endured a good deal of trauma. Often with people his age, their body will just shut down after a major surgery like this.

"You did your best, again."

"And I need a nap," said Calvert.

Sherman's watch read 1:00 a.m. He retreated to the waiting room and found Ramona asleep on the couch. Shawn had the tablet in his lap and one eye half-open, while Auntie Zil snored in the corner.

Everything hurt when Sherman took a seat. His ribs ached from getting punched. His shoulders burned from carrying Hal and his back was in knots. He very much felt his age and that number suddenly felt very old.

"How is Hal doing?" asked Ramona.

Sherman opened one exhausted eye and glanced at her. "He's still breathing, but the odds are against him."

"I'm sorry."

"No need. He picked his fight."

"And did you pick this one?"

"I could have stayed on the bus," he said. "But I'm too stubborn to leave now."

"Thank goodness for the hard-headed."

"Everyone has a streak, mine just runs deeper than others."

Ramona sighed. "I want to grab a few things from my house. Do you think it's safe?"

"No, but the odds are in your favor. The last two Russians retreated before I moved Hal."

"Again, not instilling confidence."

Sherman shrugged. Confidence was not his goal, only survival mattered. "I'll go with you," he offered.

"Thanks, I've never needed an escort home for toiletries, but I'll take one."

Sherman glanced at the empty coffee pot. "And coffee?"

"Yes, extra coffee."

"Okay, grab your jacket."

Auntie Zil stirred in the corner but didn't wake.

"We'll tell her later," said Ramona. "She's got at least a half-liter of vodka to sleep off."

"Holds her liquor like my sergeant and he's three times her size."

"Practice makes... drunks, I guess."

Sherman chuckled and grabbed a rifle.

"Shawn," he hissed.

"No not like that," he groaned.

"Shawn!"

"What?" he asked with a startle.

"We're headed out for a few minutes. Stay awake and watch the cameras," said Sherman.

Shawn yawned.

"Or else," added Sherman.

"Geez, it was just a yawn."

"People are counting on you," said Ramona.

"I'm awake, go and do whatever the heck you're doing."

Sherman motioned towards the back door. Ramona slipped on her jacket and followed.

"Are you gonna tell me what's going on with Hal now?" she asked as they slipped out into the lashing rain.

Chapter Twenty-Six

The men who arrived at the northern edge of Hilt Bay came in two boats. The same type of rubberized craft that carried Serge ashore hours earlier. Stanton watched as they pulled the boats up onto the rocky shore. There were ten men in all. Burly-looking types with beards and mustaches and empty eyes. They wore the same black dry suits to fight off the storm and frigid sea. They carried the same guns and wore the same vests—like carbon copies of the first group, only twice the size.

At least they landed in the right spot, thought Stanton.

The men jumped out and formed a brutish huddle of violent intent. A tall man with almost boyish features—save for a thick scar across his chin—approached and introduced himself as Anton.

"Where is Serge?" he asked.

"Close by," said Stanton and pointed in the direction of the vacation cottage.

"We go now," said Anton. His English was a bit broken, but his intention came across clearly.

Stanton nodded and led the way off the rocky beach under the glow of a red-beamed flashlight. The men behind followed in a staggered line snaking away from the ocean and towards the main road. They crossed the wet pavement in a great pool of darkness between two widely spaced streetlights and moved onto the dirt road leading to the cottage. The Russians moved with poise and ease despite the ever-lashing rain and howling wind.

"This is it," said Stanton, gesturing towards the structure.

Anton said something in Russian to the men and they silently moved to create a perimeter around the cottage. Half faced inward and the other half outward. It appeared they did not fully trust Stanton.

"You go first," Anton instructed and pushed Stanton towards the door.

Stanton did not like being pushed and did not like Anton for being someone who pushed others.

With the door open and Anton satisfied there was no ambush or ill-will, the Russian stepped inside. Serge lay on the couch, pale and tired. His skin had a waxy, gray look to it.

Anton knelt nearby and the men talked quietly in Russian. The conversation carried on for several minutes and Serge checked his watch on multiple occasions. The timer on his tourniquet ran well past sixty minutes.

Best to cut him out of the picture, thought Stanton, but Anton did nothing of the sort.

A man came inside and helped Serge to his one good leg.

"Anton is in charge now," Serge told Stanton. "Nothing else changes. No package equals no payment. Understood?"

"Yes," said Stanton. He understood perfectly well that

the rules remained unchanged but knew the situation had gone sideways.

"Good," said Serge. "I will coordinate from the ship."

The man helped Serge hobble out of the house and disappeared into the night. Stanton couldn't imagine Serge piloting a boat in his condition, so that left nine Russians and himself to finish the job. For the first time, doubt crept into Stanton's mind.

"Do you have more men?" he asked Anton.

"No," he replied brusquely.

"Then we should go," said Stanton, looking at his watch. "The pub closes soon, and Tom Wilder said your target will stay until closing."

Anton regarded him with a superior look. "She will be there until she finishes her bottle."

The conviction behind Anton's words fell flat. Stanton long ago stopped believing people behaved in any rational or consistent manner. There were patterns, yes, but counting them as fact invited disaster.

"What happens if she finishes before the pub closes?" asked Stanton.

Anton eyed him again, but the superiority had vanished. The man looked like he had not considered the possibility or did not understand that a bar closed for the night.

"Where is the local woman?" asked Anton.

"She lives close to the pub."

"Good, we split. You will take three of my men and get the woman. We will get the traitor."

Stanton nodded and Anton spoke to his men. A flicker of displeasure crossed their faces, but they moved in behind Stanton. They were professionals and accustomed to following orders.

All three were younger but not young. A few years past

military age, fresh off some deployment in Ukraine or Africa. The Russian army had plenty of opportunities for combat experience, but survival was not guaranteed.

Taking one last look at his map, Stanton set off for Ramona Wilder's house. The eldest daughter of Tom Wilder, soon to be released from prison if the criteria for success were met. Assuming the client had the pull he alleged, which seemed likely given the fifteen well-armed men he placed on the shore of Oregon.

They reached the driveway a little after 1:00 a.m. Well beyond any timeframe in Stanton's plan, but nothing goes to plan. By writing one down, the planner creates the unexpected. Still, Stanton did not appreciate the delay as it put his own exit strategy at risk, even with the large cushion he'd allotted.

The driveway was dark, and Stanton narrowly missed a gnarled branch that threatened to take his eye out. Anton's men pushed past him and crossed the gravel parking area towards the front door, which was palely lit by a low-wattage porch light fighting to be seen in the rain.

The house was like others they'd passed. Small, two-story homes with cedar shake shingles and little else. No lawns or landscaping, just the wilds cut back to give space.

From the shadows of dense shrub, Stanton waited and watched. If the sister resembled her brother, he expected little resistance. He was more whimper than bark. If she took after her father, the night might hold some more excitement. The rumors swirling around Tom Wilder were dark and tumultuous. Violent and brutal things. The kind of stuff that made legends and kept them in power.

The house had no lights on inside, no one up burning the midnight oil. From what he knew, Ramona Wilder worked the morning shift at the local café. Stanton expected her to be sound asleep even with the storm. A local used to such things would sleep through anything.

Two of the three Russians stacked to one side of the door, while the third tried the knob. The door didn't budge. Apparently, the residents of Hilt Bay did not trust their neighbors.

The third man took a step back and raised his boot to kick the door open. Before he could, the back of his head popped open like an over-shook bottle of champagne, and Stanton's night got a lot more interesting.

From the moment they left Doc Calvert's office, the warning bells in Sherman's mind rang unceasingly. Not a specific threat or unaccounted for shape in the night, but a general sense of unease. An itchy, crawly sensation that ran down his spine and sharpened his mind. A core bit of wiring honed over millions of years of evolution and decades of combat.

It said, *Watch out*. It said, *Be ready*.

"What happened to Hal?" asked Ramona as they slipped through the shortcut by the market.

"He ambushed the Russians on the cliff."

"Why?"

"To protect Auntie Zil's secrets and because he thinks it's 1969 and he killed communists in 1969."

"Yikes. That's a significant departure from reality."

"And then some," said Sherman, ducking under the overhanging branch in her driveway.

Ramona went straight for the front door, but Sherman directed her around back. Less light and chance of being seen. Gloria said nothing as they entered, but wagged her tail furiously against the blankets, for which Ramona rewarded her with a good belly scratch.

"We should hurry," said Sherman.

"I won't be long," Ramona replied.

"Keep the lights off."

"As if I need them," she added, heading upstairs.

Minutes passed as Ramona rummaged around in the near dark and Sherman kept Gloria company. The hound sniffed longingly at Sherman as if smelling Hal, even though her nose no longer worked as nature intended.

Sherman leaned against the kitchen wall wondering what Ramona could possibly need that took so long to find when Gloria let out a short but deep growl. A visceral sort of warning buried in her own long line of evolution.

Danger, it said.

Sherman shouldered his rifle and looked down the dog's snout towards the front door. The tingle down his spine turned to adrenaline as he eased toward a window overlooking the front of the house.

Three figures emerged from the shadows and crossed the gravel parking area to the front door. They stopped and stacked up.

Professionals, thought Sherman.

More from the same group. Not done and retreated as he'd hoped but rearmed and regrouped. Exactly as his gut had warned.

They stacked two on one side and the third on the other. The doorknob jiggled but stayed closed. Sherman knew what came next. He'd been part of an entry team more times than he cared to count. He'd even taught the course to other operators, although he despised the role of teacher. A mentor perhaps, but not an instructor holding student's hands.

The third man took a step back and readied himself to kick open the door with his boot. Sherman saw him clearly through the gap in the curtain. A late-twenties male, black dry suit, Eastern European features, a knotted nose from too many fights, and eyes full of concentration.

Sherman saw it all.

He even understood some universal truth that had brought the man to Ramona's doorstep. Part patriotism, part desperation, with a bit of boredom and pleas for purpose sprinkled in.

Without hesitation or remorse, Sherman pulled the trigger and put a bullet straight through the glass and into that pale, worn too early face. The porch light illuminated the grisly end.

Things got very kinetic from there.

Sherman switched to full-auto and sent a burst through the broken window towards the other two men but didn't have a good angle and missed. Moments after he stopped firing, the window frame and surrounding wall shredded into chunks of wood and plaster as the two Russians returned fire. Bullets hissed through the wall like angry hornets.

Ducking low, Sherman circled to his right, dumping the remainder of his magazine through the right side of the front door and wall where he'd last seen the men. He slid the last few feet into the kitchen and reloaded. Ramona's fear-stricken face appeared from the stairs and Sherman motioned at her to stay hidden.

Not wanting to be trapped in the house, he sprinted out the back door, relying on Gloria's ears to say the threat came from the front.

Sherman cleared right out the back door, finding nothing but rain and scraggly bushes. He figured the shooters were wrapping around the house to his left. That was the best tactical choice, the one he'd make, and they were professionals.

The thick bushes that surrounded Ramona's house loomed like a great shadowy wall punctuated by towering trees spreading above like bony arms. Rain slapped the ground in thick drops and the air vibrated with energy.

Sherman made for the bushes, happy to have the extra layer of darkness to wrap around himself.

Facing the back door, he slowly edged right to get a view down the length of the house on the side his gut said the Russians would go.

A few steps later, he got the sight line. Backlit by the pale porchlight stood a shape moving along the outer wall of the house. The man moved steadily, peeking through windows, looking for a shot to take.

Sherman took the shot first.

He stitched the mercenary's side with two quick bursts, eight or nine rounds in total, enough to make sure the vest couldn't catch all the bullets. The plates were only rated for three rifle rounds each. Simple math.

The guy crumbled to one side in an uncontrolled ball of limpness.

That left a question in Sherman's mind. Two were certainly dead. He'd seen to that, but the third was not confirmed. Had he gone down in the initial exchange? Was he circling the other side of the house?

The answer came a moment later with a flash and a crack from inside the house. Through the open back door, he saw Ramona standing over a body on the floor. She pointed the shiny pistol in her hand down and pulled the trigger again.

Sherman was at the back door moments later.

"Ramona, it's Frank, I'm coming in."

"He came in through a side window," she said, sliding down to the wood floor. "I thought he was you at first. I almost said something, but Gloria growled, and he turned and I-I shot him. And then I shot him again because I was scared that he'd get up."

Sherman nodded at her story and said nothing, but he'd seen more than fear in her actions. He'd seen a cold rage. The kind that smothers any moral boundary or code of conduct. The kind that leaves a taste of exhilaration and freedom followed by a long night of the soul.

"Can we go now?" she asked.

Sherman glanced out the front window and saw nothing but rain and darkness but felt more. A nagging sense of being watched. He walked back down the hall and grabbed a stinger grenade from the dead shooter's vest along with his spare magazines. All of which were speckled with blood.

Back at the shattered front window, Sherman pulled the pin on the non-lethal grenade and pitched it out the window like the high school shortstop he used to be.

The device skidded into the bushes and exploded, sending out tiny rubber balls designed to stun and disorient.

A yelp of pain drifted out of the darkness and Sherman fired an entire magazine into the bushes, eliciting another yelp—this one more visceral and primal. A hot yell of torn flesh and agony.

Yet he still saw nothing but rain and darkness.

"Out the back," said Sherman, urging Ramona towards the door. Gloria followed.

They circled away from the front and the unknown but injured assailant. Sherman led them in a wide arc through the surrounding forest and back towards the start of town near the wooden sign with the 1812 founding date.

Ramona said nothing during those minutes as they groped blindly through the undergrowth, skirting trees, both standing and fallen.

When they reached the pavement's edge and the glow of streetlights warmed their eyes, Ramona paused.

"Frank," she whispered. "What the hell is going on?"

"I'm not sure, but I think those guys were there for you."

Ramona nodded as if his words made complete sense. "The guy in the house. He saw me first and looked right at me and smiled like he knew me."

"That looked like a snatch and grab to me," said Sherman.

"Like I'm the target?"

"If not the target, then someone important enough to send four guys after," said Sherman.

"I thought they were after Auntie Zil," said Ramona.

Sherman shrugged and concentrated on the surrounding area. He didn't understand the motives or the players, but he knew the game. Kill or be killed.

Chapter Twenty-Seven

Stanton lay panting in a tall swathe of ferns somewhere near the main street. He wasn't sure of his exact location. Everything happened so quickly that he scarcely had the time to think. Running hard down the dirt road, he'd dove into the nearest hiding spot available.

He listened for movement, afraid to even shift his weight. Time dragged by. His side burned brightly with pain. Finally, when he could take no more, Stanton rolled onto his back and checked his right side.

Breathing hurt, like tiny knives sticking into his lung. Stanton moved his hand under his thick rubberized rain-coat and Kevlar vest until he felt the viscous warmth of blood. Panic ballooned in his mind and he fought to remain calm.

Focus, he thought.

He could still breathe, so no sucking chest wound, and his lung hadn't collapsed. One or two of his ribs were broken, perhaps shattered. Stanton let his fingertips dance painfully across the jagged edges of torn flesh and knew he was lucky to have run at all. A few inches further in and he'd be dead.

Stanton did not like luck or chance. He liked planning and lists and control. He wanted to shape outcomes, not swim in the cosmic river of possibilities that flowed around him.

Slipping off the small backpack he wore, Stanton removed a first aid kit. The bullet sliced right through his vest and gouged a chunk out of his pectoris major and two or more ribs, but the damage felt manageable. No direct harm to his lung or any other organs. His right arm still worked—not well or without pain, but he could move it. He made a mental note to buy better armor in the future. Something with plates that could stop a rifle round.

In the pale red glow of his flashlight, Stanton packed the wound and did his best to secure the gauze. His work wouldn't last long, but the cheap first aid kit didn't have anything else. He'd seen a doctor's office in town, and in his experience, they worked for free at gunpoint. Once he got stitched up, a bullet or two would make sure the doctor did not remember his face. His DNA would still be there, but Stanton didn't plan on staying stateside. Cash in hand, he'd travel somewhere tropical with a long history of non-extradition.

The thought flickered like a red-hot ember in a dying fire. Stanton pulled himself back into the present.

Focus, he thought again.

He stood uneasily, legs wobbling, but his mind felt sharp, and he unpacked the last few minutes, taking out each image and occurrence in an orderly fashion.

First was the breacher. He never even got his foot forward to kick the door before being shot. A single, suppressed shot. Stanton couldn't recall a loud crack.

Then came the pandemonium. The intensity of those seconds as splinters flew and the Russians desperately tried to survive. Followed by silent suspense.

Their flanking maneuver failed in spectacular fashion. From his hiding spot in the bush, Stanton had a clear view of one ex-soldier sneaking around the house. One moment, he was peeking through the windows, and then he lay dead on the ground. All Stanton saw was a flicker of movement and weak flashes through the rain.

The third Russian died out of sight. At least Stanton presumed as much. He only saw a flash through the window but heard the shot. A pistol. Unsuppressed. And the silhouette. A woman, perhaps. He wasn't sure.

Finally, images came that Stanton did want to relive. A dark figure in the window. A round object sailing out. The bang, pain, and confusion that followed. Then the gunfire and more pain. Terrible pain.

Stanton wobbled off toward the bar, swimming with questions and no answers. They'd been attacked on the cliffs and then ambushed at the house. Serge's men hadn't responded to his radio calls, so they were dead too.

Was there a third or fourth party at play? Perhaps Tom Wilder hedged his bet and found more than one buyer for his information. Perhaps the client changed things up? So many questions, so few answers.

The pub's front door was cracked open, and the neon sign was on when Stanton approached. One of Anton's men stepped out of the shadows and Stanton grimaced at not seeing him earlier.

It's the pain, he thought. *Pain dulls the senses.*

Before Stanton could push open the door and go inside, the man held up a hand.

"Wait," he said.

"Why?" asked Stanton, indignant at being challenged.

"Anton," the man called out.

Moments later, Anton emerged from inside, wiping blood off his hands with a bar towel.

"Where is the woman?" he asked.

Stanton glanced at the red towel and Anton's cut knuckles and tried to think of all the money he'd been promised for successfully completing his tasks and not the people inside.

Brevity and directness seemed best. Dawn approached, and with it, their window of opportunity.

"Your men are dead," said Stanton. He found no use in mincing words.

Anton gave away no hint of emotion. "How?" he asked.

"Someone at the woman's house. They were waiting for us. It was an ambush."

"Who?"

"It was dark, I can't say for certain."

"How many?"

Stanton wasn't sure. He'd been trying to puzzle that answer out on his slow walk to the pub.

"At least two."

"And you lived?" asked Anton. His tone carried a sharp accusation.

Stanton showed his bloody bandage and jagged wound. "Barely," he said.

Anton nodded as if the damaged flesh equaled trust, but his eyes searched the surrounding area warily.

"And the target?" asked Stanton, eager for some good news.

"Not here," said Anton.

Stanton felt all his carefully laid plans and hopes for a rich future sink. No item. No target. No money.

"Where is she?" he asked.

"The drunks do not know, but we extracted two valuable pieces of information from them. One, the target left her bottle on the bar. Two, she left the bar with the woman —Ramona Wilder."

Stanton grimaced at the news. He'd just left three corpses at Ramona's house and had no desire to go back.

"Do you think your target could be the person we encountered at Ramona's? Could they have killed your men?"

Anton scoffed. "The person we seek is an old woman far past her prime. Maybe at her best I would believe her capable, but not now. A *zmeya* fades with time."

"A *zmeya?*" asked Stanton.

"A viper."

"Oh."

"She ran many years ago. Abandoned Mother Russia. Turned on us. A traitor to the cause."

Stanton didn't need to know why, but the context felt relevant, and he suddenly wanted to know things. What were they after? How the woman figured in? Details he was paid not to know.

"Perhaps the old woman has friends," said Stanton.

"We've lost seven men. That is not a friend. That is a *ubiytsa.*"

Stanton didn't need a translation for that one. He'd been in the business long enough to know many words for assassin. None of which left him feeling better about their current situation.

"The local woman must be hiding in town," he added.

"How do you propose we find her?" asked Anton.

Stanton thought for a moment. This was not part of his plan, but he had the capacity for improvisation.

"Did you leave anyone alive in there?"

Anton nodded.

"See if they know Ramona Wilder's cell number," said Stanton. "I have a way to track calls."

The truth was that Stanton bribed a morally flexible employee at the software company used to pinpoint 911 call locations. For a significant sum, he gained access to location data for certain calls.

Anton nodded and disappeared back into the bar while Stanton waited in the rain. His side burned and tendrils of pain radiated around to his back and up to his shoulder.

The mercenary returned several minutes later with a cell phone spattered with blood. On the screen was a contact name. It read *Ramona the Reasonable*. Stanton pulled out his own phone and typed in some details into an app he was not supposed to possess and called the reasonable Wilder.

Sherman sorted through his recently acquired gear on the floor of the waiting room, swapping out and combining magazines until he was satisfied. They had two fancy Russian army rifles, Hal's Colt, the shiny pistol he'd given to Ramona, plus Shawn's shotgun loaded with an unknown number of shells. Not exactly a cornucopia of protection, but better than sharpened sticks and rocks.

Through a series of grunts and snuffs, Auntie Zil stirred to life. She sat up quickly and fixed her eyes on Sherman.

"Why did you let me sleep?" she demanded.

He looked at the red-eyed, bleary-faced woman and wondered how she had functioned at all, but merely replied, "I found Hal."

"What? Where?"

"He was out protecting your secrets."

Auntie Zil fell silent for a moment, then said, "Tell me everything."

"He saw someone snooping around your hiding spot this morning while he walked Gloria and went to investigate. The dog went home because that is what she does. Hal got spooked by the mystery man and went down to retrieve the documents for safekeeping, only, in the process, he lost his mind and doesn't remember where he put them."

"Oh," said Auntie Zil with a creeping sadness in her eyes.

"He did remember the men and decided to ambush them when they came for the list. Not a bad plan, all-in-all, but when you think it's 1969, reality doesn't live up to expectations."

"Is he alive?"

"He's got a hole through his gut, so the answer is a tenuous yes."

"Is he here?"

"In the back with Terrance."

Auntie Zil stood up and headed toward the back.

"Wait," said Sherman. "We need to find this book of secrets. I'm not one for negotiating, but this won't end until they get that list."

Auntie Zil nodded.

"And you need to part with it."

She nodded again. "Those names are equal parts curse and blessing. I took them because there was no other way out alive. I needed the leverage."

"No judgement here," said Sherman. "Just be gentle with Hal. His mental state is equally tenuous. He mistook me for my father earlier."

"I understand," said Auntie Zil and walked into the back at the same time Ramona rushed into the waiting room.

She held up her phone with a worried look. The screen lit up with an incoming call.

"It's King," she said. Then added, "The bartender at Wellerman's. He keeps calling. I'm worried."

"Did you answer?" asked Sherman.

"No, should I?"

"No, it's bad enough we have phones."

The call went to voicemail and Ramona sat down. "Can they track us?"

"Anyone can be tracked," said Sherman. "The question is, do they have the tools and resources to do it? Judging by their hardware, I'd say yes, but it requires a different skillset and technology. What I can say is the moment you answer that phone, it makes their life much easier."

Ramona looked down at the device as if it might bite her or explode. "Or it could just be King calling for help."

"Does he normally call you this late?"

"No," she said.

"Best not to answer."

"Doesn't that mean these guys are just down the street?"

"It does," said Sherman, already gearing up. Two blocks equaled too close.

"What are you doing?"

"Give me your phone," said Sherman.

Ramona handed it over a little hesitantly.

"These guys are down the street looking for you and Zil," added Sherman. "They're looking for her because she stole the secrets, and whoever is on that list is taking this personally. They're looking for you for the same reason they used Terrance. You're the local. The fixer. You would know where to find Auntie Zil because she is almost family. That's why they came to your house. This town is like a black box. Outsiders don't understand how it works. They need local intel."

"That means my dad sold out both of his kids," Ramona replied. Her tone was dangerously flat and devoid of emotion.

Sherman was not in the habit of defending crappy fathers, but he left open the possibility that Tom Wilder might not have known the full risk he'd exposed his children to. Then again, maybe he did.

"Wake Shawn up and give Auntie Zil the other rifle. She'll know how to use it."

"Good… hunting," said Ramona, after a pause, borrowing the phrase Auntie Zil used.

"You'll know it's me coming back. Anyone else, you shoot."

Ramona nodded.

"Lock the door behind me," said Sherman and he slipped out the back door into the chilling rain and wind.

Chapter Twenty-Eight

The neon hummed and Stanton waited. His first and second calls to Ramona Wilder went to voicemail, but it rang, which meant the phone was on. He considered calling her immediately back but thought otherwise. Recent events at her house must have shaken the reasonable Wilder. Maybe they were even on the move and needed to find a place to lie low. Stanton didn't mind waiting. Patience and planning were his strengths. A key to his longevity in a violent and unpredictable profession.

Anton, however, did not like waiting. He was a man of action.

The Russian fumed at Stanton for his inaction. He didn't pace or shout, that was unprofessional, un-soldierly, but Stanton knew he was in hot water.

"Call again," said Anton.

"Not yet," replied Stanton. "Give it a few more minutes. I want it to seem natural."

Anton frowned but said nothing. The rain on his dry suit refracted the neon bar signs, making him shimmer.

"Did they tell you anything else?" asked Stanton, gesturing inside, though they had still not let him through the door.

A smile spread across Anton's face. "They will tell me anything I ask. Most is garbage, anything to ease the pain, but everyone breaks."

Torture was not a skillset Stanton deployed. Torture was messy and unreliable, both of which he considered untenable. Still, he was not opposed to the process or the outcomes. Stanton was not a moral man. He lived by his own code and creed, which distilled down to *get out clean with as much money as possible*. The mission had turned pear-shaped but was salvageable. They just needed to find the item.

"Any useful information?" he asked.

"The target left with your local woman. They discussed something which no one heard and then left," said Anton.

The wound to his chest burned and Stanton focused hard on the present.

"You said the target is an old woman, that she couldn't have killed your men like that. And the local woman, Ramona, didn't do it. Someone else must be helping them. Might one of them know who that is?"

Anton smiled again and Stanton knew the man relished violence and pain. "I'd be happy to ask," he said and stepped back inside.

Before the door closed, Stanton glimpsed four or five people sitting on the floor with hands zip-tied behind their backs and various amounts of blood dripping down their faces.

A minute or two passed and cries of pain escaped from inside. The mercenary standing guard didn't flinch or even seem interested. Stanton waited and thought of the payday.

That usually helped to drive away his doubts, but this time, they lingered.

After a third scream and a brief pause, Anton stepped back outside. Once again, he wiped blood from his hands with a gray bar towel turned brown.

"They say a soldier is in town. They say he knocked out a local with a barstool yesterday."

"Do they know a name or where he's staying?" asked Stanton. From what he'd seen, knocking out a drunk with a barstool was the least impressive thing the guy had done.

"One said Hank, another Frank. No last name. He's staying with Hal Cooper. An old vet with a dog not far from your cottage."

"Oh," said Stanton. He'd seen an old man out walking his dog. He'd thought nothing of it. "When they said vet, did they mean veteran like ex-army?"

Anton grinned. "You are a very perceptive man, Mr. Stanton. I wondered the same thing. Your English language has many nuances. Often, I am not sure what you mean. They confirmed this Hal fought in Vietnam. Your great defeat."

The puzzle pieces flew around Stanton's mind in a great whirlwind of angles and possibilities.

"When I helped Serge down the hill, before your man got killed, I thought I heard someone shout, 'Godless Commies'."

Anton snorted in disdain.

"Their words, not mine," added Stanton. "What if that was Hal Cooper? I've been thinking that Tom Wilder double-crossed us, sold the location to a third-party, but maybe it was locals all along. What if Hal is working with your target? What if they're all working together? The target, Hal, Ramona, and this soldier."

Anton stared at him with mild amusement as if watching a child dance. "Who and why do not concern me. Only the item matters to me. After that, I will kill them all."

"Perhaps we should check out Hal Cooper's house," Stanton suggested. The clues pointed in that direction, and a search seemed logical.

"Fine," said Anton. "You and I will see if these rats are hiding there." He turned to his man standing guard and called him Vlad. They spoke rapidly in Russian Anton added, "They stay here."

"I don't think that's wise," said Stanton. He'd seen enough to know that more manpower was needed to neutralize this Hank or Frank. Splitting up was a bad plan. It diluted their numerical superiority.

"We don't pay you to think about that. Do as you're told, or would you rather go check out this hunch on your own?"

Stanton did not want to wander injured through the dark, so despite his misgivings over the plan, he nodded in agreement. "We can go, but do you have any painkillers? My side is killing me."

Anton laughed and tossed over an orange bottle of pills with no label. "Take two and grow some balls."

Growing a pair of testicles had no bearing on how Stanton functioned. Pain, however, did and he took two of the small white circles and swallowed them down with a gulp of rainwater.

"Let's go," said Anton, waving for Stanton to follow.

They headed north in the shadows off the main road, detouring around the intermittent streetlights and their wide pools of yellow light.

"Aren't you concerned?" asked Stanton as they stopped under a scrubby pine with low-hanging branches.

"Concerned about what?" Anton replied as his eyes darted around.

"You've lost half your men, not to mention all of Serge's."

"No, I lost three of my weakest men, which means more money for the rest of us. I am Spetsnaz; one American does not concern me."

That's shortsighted, thought Stanton.

"Now, will you call that local woman again?" said Anton. "Once we have a location, my men will take her."

Stanton pulled out the bartender's phone and his own. He pulled up the app he wasn't supposed to have and dialed *Ramona the Reasonable*.

It rang once, twice, then answered.

Stanton said nothing and heard nothing.

He waited for the app to drop a location marker on the map. With a soft ding, a dot appeared, and he hung up.

"Got her," he said as Anton peered over his shoulder.

"Where?"

"Wait…" said Stanton, looking at the map. "This can't be right. It says her phone is right next to the bar."

"Shit," said Anton.

"Oh," added Stanton.

Chapter Twenty-Nine

When the call came for a third time, Sherman stood within sight of the pub. He'd circled through the forest south then west to the main road before finding a nice dark bush between two houses to observe Wellerman's. Across those fifty rain-streaked yards, two mercenaries stood guard out front. Not the usual crowd.

Whoever was calling was not the bartender. The call was a ruse, a shiny lure to pull Ramona out of hiding. Maybe they wanted King to convince her to surface. Maybe they could acquire her location from the call. Sherman used the tech before. He knew it existed. His version was military-grade, but so was the Russian's gear. Perhaps they had other tools.

Either way, Sherman wanted them distracted to see what they would do. He answered the call and dropped the phone in the bush. He moved one more house north, putting him about forty yards down and across the street from the pub. The corner of the house fell in deep shadows from the streetlights and provided hard cover.

A minute later, the two men answered radios or calls tied into earpieces. They cupped their hands against their ears to hear over the storm and waves. They looked at each other, then looked across the road. A third man emerged from inside and light spilled out in a long rectangle. Before the door closed, Sherman glimpsed an all too familiar scene.

At least two military age males bound, kneeling and bloody. He knew their story with a glance because he'd done the same in Iraq and Afghanistan. No matter how many drones circled overhead. No matter how many calls got intercepted. Human intel never lost its value. Sometimes that required rounding up some locals and asking hard questions. Sometimes getting answers required persuasion or money, other times, it required force. Pain made people reconsider their priorities in life.

The Russians learned that lesson too. Sherman guessed they'd come looking for Auntie Zil and found her abandoned bottle of vodka and witnesses describing her departure with Ramona. Getting the bartender's phone probably required pain. King didn't strike Sherman as the sort to hand anything over without a fight.

The three mercenaries discussed their situation for a moment using hand gestures to outline possible hiding locations and avenues of attack, which meant they did have other tools and had tracked the call.

Their plan appeared simple and Sherman read the hand signals like most people read a menu. Two of the men would cross the road and search the area. A third would stay on their side of the road to provide cover. Their plan was not bad, Sherman would have done something similar. But Sherman had two crucial advantages. One, he saw them, and they did not see him. Two, he already knew their plan.

Sherman switched the rifle to his left shoulder and braced it against the corner of the house. Switching hands didn't bother him and he could shoot equally well with both like the average person switching hands to drink their coffee.

On cue, two men set off at a jog across the main road. They didn't run or throw smoke to conceal their movement or anything else they could have done. Despite losing three comrades, they acted blasé, as if they were untouchable.

Cocky and dumb, thought Sherman.

He lined up the forty-yard shot, slowed his breath, and pulled the trigger. No hesitation. No remorse. Them or him. Simple math.

Sherman hit the second guy in the line first. A clean head shot. All the lights went out at once and he crumpled like a marionette doll with no strings. The guy in front knew something was wrong. He'd heard a shot, but foolishly turned his head to look for his partner. He should have started shooting, but he didn't. His mouth opened to say something like *contact front* but didn't get the words out.

Sherman pulled the trigger again with the same results. Lights out all at once. No callout or expletive. Dead and done in a heartbeat.

The third Russian moving parallel to the road did not hesitate and the corner of Sherman's hiding spot shattered in a cloud of splinters as bullets shredded the cedar shake siding of the house.

Unfortunately for the Russian, he was still illuminated by the streetlight hanging over the pub. Doubly so, there was no cover, just an ankle-high drop to the rocky beach and a whisper of grass. Caught in the open too far from the building, his only play was overwhelming suppressive fire, which worked until he ran out of bullets in the magazine, and then his only play turned into a liability.

Sherman sensed his opportunity before it arose. Some deeply buried corner of his brain knew the shooter would reload soon. He was not consciously counting shots but had acquired the innate skill over time and experience. When the lull arrived, his window to react opened, and if the Russian was good, it would be a very small window.

Leaning out from the corner, Sherman acquired the shooter in the holographic sight. The guy was quick and slammed home the new magazine as Sherman pulled the trigger—rapidly.

Not clean shooting, he knew, but effective.

Sherman hit center mass six or seven times, over-whelming the armor by sheer volume. The Russian went down in a staggered fall that left him lying on his right side looking across the street. Sherman took his time with the last shot, leaving no room for survival. He swapped his half-empty magazine with a fresh one.

The question running through his mind was one of simple math. The first boat had five men in total. Vern confirmed that before his curiosity and stupidity cost him. Of that original group, Sherman saw one escape, limping terribly. This group was new and at least six in number. Three dead at Ramona's house and three more on the street.

How many are left? he wondered.

A boat like the Zodiac could hold six or seven if needed, but maybe not in rough seas. Too many people to be safe. That left another option. Two boats with five men each, like the first. Minus the six dead left four, plus the wounded man and the outsider named Stanton.

Six. At least six are left.

But where? Inside the bar or out searching for Auntie Zil? Perhaps at her house, which Ramona mentioned was not too far from the pub—certainly within walking distance if Auntie Zil polished off an entire bottle of vodka before heading home.

Start with the bar.

The neon lights still glowed brightly in the storm despite being an hour past closing. Glancing down the street, Sherman noticed a few more porchlights twinkling than before. The gunfire had not gone unnoticed. No one in the house next to him stirred, but further down, lights clicked on and windows shone golden in the heavy, wet air.

Sherman slipped one house closer to the bar. The lights remained off but one more down looked alive with activity. The screen door opened and an elderly man appeared on his porch. He wore a bathrobe and carried a shotgun. He surveyed the dead men in the street.

"Not this again," he grumbled.

Again, thought Sherman. *What happened before?*

No sooner had the old man spoken, the shadows on the pub's right side erupted in gunfire. The sound of which registered above the waves like popcorn popping.

The local dove awkwardly inside, cursing as chunks of wood fragmented and the screen door punctured.

Sherman aimed just left of the diminished muzzle flashes and returned fire. Ten successive shots. Quick and deliberate.

Then he sprinted hard across the road—no jogging, a legs-pumping, feet-pounding dash that didn't end until he stood on the rocky beach well past the street and on the other side of Wellerman's from the shooter.

Sherman caught his breath before angling toward the

back of the bar, which jutted out above the beach on a small pier. He hadn't noticed that piece of engineering from inside, but standing near the surging water, the raised structure made sense. There wasn't much land, and it was close to the ocean.

Light from the streetlight didn't reach either side or the back of the bar and Sherman quickly slipped into a cone of darkness. Wanting to get behind the shooter, Sherman headed to the little pier holding up Wellerman's. Waves crashed to his left and the air smelled briny. Rain still came down steadily, but the intensity waned. Even the wind had slowed down its frenetic gusts.

When he reached the pilings holding up the bar, Sherman slipped under them. His boots crunched over rocks and bits of broken beer bottles. He cleared his backside and turned a wide right, gun ready, fire-selector on full-auto. He figured the Russian would be further up on level ground, holding the corner.

He was not.

The guy came flying off the elevated berm like a linebacker chasing the ball and straight into Sherman, who got off a few shots before mass and inertia took over and sent him sprawling backward onto the rocky beach. The impact nearly knocked him unconscious, and pinpricks of light floated across his vision after his head hit the rocks. All the air in Sherman's lungs emptied out like an untied balloon being set free.

Adrenaline flooded his system in a way combat at a distance never matched. Sherman smelled the guy's sour breath and rank body odor. He felt the heat of the Russian's hands against his neck.

His rifle remained pinned under the guy's knees and Sherman too under the gun. The Russian weighed a good two-hundred pounds and Sherman felt all of it pushing him down against the rocks.

Panic seeped into the edges of his mind and Sherman tried to push it away. His senses went into overdrive. He smelled sea and decaying wood, tasted salt and bits of sand, even felt the slickness of the rocks under his hands.

All of that registered in the second before the Russian punched Sherman square in the face. Stuck against the rocks below, Sherman's face absorbed all the impact. Pain zipped through his nerves and spread across his body. He'd been hit enough to know his eyebrow had split open and felt the warmth of blood flowing down his face.

The Russian reared back and punched again. Sherman managed to get his left arm up and absorb the strike with his forearm, but that didn't dissuade his attacker from trying again. They struggled and grappled and cursed together in the wet darkness under the pier for what felt like minutes but was probably only seconds. Sherman couldn't move or toss the Russian off and the mercenary soon caught on to his upper hand. He stopped trying to punch Sherman and searched blindly on the beach for a rock with one arm while trying to pin Sherman's head to the ground.

Sherman searched too, adrenaline and panic surging in his mind.

The Russian found his rock a second too late.

Unsheathing the knife on his vest, Sherman cut through the man's tendons, nerves, and arteries around his outstretched elbow in one swift stroke.

The man howled in pain.

Sherman kept cutting. He hit the femoral artery just below the Russian's crotch and felt the warm, viscous slickness of blood on the knife. The man rocked backward in a flurry of howling curses and Sherman rolled away. He sat up in time to see the Russian groping for Sherman's rifle on the rocks.

Not a chance, he thought.

Sherman lunged at the Russian, tackling him to the ground and turning the tables. This time, he didn't waste any time. The knife in Sherman's hand did all the work, operating with surgical precision. He didn't need to think or plan. More was always better in a knife fight, and he put holes in most of the guy's vital organs within a few seconds. From there, it was only a matter of time for his heart to stop.

A minute or two was all it took.

Sherman waited with his knee on the guy's chest until he was sure. His hands were slick with blood and the scent combined with the decay from the sea. It smelled of untidy endings and the great wheel of existence.

He washed the knife and his hands in the surging tide before turning back toward the pub. Sherman recounted the bodies in his mind. Ten came ashore. Seven were dead. That left three alive from the reinforcements plus the out-of-towner named Stanton, and the man who limped away from the cliff.

Sherman really hoped they weren't all inside the pub.

Chapter Thirty

Stanton's watch read 3:30 a.m. Hours remained until sunrise and any feasible amount of light, yet the streets seemed brighter. Porchlights clicked on. Even a few windows blazed through the rain. Hilt Bay was stirring, and Stanton didn't like the reasons, even less the possible outcomes.

They never made it to Hal Cooper's house and had abandoned the idea altogether. Anton lost radio contact with Vlad shortly after calling in the warning about Ramona Wilder's phone. Apparently, the group Anton worked for happily spent money on guns but not comms, and only two men at the bar had radios. Stanton considered such an oversight negligence but didn't voice the observation.

Under the steady beat of rain, Anton paced around a pine tree, wearing a circular track into the needle-covered ground. He spoke rapidly in Russian to Serge over a satellite phone. Stanton couldn't understand the words, but he got the gist—things had gone from bad to worse, and so had their options.

Anton hung up and slipped the phone back into his vest.

"What did he say?" asked Stanton.

"He said to complete the job."

"And did he offer any freaking advice on how to do that?" asked Stanton.

"I do not need advice," Anton replied. "I am fully capable of resolving this situation."

"Bullshit," retorted Stanton. "Your men are dead."

The full weight of their situation did not penetrate Anton's ego, or perhaps he was unwilling to admit defeat. Either way, the Russian was being less than rational.

How very unsoldierly, thought Stanton.

"No list, no money," said Anton.

"List?" asked Stanton. He wondered what could possibly be worth so much blood and treasure. Such a list might contain anything, and anything might be worth everything.

"What?" replied Anton absentmindedly.

"Nothing," said Stanton. "We need to focus on making it through the night."

"Are you scared?" asked Anton, his lips pursing into a sneer.

Stanton pointed to his wound. "I'm thinking rationally. You lost your men. Our numerical superiority is gone, not that it helped. I shouldn't have to explain this to you. You're the soldier."

"And soldiers follow orders."

Stanton threw his good arm up in disgust. The job, the money… neither was worth his life. Commitment of that level bordered on delusion and Stanton was a pragmatist.

Nothing mattered more than his life. No higher calling or duty. No devotion to country or God. He thought that Anton saw the world in the same light, but Stanton realized that the Russian never left the army, not really and not in his mind.

"Don't be stupid," said Stanton.

"Don't insult me," Anton retorted. "You work for us. If you want the money, do as I say."

The money, thought Stanton.

For the first time in the last two days, the money didn't seem all that important. Getting out alive mattered, and to do so involved staying away from Anton.

"What do you suggest we do?" asked Stanton.

"We're going back to the bar," said Anton.

"To get killed?"

"To raise the stakes," said Anton.

Stanton thought survival was the penultimate stake, so the ex-soldier's proclamation sounded ominous, but he wasn't ready to cut and run. Not just yet.

Frank Sherman stepped out from under the pier covered in another man's blood. Except for his face. That was definitely his own and his split eyebrow throbbed with pain.

A few steps up the berm, on solid ground, Sherman found the dead man's rifle disabled by a bullet to the frame. The broken gun explained why the Russian tackled Sherman instead of shooting him.

Sherman checked his own rifle and, satisfied nothing was amiss, moved towards a back entrance to Wellerman's he had spotted earlier. Going through the front door of the pub was suicide with no visual until he stepped inside, and arithmetic told him there were at least three men still alive.

The backdoor was only accessible from a narrow walkway on the pier and Sherman slipped over the wooden railing and onto the weathered planks. Visible underneath him, through the gaps in the wood, was the exsanguinated Russian.

Sherman had no remorse over killing the man. The moral ambiguity of such actions vanished a long time ago. Emotions had no place in his world. He neither enjoyed nor hated violence. Where Sherman took exception was the needlessness of most situations. The Russians needn't have showed up for the list. There were other options, other avenues of recourse. But they did show up with violent intent and Sherman had no qualms about putting them all in the ground.

At the backdoor, Sherman switched to the Colt and tried the doorknob. It turned and Sherman checked the corners before slipping inside. He found himself in a storage room filled with cheap beer and cheaper liquor. The space smelled of spilled booze and the slow rot of wood exposed to salty air.

From what he recalled of his afternoon in the pub, the storage room exited on the back wall at the end of the bar. Easy enough access to keep the liquor flowing without making the bartender wander across the building.

The storage room door itself wasn't much more than a sheet of plywood with a latch on the bar side. A half-inch-wide gap ran around the door, and Sherman could see inside Wellerman's—not all the pub, but the front door and a good chunk of the main space, everything but the bar top itself.

Visible through the thin crack, Sherman saw five people sitting on the floor with their hands zip-tied behind them and their legs crossed. A classic way to prevent swift movement, one that Sherman used in Afghanistan and Iraq when detaining suspected insurgents. Some people had obvious wounds on their faces and dried blood splattering their clothes. Some kept their gaze down while others stared hard toward the bar with a burning hatred in their eyes. Sherman couldn't see what the hostages gazed at, but they all had a single focal point.

One target, thought Sherman.

Judging by the eyes following him, the last Russian paced back and forth along the bar. The walk of a worried man with diminished options. Perhaps he was reckless, scared, and unstable.

Sherman unsheathed the knife and slipped it carefully through the crack, lifting the latch on the other side. The little hook popped out of the catch and the door opened a couple of inches. None of the locals noticed except for King, the bartender. His downcast face glanced sideways toward the door. One of his eyes was swollen and blood still trickled down from a jagged gash on his forehead.

King squinted at the storage door, processing the vague sliver of Sherman visible in the crack. It didn't take the man long to come to a definitive conclusion. He held up a single finger behind his back and glanced toward the bar, then he gave the slightest of nods.

Waiting made no sense. Sherman holstered the pistol and shouldered the rifle. He aimed where he expected the Russian to be and pushed open the door with the toe of his boot, keeping his heel on the ground for stability.

The plywood door swung inward, and Sherman spotted the mercenary mid-step, pacing in front of the bar with his rifle held upward in one hand. A fraction of a second passed as Sherman put the red circle of the holographic sight over the man's head. Another fraction passed as the

Russian saw the door open, but by then, any chance of reaction was gone.

Sherman pulled the trigger and sent the intruder off to see the great mystery of death. The body hit the floor with a wet thump as chunks of skull splattered on the wall.

Some of the hostages yelped in surprise and panic, but King stood stiffly up and walked towards Sherman. He stopped short and spoke quickly.

"There were four more outside."

"They're dead," said Sherman, not mincing his words.

King nodded. "Didn't think I'd see sunrise. Thanks for dropping by. Can you do me a favor and cut these damn things off me?"

Sherman used the knife to slice through the plastic zip-cuffs and then handed the blade to King.

"Free them too," he said.

The bartender held the blood-smeared knife in his palm.

"Is that blood?" he asked.

"Theirs, not mine," said Sherman.

"Okay," said King, drawing out the first syllable.

He walked around the room, cutting hands free before returning the knife.

"I knew you were a dangerous man, but this—" He motioned around the room. "This is next-level violence."

"Do you know if there are any more?" asked Sherman, ignoring the compliment... if it was a compliment.

"Two more, I think. They left maybe fifteen minutes ago but I couldn't see which way they went. Wait, they took my phone with Ramona's number. Maybe they went after her."

"They tried earlier, but she's fine."

King had a baffled expression—half bemusement and half terror.

"Are they dead, too?" he asked.

"Yeah," said Sherman. "The two that left. Were they both like this guy?"

King followed Sherman's gaze toward the dead Russian with his vest and dry suit.

"One was like him. The boss man. A real sadistic asshole. Enjoyed beating my ass. The other wasn't. Looked like a generic middle-America white guy."

"Stanton," said Sherman.

"Yeah, they called him that."

"And those two are the only ones you saw?"

King nodded. "And these five guys, but you took care of them."

Two of the locals were already stripping the dead Russian of his weapons.

"You should go home," said Sherman.

"Not with two more assholes on the loose," said King and the others voiced their agreement.

Sherman didn't see a need to argue. It was their choice. A free country and all.

"There are three more rifles outside. Lock the doors and try not to shoot anyone. Me specifically."

King nodded again. "We've got this. They got the drop on us earlier, but not again."

"Stay inside," said Sherman and headed towards the front door.

"Wait," said King. "What the hell is going on here?"

Sherman pointed to the half-empty vodka bottle on the bar. "You'll have to ask her."

"Auntie Zil," said King. "That tracks."

"Door closed," repeated Sherman.

"Got it," said King. "Stay put. Don't shoot you."

"Keep to that," said Sherman before slipping outside.

The rain and wind had not stopped, but the storm's energy waned as morning approached.

Not much night left, he thought.

His watch read 3:35 a.m. Adrenaline still coursed through his body but was fading quickly. The coffee had worn off. Sherman felt exhausted. His head hurt and the cut stung with the wind. His ribs ached. Everything felt heavy as if his arms and legs were wrapped in lead.

Sherman looked left and saw nothing but wet pavement and the glitter of streetlights. He looked right and saw more of the same, but with bodies in the street. The locals from the bar had already stripped them of their weapons. An efficient group, fueled by a heavy dose of anger and, perhaps, alcohol.

Having no idea which direction the remaining attackers went, Sherman decided on returning to the doctor's office. He needed a stitch or two anyway as his eye continued to bleed stubbornly.

Heading straight back on the street invited unwarranted attention, so Sherman tacked south through the forest. He kept a slow and methodical pace, careful not to hurry. Impatience killed as easily as a bullet. The path back was familiar, and Sherman didn't stumble or snag on the undergrowth.

Fifteen minutes later, he crossed the main road into town within sight of the downed tree roadblock. By the time he reached the back door of Doc Calvert's office, Sherman was cold, exhausted, hungry, and in a considerable amount of pain. He knocked and stood back far enough to be sure the camera saw him.

Ramona opened the back door with a relieved look that quickly soured into worry.

"Frank, you look like hell," she said and stood aside to let him in.

"I feel worse," he replied, stepping inside.

Ramona locked the door behind him. "Are you sure? Have you looked in a mirror?"

Sherman stepped into the bathroom and took a glance. He looked beyond wild. Blood oozed from his eyebrows, and his clothes were somehow both wet and covered with gunk. Bits of slime and leaves stuck to his pants, and a pool of pink water had formed on the floor beneath his boots—amixture of the Russian's blood and rainwater.

"All right, I do look terrible," he said.

Ramona looked over her shoulder and added, "I made some fresh coffee. You interested?"

"I need a caffeine drip, but coffee sounds great. Thanks."

They went into the waiting room and Sherman sat on a plastic chair. He slipped off the vest and jacket, stripping down to his soaked T-shirt. Neither Auntie Zil nor Shawn said anything, but they both watched keenly.

Ramona returned with an extra-large mug and handed it over. "Extra cream," she said.

"Thanks," said Sherman.

He took a sip. It tasted divine, like manna for a weary soul.

All the eyes in the room remained fixated on him, waiting for an update or retelling. Sherman could feel their curiosity building, but he didn't have the energy to recount all the details.

"Long story short, there are two left," he said.

"How many did you get?" asked Auntie Zil.

"Five," said Sherman.

Shawn's jaw would have hit the floor had it not been attached.

Auntie Zil nodded in muted admiration.

"Five," repeated Ramona.

Sherman took another sip of coffee. "Three on the road outside the pub. One under the pier and one more inside. Your bottle is still on the bar, by the way."

Auntie Zil shrugged, "Not all traditions last."

"How is King and everyone else?" asked Ramona.

"Traumatized but alive," said Sherman.

Ramona let out a torrid breath. "Thank you, again."

"How's Hal?" he asked.

"Still alive," said Auntie Zil.

"Stable but critical," Doc Calvert corrected, stepping into the waiting room. "Looks like you need some help."

Sherman gave a tiny nod. Moving his head hurt.

The doctor disappeared for a moment and returned with a small box labeled wound care. He knelt next to Sherman and cleaned the cut on his eyebrow.

"This is pretty deep," said Doc Calvert. "I'm going to place some butterfly strips to keep it shut. Try not to get punched again."

"How did you know?" asked Sherman.

"I can see the bruising from the knuckles."

"He had a hard fist."

"And a good deal of blood," said Calvert.

Sherman tried not to move.

"The other side of your face is covered in it," said the doctor as an explanation.

Sherman nodded. "That too."

Doc Calvert finished and stood up. "It's a pretty clean cut, should heal up nicely and blend in with all the other scars."

"Thanks, Doc."

"If there is nothing else, I'm going to take a nap," he said and wandered off to the dentist's chair.

Sherman leaned back and finished his cup of coffee in greedy gulps.

"What about the last two?" asked Ramona.

"Two or twenty, they'll keep coming," said Sherman. "Whoever is left on that list has deep pockets. They won't stop until they have what she took." He nodded toward Auntie Zil.

"Are you willing to part with your secrets?" asked Ramona.

The old woman nodded slowly. "I'm ready."

"How are you gonna do that if old man crazy lost it?" asked Shawn, interjecting himself into the conversation.

Ramona shot him a look that said, *The adults are talking.*

"Just asking," he added.

"Young Shawn has a point," said Auntie Zil. "We can do nothing without the documents."

"Before Hal started shooting, the mercenaries opened a box, but it was empty," said Sherman. "How many documents are we talking?"

Auntie Zil held up her hands and mimed a rough size. About two reams worth of paper.

"That's a lot of secrets," said Ramona.

"Some files have many pictures," said Auntie Zil.

"You know all the proverbial skeletons," added Ramona.

"And more."

"Any copies?" asked Sherman.

Auntie Zil tapped her head. "Just the ones up here."

"We better hope they accept just the hard copies," said Sherman.

"Assuming Hal didn't dump them at sea," Ramona said.

Sherman shook his head. Despite Hal's outwardly irrational behavior, inside his own mind, he was acting very rationally. He just happened to be stuck in the distant past.

"Look, Hal is losing his mind, but right now, he thinks it is 1969 and is acting accordingly. He's not crazy... well, he is, but you get what I mean."

"He is doing what he did fifty-plus years ago," said Ramona.

"Exactly," said Sherman.

"And what was Hal doing in 1969?" she asked.

"Fighting in Vietnam."

Chapter Thirty-One

Even in the pre-dawn darkness, the bodies in the road were clearly visible—contorted wet forms bathed in the dusky yellow streetlights. Stanton saw them from a good distance out, but Anton wanted to move closer.

"They're dead," said Stanton. He didn't think saying more mattered.

"The soldier did this," said Anton.

The truth of his statement seemed obvious to Stanton. Of course, the soldier caused all the trouble. He wanted to remind Anton this was par for the course, an inevitability, but his side ached and his mind suddenly felt fuzzy from the painkillers.

"We should leave," said Stanton. The words tumbled out before his brain could wrangle them back.

"Leave!" growled Anton, and Stanton knew he had made a mistake in suggesting retreat.

"You must have more men," added Stanton, trying to recover. "Come back with them and try again."

"This was your plan, Mr. Stanton. You must fix it."

Stanton desperately tried to fabricate some response, but his mind felt heavy and foggy.

The painkillers, he thought, feeling out of control.

Anton scoffed at him. There was real venom in his eyes. A hatred of sorts that Stanton did not understand.

"Make yourself useful," said the Russian, who was double-checking his own rifle and gear.

"What are you doing?" asked Stanton, feeling suddenly vulnerable as if his position in the grand plan teetered precariously.

"The soldier knows. I bet he took the list for himself. I'm going to find him and cut the information out of him, slowly, painfully."

Stanton agreed with the first statement. The soldier knew what was going on. As for the second, he wasn't sure, but anything was possible. The usefulness of torture, however, did not interest him. Too unreliable and messy.

"Where are you going?" asked Stanton.

"The bar," said Anton. "Those drunks must know where he went."

Stanton wanted to say how bad of a plan it was, but Anton was already marching down the road. It was a terrible plan, even with a foggy mind, Stanton understood that much. The man was marching up to the building in which his men lay dead or dying. That seemed, to Stanton, to be the very definition of insanity. Doing the same thing again and expecting a different outcome.

From the protection of a cedar, Stanton watched as Anton slipped his way along the street and to the door of Wellerman's Pub. The Russian stopped at the door and tried the knob, but it did not budge.

"Don't do it," whispered Stanton into the night.

Anton, of course, couldn't hear him and wouldn't have

listened. He stepped back and kicked open the front door with a clatter of broken wood. He managed one step forward before everything around him lit up in the pale glow of gunfire.

Dozens of rounds hit Anton and he crumpled into a messy heap at the pub's doorway. At least one person from inside came out and shot Anton again from very close range.

Overkill, thought Stanton.

Then it happened again.

And again.

And again.

Normal people don't act like this, thought Stanton, and he was right. But Hilt Bay was not populated by normal people.

The vindictiveness of the locals, combined with the loss of the only remaining mercenary, made Stanton's next choice easy. He would leave the wretched town as soon as possible. His employer might not even know he'd quit. With any luck, they might assume he got killed too.

Stanton knew he couldn't work again. Not with his name and his face, but those things could be changed. Starting new bothered him, but worse fates awaited him if his employer found out he'd cut and run. Failure was a poorly tolerated outcome in his line of work, and he'd over promised on this job. The money had blinded him to the risks. Happenstance had brought the soldier to town or maybe Anton was right. Maybe he was after the list as well.

Only one more task remained—escaping Hilt Bay. He'd planned on hiking south to the defunct lighthouse and getting a ride from the main road. Unfortunately, his ride was likely halfway back to Idaho by now. His backup plan was a bus stop. The bus ran regularly and connected to a larger town where he could find transport to Portland and the airport.

That was Stanton's plan.

Plans, as he'd discovered, never worked out so smoothly and the pain radiating out from his side changed the order of operations.

Doctor first, thought Stanton.

He would get the local to patch him up and, in turn, Stanton would put a hole in the doctor. One more body wouldn't matter.

Doctor first, then escape. A straightforward plan.

Chapter Thirty-Two

The exact details of his father's and Hal's service in Vietnam were a mystery to Sherman but he understood the broad strokes of their mission. They killed Vietcong—lots of them according to the meager stories his father hinted at after one too many longneck bottles.

Ramona still looked confused by his train of thought. "What did Hal do in Vietnam that could possibly help us now?" she asked.

Auntie Zil sighed with a faraway look in her eyes as if she was gazing into the past.

"Ask her," said Sherman.

"Auntie Zil," said Ramona. "Do you know?"

"I was much younger then," she began. "My first assignment for the KGB. Moscow sent us to north Vietnam as advisors, much like the Americans years before. They thought sending a woman would be less noticeable. The war was everywhere back then. North or south, it didn't matter. My orders were simple. Help coordinate the Vietcong activities in the south. We devised all sorts of strategies to keep things organized and things went well until all the local leaders started dying, usually from a sniper's bullet."

"Hal?" asked Ramona.

"And others," said Auntie Zil. "We didn't know their names back then. They weren't infamous like Hathcock, but just as deadly. The problem we faced was that our intel disappeared the Vietcong."

"What do you mean by intel?" asked Ramona and Sherman smiled at her acumen. She asked the right question.

"Maps, lists of collaborators, weapon counts, troop strengths. All manner of documents. You must remember, communists love documentation. The more, the better, in a bureaucratic state. Important information to have when fighting a war, so it was even more galling to have it fall into enemy hands."

Auntie Zil Paused and gave a brief chuckle before continuing.

"It wasn't because the Vietcong lacked resourcefulness, they could do just about anything if they set their minds to it and with a quarter of the parts. But they kept hiding things in their houses."

Sherman and Ramona both leaned forward sensing the importance of Auntie Zil's previous laugh.

"At first, they hid documents in rice bags and floor-boards, but the Americans figured that out quickly. Then they hung documents down their wells, but that didn't work. They buried guns and ammunition at the edge of the village, but secrets they wanted to keep close."

"What was your third best solution?" asked Sherman. The top two were likely too successful for Hal to have known about, but the third seemed a reasonable place to start.

Auntie Zil smiled. "Smart of you not to start with the best. The Americans never figured those out. One of my first designs, one that worked for a few months, involved a narrow diameter metal pipe capped at both ends, but long enough to fit whatever maps or papers went inside. The Vietcong leader would slide it inside one of the bamboo struts in their hut. Even if it burned down, like many villages did when the Americans came, chances were the contents would survive."

"I don't think all your documents would fit in a steel pipe," said Ramona.

"No, they wouldn't," said Sherman. "But I think I know where Hal might have put them."

"Where?" asked Ramona and Auntie Zil.

Before Sherman could answer, he heard the distinctive pop of suppressed rifle fire in the distance and jumped to his feet.

"Did you hear that?" he asked.

"Lots of gunfire," said Auntie Zil.

"From the west," said Sherman, peering through a crack in the curtains.

"The pub?" asked Ramona, her face contorting with concern. "They came back."

"Not without consequence," said Sherman. "Those guys were armed and angry when I left."

Ramona ran to the office phone and quickly dialed a number without pause.

"Hey, it's me. We heard gunfire. Are you okay?"

Sherman couldn't hear the response, but Ramona let out a long sigh of relief and smiled.

"King says the Russian is dead," she conveyed with one hand over the receiver.

"Only one?" asked Sherman.

Ramona repeated the question and nodded. "Only one."

"Tell him good work," Sherman added.

Ramona did and gratefully hung up the phone. She caught Sherman looking at her in curiosity.

"King is an old friend," she said as if her worry needed explaining, which it didn't. "He helped me move out after Jack died, which took some guts considering Colby threatened to beat the crap out of him." She laughed. "I don't think King even blinked and no one called his bluff."

"Friends like that are hard to find," said Sherman.

"I must be lucky," said Ramona and smiled again.

Auntie Zil cracked her knuckles and Sherman turned back to face the old woman, suddenly aware he had been looking at Ramona a few beats too long.

"There is still one more, correct?" she asked.

"Stanton," said Ramona, the smile disappearing.

"Fleeing is the smart play," said Sherman. "He is on his own now—no hired guns for backup. He doesn't strike me as a zealot. This was carefully planned, and all good plans have an exit."

"Do you think he'll run?" asked Shawn.

"I don't pretend to know what he'll do, but that's the smart move. Why?"

Shawn held up the tablet. "Because there is a dude walking toward the front door and I ain't ever seen him before."

Sure enough, the camera showed a single figure hugging the edge of the buildings and headed their direction. The man wore a thick rubberized raincoat with the hood up, but his head swiveled about with worry, and he clutched his side with one arm.

"He's leaving town," said Ramona.

"No," said Auntie Zil. "He's hurt."

Sherman grabbed his rifle and rushed to the front door, pulling Shawn along with him. "Hold that up so I can see," he instructed.

With the tablet in view, Sherman waited to open the door as Stanton passed, but to his amusement, the figure stopped and rang the emergency doorbell like anyone else. There was a clamor and the dentist's office and Doc Calvert shouted, "*Coming*," out of habit.

The man outside looked back toward the bar and Sherman pulled open the door, rifle raised. When he turned back, his eyes ballooned in surprise.

"Move and you die," said Sherman.

Stanton's pale blue eyes danced around the room before landing back on Sherman. His left arm crossed his body, clutching at his right side just under the armpit. His right hand was in his pocket, unseen, no doubt holding a handgun of sorts.

"You're not that quick," said Sherman, his finger already exerting a few pounds of force on the trigger. "Show me your hands slowly if you want to live."

Stanton didn't move, but his eyes burrowed into Sherman, who dug right back.

"I'm not gonna count," said Sherman, who began to think he should have shot the stranger in the face straight away and been done with the sordid adventure, but they would keep coming for the list, so he tried a diplomatic approach.

Stanton blinked and carefully held up his hands above his shoulders, wincing in the process.

"Shawn, search him," said Sherman.

"I'm unarmed," said Stanton.

"Then you're stupid," said Sherman.

Shawn retrieved a Glock 19 from Stanton's right jacket pocket and held it up along with two phones from another pocket.

"Ankles too," said Sherman and Shawn checked and came up with a five-inch fixed blade.

"Take the jacket off," instructed Sherman.

Stanton winced again as Shawn tugged the heavy raincoat off, revealing soft body armor torn on one side.

"Armor too."

When Sean removed the armor, they all saw why Stanton clutched at his side. A bloody wad of gauze attached by a good deal of tape wrapped around his chest. A bullet wound. Through and through, judging by the looks of it, but bullets never travel without creating damage.

"You're the soldier," said Stanton, his gaze fixed on Sherman.

"And you're the planner," said Sherman. "Take a seat on the floor."

After Stanton complied, Sherman pulled a zip-cuffs off the vest and tossed it to Shawn. "Hands behind his back. Keep your feet out front. Pull it tight."

Shawn hesitated as Stanton slowly pulled his arms back like the man might bite, but eventually got everything secured.

Doc Calvert stepped forward and tapped Sherman on the shoulder. "I'd like to help him, unless you plan on executing a man in my office."

"For the record, I bet my house he planned on killing you after," said Sherman.

"I don't doubt it, but I took an oath."

"Suit yourself," said Sherman, glad people like Doc Calvert still roamed the earth. That kind of chivalry was a dying ember.

As the doctor worked, Ramona leaned forward and asked, "Do you even own a home?"

"No, but it seemed a good figure of speech," whispered Sherman.

After cleaning and repacking the wound, the doctor rejoined Sherman. "He needs surgery to remove the bone fragments."

"Not going to happen here," said Sherman.

"I assumed as much. I also assume I don't want to see what comes next."

"Probably not, it might stretch your oath."

"I'll be in the back if you need me."

"Thanks, Doc."

Sherman turned back to Stanton, who seethed with a cold fury that radiated out of his pale blue eyes. He was a dangerous man. A man of violence, cruelty, and indifference but also a man of intellect and self-preservation. He could have gone down swinging with the last Russian but chose to save himself or at least try. Sherman thought that quality would be useful in the coming hours. A true believer wouldn't help the enemy, but a rational planner might if the incentives were right, and what better incentive was there than life itself.

Sherman knelt in front of Stanton, so they looked eye to eye.

"This next part isn't my forte. I'm a take action kind of guy and not much for the questioning bit, but I'll try my best, and if we don't get anywhere, I'll turn it over to her," said Sherman, pointing to Auntie Zil who sat quietly on the couch.

Stanton gazed at her with icy eyes, devouring every detail. Then he switched to Ramona and she shifted uneasily.

"You've been here the whole time," he said.

"Ever since you—" Ramona began, but Sherman held up a hand.

He knew what she would say and didn't want Stanton to know Terrance was still alive and didn't die in that ravine.

"Since when?" Stanton prodded.

"Since your friends landed their boat in the wrong town," said Sherman. "How many more of them are out there?"

"Dozens," said Stanton.

The lie came smoothly, without effort or hesitation. At least, Sherman thought it was a lie.

"They're probably surrounding this dismal building as we speak," added Stanton.

Sherman picked up the tablet and glanced at the camera feed. He saw nothing but rain and empty streets.

"Afraid not," he said. "I think they're all dead, save for one or two who went back with the guy shot in the leg. Looked like a pretty bad injury. Probably tourniquet worthy, which means he needed medical attention within the hour. You're alone, hurt, and trying to get out."

Stanton said nothing. His face revealed nothing, as if carved from stone—a smooth professional.

Auntie Zil stood up and pulled a chair across the room, letting it drag and squeak. She set it down in front of Stanton and sat.

"Mr. Stanton," she began, and Stanton's eyes twitched at the use of his name. "Yes, we know who you are. I also know the men you work for are after me."

Those pale blue eyes widened with interest.

"You can still hand over the list," he said. "Give it to me and no one else gets hurt."

Auntie Zil gave a crinkled smile. "Call the man who hired you and you might live."

Stanton hesitated.

"Or don't and the soldier here will dump your corpse in the ocean for the sharks to deal with."

Sherman hadn't agreed to that but didn't mind the idea.

"That's not much of a choice," said Stanton.

"I didn't say you had one," retorted Auntie Zil. "You have an opportunity to see the sunrise if you call the person funding this misguided operation. And if you do as I say."

"And you won't hurt me?" asked Stanton. His expression said nothing of his fears, but the question laid them bare.

"I won't," said Auntie Zil and she sounded convincing, but she also pushed a man off the cliff hours earlier, so Sherman wasn't sure of her authenticity.

"What about him?" asked Stanton and nodded in Sherman's direction.

"I've got no intention of hurting you if you make this call."

"And her?"

This time, Stanton nodded toward Ramona who stood in the back seething with anger but trying to hide it. Sherman sympathized. The guy who shot her brother and left him for dead was tied up on the floor asking if he was safe in her presence.

"Does she have any reason to harm you?" asked Sherman before Ramona could answer.

"No," said Stanton a little too firmly as if hoping no one knew about Terrance.

"Are you satisfied with our intentions?" asked Auntie Zil.

"Not in the slightest, but hand me the flip phone and I'll make the call."

"A few ground rules first," Auntie Zil continued. "There will be no mention of your current location. You may retell events in broad strokes, but no specifics related to anyone in the room besides me. We give them the list and they leave us alone. Am I clear?"

"They want your blood," Stanton added.

"They want the list more," she replied. "Am I clear?"

"Yes, no specifics, except for you."

"Good. Shawn, would you open the flip phone and dial whatever number Mr. Stanton requires but put the call on speaker."

Shawn did as asked and, soon enough, they heard the call ringing. It kept ringing without answer until it should have gone to voicemail. Right before Shawn bent forward to hang up and try again, someone answered.

"It's Stanton," said Stanton.

"This is a dead number, Mr. Stanton. Why are you calling me?" asked the voice, which sounded Eastern European to Sherman. Probably Russian, but he wasn't sure. Lots of Slavic languages sounded alike to the untrained ear.

Auntie Zil shifted uncomfortably in her chair, looking like she recognized the voice.

"The situation warrants direct contact," said Stanton. "Have you heard from Serge?"

There was a pause on the other end. "Not recently."

"That's because all his men are dead, and the mission is a failure."

"How?"

"Locals," said Stanton simply.

Sherman gave him credit. The man was an experienced operator.

"You have not answered my question. Why are you calling?"

"The situation has changed but I believe the item you want is still attainable."

"Go on."

"The woman you're after is willing to give up the list on the condition that you leave her and this town alone."

Another pause ensued.

"Hello, Nadia."

Auntie Zil sat up straighter as if bracing for an unpleasant conversation.

"Viktor," she said.

"You remember."

"Some things cannot be forgotten."

"Tell me, Nadia, what do you want?"

"You can have the dossiers," said Auntie Zil.

"And in return?" asked Viktor.

"You forget about Nadia and this town. I haven't been that woman in forty years."

"Once KGB, always KGB," said the man.

"No, Viktor. I moved on with life."

The man laughed hollowly.

"Fine. I will not contradict your delusion. Deliver the list to my man and you and that town will be forgotten like all the others."

Auntie Zil grimaced but said, "It will be done."

"Always the professional. Now, Mr. Stanton, are you still breathing?"

"Yes."

"Fascinating. Serge will call you to arrange the retrieval. Do not bungle what opportunity remains."

"Yes, sir."

The call ended without another word and both Auntie

Zil and Stanton let out collective sighs. Sherman had no idea of Viktor's identity, but he certainly inspired fear, which meant he had considerable money and power and the will to wield it.

"Well," said Auntie Zil. "I guess the only thing left to do is find the list."

Stanton's pale blue eyes went mad with surprise.

Chapter Thirty-Three

The first pale glow of day filtered between the trees in a dull silver. Sherman's watch read 5:25 a.m. He'd been awake for almost twenty-four hours, but it felt longer. His face ached, his ribs hurt, and his body wanted to shut down. Ramona looked a little better but wasn't covered in dried blood and butterfly bandages.

They stepped out of the doctor's office and into Ramona's SUV, still parked in the wrong direction for that side of the street. Sherman kept his vest on and still carried the rifle, despite the illusion of safety. Old habits from years in places where the danger never left.

"Do you think Auntie Zil will… you know, break her word?" asked Ramona.

"And shoot Stanton?"

"Or worse. She did push a guy off the cliff."

"Do you care?" asked Sherman.

"Maybe."

"As in you don't approve or you want to be the one to do it?"

Ramona started the Toyota but said nothing as they turned around and headed towards Hal's house.

"He did shoot Terrance," she added after turning right at the T-junction.

"That he did," said Sherman.

Ramona remained silent, but she seemed to struggle with some internal conflict like the binding ties of family.

"We Wilders have a code," she added.

"One that you follow?" asked Sherman.

"Not with any regularity, but collective defense and retribution are held in high regard."

"Sounds like a lot of personal codes I've heard over the years," said Sherman.

"Do you have one?" she asked.

"Survive," said Sherman simply.

Ramona waited for more, and when none came, she glanced in his direction quizzically and asked, "That's it? No country or duty or mission?"

"Some of that," said Sherman. "But survival matters most. Hard to fight if you're dead."

"Doesn't that go against the idea of being a soldier?"

Sherman considered her question carefully. "Am I afraid to die? No. I expect to meet a violent end one day. Simple math, really. Do this long enough and the odds stack against you. But that's not the point of survival. It's not outrunning the inevitable but being effective for as long as possible. I've lost a lot of friends, good men and women, and I would trade with them in a heartbeat, but they're dead and I'm not, so I'll keep on surviving for as long as possible."

Ramona sighed in a strange understanding sort of way. "You certainly have my thanks. We'd all be fish bait if you weren't around."

Somehow, Sherman doubted that but took the compliment and smiled.

Ramona pulled up in front of Hal's darkened house and they exited the SUV. Rain still drizzled from the swirling clouds overhead.

"Where do you think Hal put the documents?" asked Ramona.

Sherman moved around the house and towards the shed out back. He motioned for Ramona to follow.

"This wasn't thrashed like the rest of the house," he said as they stood in front of the still-open shed doors.

"Maybe Hal forgot he had one," said Ramona.

"I was thinking something similar," Sherman added.

He pulled the string in the middle of the shed and a pale-yellow light washed over the space. On the left side was a small built-in wooden bench, and below that, the toolboxes that Sherman had found the Colt in. Woodworking tools hung from a pegboard above the bench and the shed had the earthy aroma of sawdust and sap. It reminded Sherman of his friend, Tillerman. He and Hal would have gotten along, with their shared interests and hermit-like proclivities.

"I looked through the toolboxes earlier," he said and turned to the right side of the shed. "But this deserves a search."

There were old file boxes stacked in one corner and piles of lumber against the wall.

"I'll take the boxes," said Ramona.

Sherman nodded and began sifting through odd bits of construction material. He turned over planks and chunks of wood, none of which could have concealed anything like what Auntie Zil described. Sherman even checked the extra lengths of PVC pipe, but they were empty of any paper.

"No luck here," he said.

"Lots of old newspaper clippings but nothing that looks like Soviet secrets. Oh, you're in this one." Ramona held up an old picture cut from a local paper when Sherman was in high school. It showed the baseball team and the title read, *Back-to-back County Champions*.

"I find it hard to imagine you as a teenager," Ramona added.

"And here I don't feel a day over twenty-two," Sherman joked.

"I hate to break it to you, but you look old and haggard right now."

"I feel it too," said Sherman.

"Afraid I've got nothing here," said Ramona.

Sherman took a step back to survey the scene. "If Hal is stuck in the late sixties, but not Vietnam, where would he hide something?"

"That's a rhetorical question, right?"

"Maybe. Where does your father hide things?"

"In the Smuggler's Vault, so we never found anything," answered Ramona.

"I see," said Sherman and scratched his beard. "Mine used to hide booze in the rafters of the garage. I never knew if he hid it from me or my mother."

"I raided my share of liquor cabinets, but after my mom died, my dad didn't say anything. I think he knew we needed a release but couldn't bear the thought of genuine emotional support."

"The shitty fathers' club," said Sherman.

"Indeed," replied Ramona.

"Hand me that stool," he said, and Ramona gave him a stubby stepping stool.

The shed had an angled roof and exposed 2x6 rafters

for a ceiling that was never built. Sherman guessed Hal wasn't climbing up between the exposed rafters at his age, so he poked his head up and looked around. He didn't see any hidden parcels and was about to step down when an incongruity snagged in his mind. The walls of the shed were oddly insulated, and each wall had a 2x4 running along the top, except for one section towards the back.

Sherman stepped down and slid the stool towards the odd section.

"What is it?" asked Ramona.

"Bad construction practices," said Sherman as he reached his arm down between the sheets of plywood. He found no insulation, but two heavy rectangular objects wrapped in plastic. "And a good hiding spot," he added, pulling out his prize.

The two parcels thumped heavily as Sherman placed them on the workbench. Wrapped in clear plastic were a series of old brown file folders—hundreds of them, decades of surveillance and counter-surveillance, secrets upon secrets, all carefully labeled and categorized.

"All this bloodshed for some paper," said Ramona.

"It usually is," said Sherman. "Treaties, money… it's all paper."

"And it's worth nothing," she said.

Sherman couldn't argue with that. Of all the war he'd seen, very little of it made any sense. Driving the Taliban from Afghanistan could have been an exception, but now they were back. Things had come full circle, back to bad.

"Do you want to know what's inside?" asked Ramona, turning the plastic-wrapped collection over in her hands.

"No," said Sherman. "I don't."

Ramona tilted her head and looked at him with those curious eyes. "Not even a little?"

"Nope. In my experience, secrets don't end well."

"No, I suppose not," added Ramona, but she didn't look convinced. Some small part of her wanted to know. Sherman could see as much.

"You can always ask Auntie Zil," he suggested. "She might share a scrap or two with you. Or maybe Hal can provide some clarity... if he ever wakes up. I'm sure he knows lots of skeletons."

"And you? What secrets do you have?"

"Plenty," said Sherman. "But most of them aren't worth sharing."

"I doubt that," said Ramona.

"Come on, let's get these back," said Sherman.

Even having them gave him a sense of foreboding, like the ghosts of Soviet Russia might reach out and pull them under.

They left as the pallid light of morning began to filter through the trees of Hilt Bay. By the time they got to the T-junction, Sherman could see the waves crashing onto the rocky beach. The glittery, wet pavement of last night looked a dull charcoal.

What Sherman didn't see on the road in front of the pub were the bodies. They had disappeared.

"Where are they?" asked Sherman.

"Who?"

"The dead," said Sherman.

Ramona pointed to a porch where an old couple were busy taping the ends of a tarp. A tarp big enough to hold a corpse.

"Hilt Bay takes care of its own. I'm sure King told them everything. My guess is, those men will be down the Smuggler's Vault by lunch."

The old couple gave Ramona a solemn nod as they turned left toward the doctor's office.

Further down, a trio of trucks were parked by the downed trees. Men with chainsaws drank coffee from thermoses and sized up the challenge.

"That might take them until lunch too," added Ramona as they parked.

Everyone was still inside where they had left them earlier. Auntie Zil sat very still on the couch, glaring at Stanton, who glared right back with his pale blue eyes. Only Shawn had changed spots and was now asleep in the corner.

"Did you find them?" asked Auntie Zil.

Sherman handed over the plastic-wrapped documents. "He hid them in the shed wall," he added.

Auntie Zil nodded and took the thick collection, placing it next to her on the couch. She looked across the room and said, "Time to call your employer, Mr. Stanton."

Stanton frowned, but by then, he had no choice in the matter. Auntie Zil opened the flip phone and redialed the last number with the call on speaker.

The call connected, and Stanton went through his usual introduction before the man Auntie Zil called Viktor spoke.

"Do you have the documents?" he asked.

"They do," said Stanton, whose hands were still bound behind his back.

"Good. Serge will be there in an hour to collect everything. He will meet you on the beach. Make sure no one interrupts."

"Of course," said Stanton, and Auntie Zil closed the phone.

Ramona continued to glare at Stanton from the edge of

the room, hatred burning in her eyes. Her hands fidgeted and flitted.

Chapter Thirty-Four

The hour passed slowly until Ramona suddenly looked at the clock and squeezed Sherman's shoulder.

"The cafe just opened. I bet you could use a hot meal," she said.

"And coffee," added Sherman, acknowledging his low energy reserves.

"Of course," said Ramona.

"Are you good watching him?" Sherman asked Auntie Zil.

"I am up to the task," she replied.

"I'll wake Shawn up, too," said Ramona.

"I am fine," said Auntie Zil.

"Extra eyes won't hurt," said Sherman.

"I'll bring you all to-go boxes," Ramona offered.

"Extra cabbage," said Auntie Zil before adding, "please."

Stanton said nothing, which was all he would have gotten anyway.

Sherman and Ramona left the office and drove the two blocks to the café, just in case they needed the vehicle.

"You might want to take that off," said Ramona and pointed to the tactical vest Sherman still wore.

He slipped it and his wet jacket off and put it in the back seat next to the rifle but tucked the Colt into his waist. The task was incomplete, and Sherman didn't like the feeling. That buried core of survival instincts said *stay sharp*.

Ramona did not comment about the pistol, and they walked into the café minutes after it opened, yet the place was already full.

Most of the group from Wellerman's Pub were there, including King, who nursed a cup of coffee at the counter. Two men, who Sherman recognized as hostages from hours earlier, vacated their seats at the counter without a word and offered them to Sherman and Ramona.

Ramona thanked them and they sat next to King. A woman in her late fifties emerged with two mugs of coffee and wordlessly put them down.

"Thanks, Barb," said Ramona.

Sherman felt the collective gaze of the restaurant on his back, but the energy did not feel negative. They seemed welcoming, almost appreciative.

"They all know," said King, looking over at Sherman. "They won't say a thing, but they all know."

The idea of the entire town knowing he'd shot a bunch of guys, even bad guys, did not sit well with Sherman.

An older man that Sherman thought could be the one he saw dive for cover on his front porch, finished his meal and patted Sherman on the shoulder before he left. The man said nothing, but there was gratitude and respect in his expression.

Barb emerged with two blue-plate specials, and as they

ate, several more locals stopped to give Sherman a squeeze or pat on the back.

"See," said King. "This town doesn't give up its own and you've certainly earned their respect."

Barb didn't even bring a check when they'd finished eating. She placed three to-go boxes down and smiled at Sherman.

"If you're ever hungry, just stop by, it's on the house," she said.

Sherman nodded. "Thanks."

"Beer too," said King.

They stood to leave, and Sherman tried to leave a tip, but Ramona shook her head and said, "Don't insult Barb's generosity. This is her way of showing gratitude."

"Her husband was in the pub," said King.

"Oh," said Sherman, putting his wallet away.

By the time they got back to Doc Calvert's office, half of the downed trees were cut and cleared from the road.

Ramona handed out boxes of food to Shawn, Auntie Zil, and Doc Calvert, who emerged from the back room with bleary eyes. They ate in silence, ignoring Stanton's steady glare.

With fifteen minutes to go, Sherman retrieved the vest and rifle from Ramona's SUV and geared up. He had no intention of meeting Serge unprepared.

"Time to go," he said.

Ramona and Auntie Zil both stood.

"No offense, Auntie Zil," he said. "I think it is best that you stay. I don't want them getting any ideas."

The woman furrowed her wrinkled brow but nodded, "I'll stay here with Hal," she said.

"I'm coming," said Ramona.

Sherman didn't argue and pulled Stanton to his feet.

They shuffled out to the SUV and Ramona turned south at the T-junction. They passed the salvage yard, which had a newly acquired, albeit damaged, Zodiac boat out front. The lumber mill was buzzing with activity as well, processing freshly cut trees from the roadblock.

They kept going to the southern edge of the beach and got out. Only a drizzle remained and the three of them stood in the bracing sea air waiting for Serge to arrive.

Stanton was not pleased with the plan as it wasn't his plan, but his luck still held. Despite the collective failures of Serge and Anton, he was on the verge of getting paid. He just needed to survive the next few minutes and his obligations would be fulfilled. His employer might find cause to reduce his fee, but even seventy percent of rich was still rich.

Of course, he didn't let any of those thoughts show—not so close to the end.

Stay calm, he thought. *No sudden movements*.

The soldier wasn't jumpy, but the Wilder woman had not stopped with the death glares for hours. Stanton did his best to ignore her without looking away or showing fear.

Finding Terrance will take time, he told himself. *She doesn't know... yet*.

Still, the risk of discovery existed. *Yet* did not mean an allotted time. *Yet* was not a guarantee of safe passage. It was the absence of facts, and facts might emerge at any moment.

A tingling sense of relief radiated down Stanton's back as a boat emerged into view. The black Zodiac motored up to the beach, but Serge made no effort to pull it in any further. Another Russian sat by the till. The one who helped Serge back.

Lucky bastard, thought Stanton.

Just two remained to split their substantial payday.

Serge limped up the rocky beach. His leg was stiff and wrapped in a cast. He eyed the soldier and the woman before scoffing at Stanton.

"You got caught," he said.

"Better than dead," Stanton replied indignantly.

"Perhaps," said Serge before addressing the soldier. "Do you have what we want?"

"She does," he answered with one hand still on the rifle. The soldier wasn't taking chances, but from what Stanton knew, the Russians wouldn't last long in a fight.

Ramona Wilder handed over the two thick stacks of folders and papers. Serge took them, peeled off the plastic, and began flipping through the ancient brown folders until he stopped. Serge didn't open the file but took a picture of the cover with his phone and sent it into the ether.

He answered a call moments later. They spoke in Russian. Stanton didn't understand a word, but Serge nodded throughout and hung up with an odd look of triumph.

"Is it all there?" he asked.

"She said it is," said Ramona.

Stanton assumed they spoke of the old woman everyone called Auntie Zil.

"You won't like it if we have to come back," said Serge.

"Neither will you," said the soldier.

A statement Stanton found rather trite. Of course, he wouldn't, nor would Serge return with anything less than a battalion of men.

Serge gave a muted laugh that died in his throat. "We're done then," he said and headed back to the boat.

"What about him?" shouted the soldier. He was pointing at Stanton.

"Not my problem," said Serge and turned away.

"We made a deal," said Stanton, wanting to be freed while Serge was there. His presence felt like an added guarantee. A witness or enforcer of the agreement.

But Serge didn't stay.

The boat roared away into the drizzle and choppy waves, leaving Stanton standing on an empty beach with Ramona and the soldier.

"Did my father know?" asked Ramona.

Stanton didn't like family questions and he turned tentatively in her direction.

"Did my father know what would happen?" she elaborated.

"You'll have to ask him," said Stanton, not wanting to get involved.

"I'm asking you," she replied.

"He knew enough."

"And what did he get out of this deal?"

"His freedom," said Stanton.

"He's got seven years left on his sentence," said Ramona.

"And now it is days."

Ramona frowned and Stanton knew he was walking a delicate line.

"Can you cut these cuffs off?" he asked, looking at the soldier.

"I said I wouldn't hurt you, but I have no intention of helping you."

Stanton suppressed his rage. The cuffs would make his hike out harder, but he'd find a way to get them off. A sharp rock or a piece of metal would work.

"I'll be on my way then," said Stanton. He didn't want to risk any more time with those two.

The soldier held up a hand and pushed him in the chest. The force staggered Stanton backwards.

"She's not done," said the soldier.

I am, thought Stanton, but waited quietly.

"Did my father know what you would do?" she asked.

"I just gathered the gear," said Stanton, trying to sound unimportant.

"No, Terrance gathered the gear. We saw it in his car."

Her brother's name sent a tiny chill down Stanton's neck, but he didn't let his fear show. They couldn't know. Not yet.

"He helped because your father told him to," said Stanton.

Ramona nodded, slowly bobbing her head up and down, but her face had the tight lines of rage.

"He helped you, and then you shot him—left him for dead in a ravine."

"No," said Stanton, his stomach dropping with a dark rampant fear.

"We found him. He's in the back room of the doctor's office. Alive and stable."

At least he's not here, thought Stanton.

"You shot him," she continued. "For what? The fun of it?"

Stanton couldn't think of a reasonable excuse or a palatable truth. His only hope lay with her nickname on the bartender's phone. Perhaps she truly was reasonable.

"Employer stipulation," he offered.

"Cleaning up loose ends," added the soldier.

"Something like that," said Stanton.

"Well, I guess that has a similar outcome to family

pride," said Ramona and raised a shiny pistol from behind her back.

Nothing registered in Stanton's mind—it went blank—then Ramona pulled the trigger, and he was gone.

The gunshot didn't surprise Sherman. He guessed the pistol was still in Ramona's coat. The real question was, would she pull the trigger? Up until the attack at her house, Sherman would have said *maybe*.

Maybe is a good guess for most people. *No* only applies to the truly zealous. Most people, when pushed hard enough, snap. It's human nature. After the attack at her house, after she put the Russian down with an extra bullet, Sherman changed his answer.

Ramona was a strong *yes*.

Click. Bang. Done.

Stanton crumpled to the ground.

"Was that part of the Wilder code?" asked Sherman.

"Probably, or maybe he was just an asshole."

"Definitely an asshole," said Sherman, who held no judgement against her actions.

"Are you all done?" said a voice from behind. The old couple from the porch stepped off the road and onto the beach.

Ramona waved. "Thanks, Howard. I'm all done."

"Howard?" asked Sherman.

"He used to be the mortician," she answered.

"That explains the body bag," he replied.

They left Howard and his wife to clean up what remained of Stanton and headed back to the doctor's office.

Chapter Thirty-Five

Hal came out of his fever-pitched dreams a couple of days after the dust settled and the bodies disappeared. Even the bullet-ridden window and door at Ramona's house had been replaced, a gift from Ms. Bleeker's guest, Mr. Mendoza. Only Vern's brief funeral suggested anything had happened in Hilt Bay.

Sherman happened to be in the room when Hal woke. He gave him a warm smile and Sherman wondered what version of Hal had surfaced.

"Franky," he croaked.

"Uncle Hal," said Sherman and took a seat next to the bed. "How are you feeling?"

"Like I got shot," said Hal, his eyes dancing around the room.

"That's because you did," said Sherman. "Do you remember anything from the last few days?"

A mixture of confusion and embarrassment crossed Hal's haggard face.

"Everything is hazy," replied Hal with a deep sigh.

"I bet the painkillers don't help," Sherman added.

Hal gave a lopsided grin.

"I remember taking Gloria for a walk," he said.

Upon hearing her name, Gloria got up from her bed in the corner of the makeshift surgery room and came over to lick Hal's hand. Hal lit up with joy and scratched her head.

"We were out walking, and I saw... someone," he continued. "After that, things get all jumbled in my mind." He looked away for a moment then snapped back to Sherman. "Wait... how did I get shot?"

"That's quite a tale," said Sherman.

Hal gestured around impotently. "I'm not going anywhere."

Sherman refreshed his cup of coffee and told the story as he understood it, beginning with Gloria's unaccompanied arrival at the door. Hal listened and nodded along as if it all made complete sense.

When Sherman retold Terrance's ordeal, Hal said, "I ain't surprised. He's been looking for trouble since he was a boy, but who can blame him. With a father like that and his poor mother. Plucks at the heartstrings if you think about it. And you thought he hurt me?"

Sherman shrugged and continued, arriving at the conversation with Doc Calvert about Hal's diagnosis.

"I should have told you sooner," said Hal. "But losing one's mind is not the easiest thing to admit, let alone share."

"I don't blame you," Sherman replied. "You're under no obligation to share anything with me."

"I've got a bleak road in front of me, Frank, and you're the closest thing to family I have left, so I'll try to be straight with you... until I forget we had this conversation."

Sherman smiled at the self-deprecating truth of Hal's statement and continued the story through Auntie Zil leaving her half-finished bottle and the gunfight on the cliff. He ended with the trek to Doc Calvert's office.

"That was not my brightest moment," said Hal.

"It could have gone worse."

"Did you know I once carried your father off a mountain?"

"No," said Sherman, curious for the story.

"This was back in Vietnam, well before you were born. Heck, before he ever met your mother. Anyways, the war was all but over, the writing on the wall, and the brass decided they wanted to take a few high-ranking Vietnamese with them on their collective ride to defeat."

"Unsurprising," said Sherman.

"Your father and I were helicoptered far into the bush to chase down some important NVA general who was particularly close with the Russians. A parting snub in their eye from the CIA before we left for good. We humped around in that jungle heat for two days before we found their camp. Never felt so hot and so sweaty in my life. Your father picked this mountain, a hill to people who didn't have to hike up it, to take the shot."

"Not a bad plan," said Sherman.

"No, your father never made a bad plan. Neither was the execution. He sent that NVA general to the next life one clean shot. None of that was the problem."

"Did the NVA find you?"

"Nope," said Hal with a grin.

"What then?"

"Your father got bit by some multicolored jungle spider the size of a golf ball. His leg swelled up like an overfilled sausage and turned all shades of purple. We were too far out to call for evac without giving away our position to the enemy, so I had to carry his delirious ass off the mountain and down the valley until we could get picked up by a Huey."

Sherman couldn't stop laughing. "That's a good story. Why did I never hear it before?"

"Your father was too embarrassed to tell it outside our unit. That spider nearly killed him. He never went back to Vietnam after that."

"Maybe the spider saved him," said Sherman.

"Sounds like you saved me," said Hal. "About time a Sherman returned the favor."

They laughed together because laughter was a tonic for all the trauma they'd seen and caused. Sherman continued the story as Hal listened intently to every word, right through the five dead men at the bar and up to finding the hidden stash in Hal's shed.

"I made that nook years ago, just in case I came across something worth hiding," said Hal.

"And you did."

"Too bad I didn't recall it earlier. Might have saved me from wrecking my house."

"Your neighbors put it back together," said Sherman.

"Good people," said Hal, almost wistfully. "And this Stanton character? Did Zil let him leave?"

"Yes, but Ramona didn't."

Hal's eyes narrowed but there was a small crack of a smile on his face. "She did it?" he asked.

"Very effectively," said Sherman.

Hal fell silent for a minute, lost in some thought or maybe the thought was lost in him.

"I know you and your father didn't get along, but, by God, he would be proud of you."

Pride was not something Sherman remembered his father showering on him.

"Why, the body count?" asked Sherman.

"No, nothing to do with that, but you're a far better soldier than we ever were. He would have been proud of you for making the hard choices and doing the necessary evil."

"The necessary evil?" asked Sherman. The phrase sounded oddly familiar.

"Your father used to say that about our missions. We were the necessary evil that kept others safe."

The more Sherman thought about the phrase, the more it made sense.

"Can I ask you a personal question?"

"Sure," said Hal.

"In your bedroom, there are sticky notes covering the wall, which I get is for remembering things, but we found one missing. I thought it was related to your disappearance, but now I want to know what you are trying to solve. There are a lot of old names and dates."

Hal said nothing for a moment and Sherman wondered if he even remembered the notes at all.

"I suppose that is what I wanted to tell you about this whole time. Why I wrote to you in the first place."

"Okay," said Sherman, suddenly confused.

"Do you remember high school?"

"I try not to," said Sherman.

"We all got transferred your junior year."

"That happened a lot growing up," said Sherman.

"I know, but this was different," said Hal.

"Why?" asked Sherman. He remembered moving and being angry with his father and otherwise moody from being a teenager, but nothing out of the ordinary.

"There was a colonel on the base back then. A real hotshot, ass-kissing type that had general material written all over him. Your father despised the man, and the feeling was mutual. One day, the colonel didn't report for duty. Alarm bells rang as they do for important people and the MPs searched his house but found nothing. No trace of him at all."

"You think my dad had something to do with that?"

"I didn't, but the MPs did. Someone saw the colonel flirting with your mother at a base party. That someone also saw your father issue a stern warning to the man."

"I imagine the threat was graphic," said Sherman.

"Your father wasn't a man of many words, but he used some very descriptive phrases in his rebuke. Words that the MPs found very suspicious. Of course, they couldn't find a body or evidence of a crime, but the brass thought it best to transfer us out to bury any rumors of wrongdoing."

"Okay, but how does that tie into the notes on your wall? My dad died years ago."

Hal leaned forward as if someone was listening. "I saw the colonel's name on Zil's list."

Sherman said nothing for a moment, trying to find a place to begin. He asked, "Out of misplaced curiosity, why would his name be on her list?"

"Do you know what was in the list?" countered Hal.

"No, and I'm not sure I want to."

"Foreign assets, double agents, triple agents, you name it."

"That sounds above my pay grade," said Sherman.

"Mine too, back in the day, but now I'm retired, and I don't give a damn."

"Okay," said Sherman. "That makes this colonel some sort of sleeper agent for the Russians, right?"

"Very much so."

"But he disappeared, so why bring it up now?"

"Zil and I were flipping through the files not long ago and his popped up. I didn't say anything at the time, but there was an alias listed."

"He didn't flee to Russia?"

"No," said Hal.

"Alright, I'll bite. Where is he now?"

"It took me a lot of digging and sticky notes to remember it all, but I found him. He works for an aerospace contractor in Seattle."

"Do they contract with the government?" asked Sherman.

"They build guided missiles," said Hal.

"Do you have a name?"

"I do," said Hal and relayed the alias.

Sherman nodded his head and thought about his next move. He'd have to call Major Sanders but didn't want to reveal where or how he got such information. He needed to walk a fine line not to get anyone into trouble.

"I'll make some calls," said Sherman. "Get some rest, we'll talk again soon."

Chapter Thirty-Six

The next few days passed slowly. Sherman spent most of the time with Hal in the back of Doc Calvert's office. They shared stories and laughed. The old Marine had never softened, and despite his best efforts, otherwise appeared primed to make a recovery. Not a full recovery, that didn't happen at his age, but he was working towards solid foods and that was progress after getting shot in the gut.

Terrance also moved beyond *Stable but Critical* to *On the Mend*. He stood a better chance physically, but Sherman wondered about his mental trauma. Ramona tried to play it off, but her brother's eyes looked hollow and joyless.

On day four, after a blue-plate special on the house, Sherman found himself on a bar stool at the pub thinking he could get used to free food and beer. The air was cold, with a strong and early winter wind. The trees rustled and swayed and creaked.

King's face still had a bandage, and the swelling was reduced but the bruises remained. In many ways, Sherman looked no better, and they appeared like two bruised and battered boxers after a match.

Sherman's phone rang.

He knew why with one look at the number.

A Pentagon phone number. Major Sanders recalling him to duty.

"Hello, Major," he answered.

"Captain, I trust nothing else has happened since we last spoke."

"Just my vacation," said Sherman, glad to have found one at last.

"Good. I wanted to inform you that the appropriate authorities are looking into the matter at hand. It appears your suspicions are correct."

"That's unfortunate," said Sherman.

"Depends on how you look at it, Captain. Better to catch him now than never."

"True," said Sherman. "But I'm guessing that's not why you called."

"No. There is a C-130 leaving Vandenberg Air Force Base in forty-eight hours. You need to be on it."

"Understood," said Sherman. "Do I need to know where I'm going?"

"Full briefing on the plane," said Sanders.

Top secret, thought Sherman.

"I'll be there," he said.

"See you on the tarmac," said Sanders and hung up.

Sherman finished his beer and started looking at flights. One leaving Portland the next morning allotted him enough time to make the C-130. He quickly booked it as King watched.

"Duty calls?" asked the bartender.

"Something like that," said Sherman as the front door opened.

"I hope that ticket is refundable," said King.

Sherman turned to look at the new arrival and found a raven-haired man with a ruddy complexion and a body built for violence. Not much taller than Sherman, the man was wider than a redwood and sinewy from years of work. He looked to be in his fifties and his presence commanded the room.

"Who is that?" asked Sherman.

"Tom Wilder," said King.

"Oh," said Sherman.

Tom strode up to the bar and took a stool. Without a word, King poured him a dark and set it down.

"No grand welcome party, King? The prodigal son has returned," said Tom, waving his arms self-importantly.

King did not look pleased to see the man but there was a look of respect in his eyes, like one might respect a wild animal with sharp teeth.

"Did you break out or are you on parole?"

Tom finished the beer in two greedy gulps and motioned for another. The bartender begrudgingly obliged.

"I am a free man. Charges dismissed. Sentence vacated. A miscarriage of justice overturned."

"You're a lucky man, Tom."

"Ain't never believed in luck. I make my own."

"You should check on Terrance," added King.

Tom raised an eyebrow. Was it in surprise? Sherman couldn't tell.

"What did that boy do now?" asked Tom.

"Got shot," said King.

Tom regarded the answer without expression. No worry

or dismay. "That news has been a long time coming," he replied.

Sherman stood to leave and gave King a wave. He needed to find Ramona and give her a double dose of bad news.

Sherman caught her at the tail end of the morning shift at the café. She smiled when he walked inside, and Sherman didn't like to admit how much that smile was growing on him.

"I'm almost off," she said and leaned over to kiss him across the counter.

He was going to miss that for sure. Other things too. The curve of her hips. How she smelled in the morning. Her tilted looks of inquisitiveness. But all things ended eventually—that was life.

"We need to talk," he said.

She smiled back but there was a tinge of sadness in her eyes. "You have to go back."

"I do," said Sherman. "But that's not what we need to discuss."

She tilted her head and asked, "What then?"

"Your dad is back in town."

Ramona's face turned a dull grey and she untied her apron and hung it up behind the counter.

"I've got to run, Barb," she shouted back into the kitchen.

Barb's voice floated out, "Everything okay?"

"No, my father is back."

"Oh," came Barb's reply. "Oh, no."

They left and walked to Ramona's house as cold autumn winds whipped down the road. She looked forlorn in the leaden light.

"No one seemed pleased to see him at the bar either," said Sherman as they went.

"Before he went to prison, my father was the de facto law around here. Had been for years. It gave the town structure, but not everyone agreed with him or his methods. Most people liked the old ways, where people minded their own business and said nothing. Disputes got settled over a pint and ended with a handshake or a visit to the doctor's office. Tom Wilder didn't appreciate the old ways. He wanted more—more money, more drugs, and guns to smuggle. He is and always has been a hungry man."

"Do you think he knows what happened?" asked Sherman. "King told him Terrance got shot, but he didn't look all that upset by the news."

Ramona pondered his question for a moment before replying with another. "Do you think he sacrificed us for a ticket out?"

Sherman had no idea if that was true, but the more he knew about Tom Wilder, the less outlandish her claim seemed.

"Maybe," he answered. "What do you want to do about him?"

"Nothing right now," she said with a smile. "I want to enjoy you while you're still here."

The afternoon passed pleasantly. Soon enough, the light grew thin and steely, and Ramona slipped her naked frame out of bed to make tea. Sherman enjoyed the splendid impermanence of the moment.

A loud banging on the door made Sherman pull on his pants and hurry downstairs. He found Ramona slipping into a bathrobe with her phone in hand.

"I guess King kicked him out early," she said. "You can slip out the back if you want."

"I'm fine right here," said Sherman.

She opened the door and Tom Wilder rumbled in like a freight train trying to make up time. His eyes were narrow and watery. Sherman smelled stale beer from across the room.

"What are you doing here, Dad?"

"That's no way to greet your father," he bellowed and headed for the kitchen.

Tom stopped when he saw Sherman.

They stood a dozen feet apart, sizing each other up like rival predators meeting on the savannah. Sherman saw a drunk man on the slow downward slope of age trying to will himself back to the top. It reminded him of a saying his mother used: *The first forty years is a gift, and the rest is earned.*

"Who are you?" Tom growled, guttural and slurring.

"A friend of Ramona's," said Sherman, still only wearing a pair of jeans.

"What kind of friend?" asked Tom. "Have you been playing fast and loose with your virtue again, young lady?"

"Dad!" yelled Ramona.

"I don't think that concerns you," said Sherman.

"This is my house!" he bellowed. "Paid for with my money. Don't you dare tell me what I can or can't say in here."

Sherman glanced over at Ramona, who glowed red with embarrassment and anger. He hadn't given an inch to Tom and didn't plan on stepping back.

"Dad, you need to leave," said Ramona, trying to keep her voice easy and reasonable.

"No, this is my house. You're trespassing," Tom said with a sneer.

"You're drunk," said Ramona.

"Can you blame me? I haven't had a drink in years or

maybe you forgot all about me locked up in that cesspool. You never did come to visit. Only Terrance came out to see me, God rest his soul."

"He's not dead," said Ramona.

"What?"

"Your son... he's not dead. The guy you gave him up to, Stanton, shot him and left him for dead, but Terrance survived."

"Whoa," said Tom, pointing a finger at her. "What are you accusing me of?"

"I'm accusing you of selling out your own family to get out of prison, or do you have another reason for your sudden and inexplicable release?"

Tom tried to steady himself and shake out the booze clouding his mind.

"No, no, no, no," he muttered. "Don't you dare go spreading rumors like that around town. I have a reputation and I won't have your falsehoods darkening my good name."

"They're all dead," said Sherman and Tom eyed him uneasily. "Stanton and the guys who came to collect the secrets Auntie Zil hid up there. They are all dead."

"Not everyone," added Ramona.

"Right, we did give the two still alive the secrets in exchange for leaving Hilt Bay alone. Heck, I guess they even held up their end of the bargain and got you out of prison."

Ramona continued, "Here's the thing, Dad. The guys who showed up because you squealed... well, they hurt a lot of people. They shot Terrance, killed Vern, beat up and shot at a dozen more people. The town was almighty pissed and out for blood, and you know who they blame?"

Tom looked on blankly.

"They blame you, Dad. This was all your fault because you couldn't do the time."

"You little slut," yelled Tom and pulled his arm back to punch Ramona in the face.

Sherman took three rapid steps forward and caught Tom's arm before it could do any damage. At the same time, Sherman kicked Tom's feet out from under him and the drunk landed with a dish rattling crunch on the hardwood floor.

Sherman wasn't done. Twisting at the wrist, he pulled Tom across the living room, out the front door, and down the porch steps. Sherman didn't stop until they were both in the gravel driveway.

Tom rose to one knee and glared at him with pure rage. He held his wrist gingerly with the other hand.

Should have twisted harder, thought Sherman.

"I'll kill you for this," said Tom in a low hissing voice.

"I've done a lot of killing in the past week, some of it right where you stand, but this ain't my fight," said Sherman.

Tom mistook Sherman's statement for weakness and sneered. "Not man enough to face me?"

"I said it wasn't my fight. It's hers." Sherman pointed behind him.

Tom swiveled and found Auntie Zil standing in the shadows of a cedar. Her hands were clasped behind her back, and she wore black pants and a dark blue knitted fisherman sweater.

"No, no, no," he spluttered and fell backward.

"Tom, walk with me," said Auntie Zil.

"I ain't walking anywhere with you," said Tom, shuffling away from her on his butt.

Auntie Zil unclasped her hands and brought them

around to the front. They held a suppressed pistol—a 9mm Makarov or similar model. A compact gun. A spy's gun.

"Listen, Zil, I didn't have a choice," said Tom. "They said no one would get hurt."

"Thomas, no more lies. We will walk together and let nature absolve us of our sins."

"I don't need absolving."

"We all need absolution," said Auntie Zil. "Now, come with me."

Tom Wilder looked at Sherman, who would have gladly beat him to a pulp, and reluctantly stood. Even more reluctantly, he followed Auntie Zil north towards the cliff overlooking the ocean and the dark hole in the ground. Sherman watched them disappear into the gloaming. Old friends, now enemies. A mirror of her journey with Hal.

"I'm sorry it went that way," said Sherman as Ramona joined him outside.

Ramona put her arm around his waist and squeezed tightly. "I don't think it could have ended any other way."

Three weeks passed and Sherman found himself sitting on another cot in another plywood-covered room cooled by an overactive air-conditioner. The mission was identical to Mali. The location was adjacent. Almost like the higher-ups had put the genie back in the bottle. Not the same, but close enough for senators serving on committees in Washington to call it a victory. *Regional security preserved*, the headlines might read.

Major Sanders poked his head into the room and announced, "They caught the guy in Seattle red-handed."

"Glad to hear," said Sherman.

"The brass wants to know where the tip came from," said the major.

"I overheard it at a bar," said Sherman.

Sanders laughed. "Uncle Hal?"

Sherman said nothing.

"Have it your way, Captain. A man at a bar."

Sanders left chuckling to himself, and a Staff Sergeant tossed a letter onto Sherman's cot before moving on. Sherman turned it over in his hands. The return address read Ramona Wilder, Hilt Bay, Oregon. No address or zip code.

Inside was a note that read:

Frank,

I don't know where this will find you, but Hal wanted to send it out while his mind was still clear. Come and visit again soon.

Good hunting,

Ramona

Tucked inside the envelope with the note were several sheets of thick notarized paper bearing Doc Calvert's signature. Sherman unfolded the official documents. They contained the deed to Hal's house and property. All paid off and loan-free. Everything had been transferred to Sherman.

Scrawled on a small scrap of paper was a handwritten note from Hal: *When you're in need of a place to call your own.*

Sherman set the note down and smiled. For once, the idea of permanence didn't sound so bad.

Next in the Frank Sherman Thrillers Series

vinci-books.com/TheOldWar

The war never ended. It just went underground.

When a neo-Nazi is murdered near a U.S. Army base, Captain
Frank Sherman uncovers a hidden cache of chemical weapons.
Teaming with a ruthless CIA operative, he races through a web of
extremists and betrayal to stop a conspiracy that could ignite
global war.

Turn the page for a free preview…

The Old War: Prologue

Two Weeks Prior

Rarely did all of them meet. The confluence of that many people drew suspicion, but they had an overlapping day of leave, and the town pub seemed a reasonable gathering place. No one was surprised to see Americans drinking away a free day in the village.

Steins of beer and plates of sausage covered the table.

Jared spoke first. "You all know my sister, Gretchen. I invited her here to help with our current situation. She's up to speed on the recent proposition from you know who."

Gretchen nodded. "The problem needs addressing."

"It needs a permanent solution," said another.

"We're not killing anyone," said Gretchen, lowering her voice.

"That's right," the others agreed.

"You guys have a fine racket here. Easy money, by all accounts. Maybe we should view it as an opportunity," said Gretchen.

"It's blackmail," said Jared. "She's threatening to blow the whistle if we don't help. I'm leaning toward the permanent solution too."

"Look," Gretchen started. "This could be big. No, not big. It could be a huge payday."

The men around the table looked at her with hungry but skeptical eyes.

"How big?" one asked.

"Depends on the buyer," said Gretchen. "Maybe seven figures."

A low whistle followed as the group counted into the millions.

"But we need the right buyer," Gretchen continued. "You can't just sell this stuff to street thugs. What about the people you've been working with?"

Jared shook his head. "I don't think they'd want it. Besides, Alfred said he has a potential buyer for any unique items we find."

"The German? Do we trust him?" asked Gretchen.

"No further than I can throw him, but he helped us secure storage," said Jared. "He's a bit of a loner and has contrarian political views, but he likes to be liked."

Gretchen frowned. Outsiders were trouble. Foreigners were worse.

"And no issues with him thus far?" she asked.

The men shook their heads.

"Look, I know you've been pulled into this surly bunch haphazardly," said Jared. "But I think we can trust him."

"Haphazardly?" asked Gretchen. "Is that what you call involving me in potential treason?"

"Not treason," said Jared. "The items don't even exist on paper."

The others nodded.

"Despite the potential payday, I still don't like it," said Gretchen. "There are too many risks to control. This will take a good deal of planning."

"But you'll help," said Jared.

Gretchen looked at her brother and smiled. "I suppose I don't have a choice."

The Old War: Chapter One

Germany, Western Europe

The phone clanged away mercilessly in the dark kitchen. Morning remained hours away, and Otto Faust begrudgingly wrapped his aging body up in a robe and trudged towards the racket. Early morning calls never brought good news. In all his years as a police officer in Stuttgart, and now police chief in his hometown, he'd never found a pleasant conversation waiting for him on the other end of a call arriving before dawn.

Otto picked up the heavy receiver and said, "It's early, Elke."

"I'm sorry to wake you, Chief," his deputy replied. Elke's ever-present cheerfulness shone through despite the hour.

When he hired her, Otto had his doubts about her longevity in their profession. She was his niece, after all, and hiring her was a favor to his brother, but she continued to impress him.

"It's fine, I was awake," said Otto with a smidge of truth. He'd been awake because, at this stage of life, he got up to pee three times a night. A weak bladder, as his doctor liked to say.

"I've got bad news," Elke continued.

"It always is at this hour. What happened?"

"There's been a murder."

"What?" Otto asked.

Achenburg had not seen an unnatural death since the war. The town was small and quiet. People said hello to each other on the cobblestone streets. Neighborliness was more than a word. It coursed through the town's very fabric. Otto knew everyone by first name. He knew their stories, quarrels, habits, and vices. But murder... that did not happen in Achenburg.

"Who is the victim?" asked Otto.

"Alfred Hoffman," said Elke.

That Alfred died did not surprise Otto. The young Hoffman's troubled streak ran far and wide, a bit like a river if the river twisted down the wrong side of history and stank of cheap vodka. For years, Alfred drifted further away from the village norms until he shattered them altogether. Otto's only solace was that Alfred's parents had not lived long enough to see their son turn into a rabid neo-Nazi.

"There must be some mistake, Elke," said Otto. "You can't just declare a death, however deplorable the victim, a murder."

"He was shot, Chief."

Otto sighed deeply upon hearing the news. "Where are you?"

"Just south of the forest road."

"Okay, seal off the area. I'll be there in twenty minutes."

Otto drove slowly through the still slumbering village of his birth—past the colorfully adorned bakery and drab butcher, past the wooden bar and stone churches. His headlights wobbled over the cobblestone streets and caught in the narrow alleyways, casting long, angular shadows. He made it to the outskirts of town in thirty minutes. His mind had not caught on to the languidness age bestowed. He moved slower. Muscles ached, knees cracked and throbbed. Getting old was not for the faint of heart.

Dim rays of sunlight crested over the towering spruce and fir trees, their silhouettes rising like a foreboding green wall, ancient and watchful, hiding long-buried secrets. Otto parked next to Elke's police car. She stood next to the flashing lights, bathed in blue and red.

"You can turn those off," he said.

"I wanted to warn off any passersby."

Otto flung his hand dismissively. "If anything, the lights will attract Mrs. Schiller. She loves to stick her nose where it does not belong."

Elke giggled. "She does have a big nose."

"That she does," said Otto. "Now, let us focus on the task at hand. Where is the body?"

Elke pointed down the dirt road beyond a wooden gate older than Otto.

"Mr. Stücke found him an hour ago when he went to let his sheep out for the day."

Otto glanced back towards the town about a mile away, wondering why Alfred would bother coming out here.

"You ready, Chief?" asked Elke.

"Yeah, lead on."

Elke and Otto slipped past the old wooden gate and walked another hundred yards up the dirt road. A late spring chill hung in the air as the great swathe of trees that formed the Schwartzwald enveloped them like an evergreen curtain.

For Otto, it was a spiritual place, as good as any church or temple. His ancestors walked between those trunks, felt the rough bark, and sat on sturdy limbs. The trees, the village, and life were all intimately intertwined.

"He's up there," said Elke, pointing toward a bend in the road.

The silvery pre-dawn light slipped through the trees, growing brighter with every minute. Alfred's body lay half on the road, his head and chest crushing a bed of ferns. His legs stuck out over the dirt road, clearly visible to anyone driving by. Alfred's boots pointed up towards the sky, and Otto saw he'd fallen backward into the lush green undergrowth.

Otto leaned over for a closer look, careful not to disturb the body. Alfred looked almost peaceful, hands to his sides, palms up, just laying there, staring up into the trees.

Almost, thought Otto.

Except there was a bullet hole in his forehead. A perfect red circle just above his right eyebrow. Leaning further, Otto soon discovered that perfectly small entry wound left a ghastly exit—bits of Alfred that Otto hoped never to see.

"Well, Chief, what do you think?" asked Elke, glancing over his shoulder.

Otto stood up, his knees cracking, and looked around. "You're right about the murder part. No one shoots themselves in the forehead, and I don't see a gun nearby, although I want a full search of the area."

"Will do," said Elke.

She sounded excited, and with good reason. This was real police work, the kind that Otto experienced as a young cop in Stuttgart, but the kind he dreaded as an old man nearing retirement in his hometown.

"Did you or Stücke find Alfred's car nearby?"

"No," said Elke.

Otto glanced back towards the village again. "I suppose he could have walked here."

"Alfred wasn't much for walking," said Elke.

"No, he loved that damn car too much."

"Maybe he got a ride."

Otto shrugged. There were a lot of maybes swirling through his mind. Questions with no answers—not yet and maybe not ever. The biggest question did not involve the victim but the dirt road itself. There were other ways through the forest, paved roads with wide lanes and faster speed limits.

Why this road?

"I'll call the coroner," said Otto. "Don't touch the body until she gets here."

"You didn't have to remind me," said Elke curtly.

"I know," said Otto. "Search the area and take pictures of anything you find."

"I knew that too," said Elke.

Otto smiled and turned to leave.

"Where are you going?" asked Elke.

"To talk with the Americans."

"Why them?"

Otto pointed to a fork in the road they'd passed just beyond the wooden gate.

"If you turn right at the fork, you'll end up at the back entrance of the American army base."

"Oh."

"And the last person to get shot here died in the war."

"Right," said Elke.

Otto smiled at his niece again. She was smart and capable, but so very young. The war wasn't tangible to her. Otto never knew of it personally, but his father had fought in *Wehrmacht* and came back a shattered man. A shadow of his former self. War, Otto learned, broke not only nations and soldiers, but families too.

Colonel Eileen Barber sat behind her desk, sipping on a cup of acidic black coffee, wondering if she should go back to sleep. Working early always suited her. She relished challenges, and that attitude served her well in the army. She rose through the ranks, earned respectable posts, and commendations. But that was all in the past. Now she was the commander of Hamilton Barracks—a soon-to-close base in the middle of nowhere southern Germany with no strategic value. A demotion would have stung less. All because of one transgression, a lone blemish, a singular moment of poor judgement and moral rectitude that cost her a promising career.

Back to bed, she thought and stood to leave before her desk phone rang.

"This is Colonel Barber," she said.

"Colonel, this is Sergeant Mack at the rear gate. A local policeman is here to see you."

"What is it regarding?"

"He says a murder, ma'am."

Barber rubbed her temples, trying to push back an approaching headache. "Escort him to my office, Sergeant."

"Yes, ma'am."

Colonel Barber sat back down and took another sip of coffee. Going back to bed was no longer an option.

A few minutes later, Sergeant Mack knocked and

ushered a slightly disheveled man into her office. Barber guessed he was in his early sixties with mostly gray hair and a slight paunch that came from too many plates of *schnitzel* washed down with beer.

"Good morning, I'm Colonel Barber. How can I help you?"

"My name is Otto Faust. I'm the chief of police in Achenburg."

"Ah, it's a pleasure to meet you, Chief. My apologies for not coming earlier to introduce myself. I only took command here a few weeks ago."

The chief nodded in understanding and said, "I'm sorry to bother you this early, but I wanted to inform you of a murder in the village."

Barber did not like the direction their conversation might lead if an American was involved. "Who is the victim?"

"A local man, Alfred Hoffman."

Barber let out a tiny sigh of relief that it wasn't one of hers. "With all due respect, Chief, why does a dead German national concern me?"

"He was shot."

Barber frowned at another idea. The perpetrator might be an American.

"And?" she asked.

"We haven't had a murder in Achenburg since the war."

She assumed he meant World War Two, which was a long time not to have a murder, even in a small, provincial town.

"What's your point?" asked Barber.

"American cities have lots of shootings."

"Do you have any evidence linking one of my soldiers to this alleged crime?"

"Nothing yet," said the chief.

"Then what brings you here? If the deceased is a German and you have no suggestion that an American is involved, I don't see how I can help."

"We found his body on a road that leads to the rear gate of this base. This is a courtesy meeting."

"I see," said Barber, although she didn't want to. Her new posting was already bad enough. A guilty American would only make her look worse. "I'll open an inquiry with the Military Police and report this up to Stuttgart."

"Will that help?"

The question caught Barber off guard. "It's the army, Chief. Only time will tell."

"Thank you for your help, Colonel," said the chief as he turned to leave.

Barber waited until he and the sergeant were gone before picking up the phone and dialing her own staff sergeant—the one person she got to take with her to the new posting, the only person she trusted.

"Colonel, how can I help?"

"Can you pull the rear gate logs for the last two weeks?"

"Yes, ma'am. Anything you're looking for?"

"A local man was murdered last night in Achenburg. Pull the logs and bring them up here. Keep it quiet."

"Understood."

Barber leaned back in her chair and looked out the window. Hamilton Barracks expanded out below her second-story office, coming up from the valley and stopping at the forest. It remained a small complex of brown brick buildings built on the heels of the Third Reich's defeat and the rise of the Soviet threat—more of a glorified ammo depot than barracks. The base was set to close in the next year, with Barber as the last commander. A dead-end post to a dead-in-the-water career.

Hours slid by and Colonel Barber busied herself with reams of paperwork on transfer orders. A knock on the door brought her into the present. Staff Sergeant Wendel slipped inside, her short red hair tucked under an army-issued hat and her freckled face devoid of emotion. She carried a stack of folders a foot high.

Not two weeks of logs, thought Barber.

"Colonel, I think we have an issue."

"Judging by the fifty years of paperwork in your arms, I'm guessing it's more than an issue."

Staff Sergeant Wendel set down the files on the colonel's desk with a small thud and a tiny puff of dust.

"Stuttgart messaged us this morning. We sent the wrong crate. I pulled the last few months of logs and noticed an irregularity of sorts. Transfers going out to Stuttgart... except, when I checked with them, the shipments didn't match."

"What do you mean, didn't match?" asked Barber.

"We would transfer over a certain batch of crates, mostly Cold War munitions, and on at least five separate occasions, they got the wrong crates."

Barber was not in the habit of jumping to conclusions. She liked to play through all the possibilities before passing judgment.

"Mistakes happen. We're offloading an entire base."

Wendel nodded. "We are."

"But you're going to tell me the boxes we should have sent are..."

"Missing, ma'am."

"You looked?" asked Barber.

"I checked their last known location in storage but found nothing, and our system thinks they are in Stuttgart."

"So, no one is looking for them here."

"Correct, ma'am."

"What are we missing?"

"Mostly rifles and ammunition of various calibers."

In the grand arsenal of freedom, that didn't sound so bad to Colonel Barber.

"Have you formed a hypothesis regarding the nature of these disappearances?" asked Barber.

"The army didn't train me to guess, ma'am."

"Just the facts."

Wendel smiled, freckles arching over her cheeks.

"I'll take a stab," said Barber. "One or more of our base personnel realized a business opportunity and arranged for this mistake."

The staff sergeant nodded. "A possibility, ma'am."

"Do you have the names of the transportation crew?"

Wendel slid over the list. "The serial numbers are on there too."

"When were the transfers?"

"Of the five I identified, four happened months ago."

Barber nodded with a slight smile. They happened before her time. Not her fault. Easy to lay the blame at the previous commander's feet.

"And the fifth?"

"Two days ago, ma'am."

"Shit," said Barber. "Okay, I'll run this up the chain and open an investigation. Good work, by the way."

"Thank you, ma'am."

"Best to keep this to yourself for the time being," added Barber. "We are already in choppy waters. No need to rock the boat any further."

"Understood, ma'am," replied Wendel.

"Oh," replied Barber, having almost forgotten the murdered local in the swirling stink of larger issues. "Did anyone leave out the back last night?"

"No, ma'am," said Wendel before slipping out of the room.

Colonel Barber picked up the phone and made a call she did not want to make, one that might endanger her already fragile career.

The surreptitious meeting happened quickly in an old building. Two people entered from opposite doors and met in the middle. The empty building provided privacy—a much-needed commodity in times of peril.

Gretchen spoke first.

"Alfred is dead."

"How?" asked Jared.

"Shot in the head."

"Shit. Do you know who did it?"

"If I knew that, our problems would be strengths. The guy wasn't exactly popular around here."

"Not us then," said Jared.

"Unless you did it."

"Not that I didn't want to at times, but no. Do you think he gave us up?"

"No idea, but we should move things along," said Gretchen.

"If you say so."

"I do."

"Maybe one of the other buyers is sniffing around," said Jared, still stuck on the subject. "Or maybe Alfred tried to cut his friends out of the deal."

Gretchen paused for a moment in consideration. "Even more reason to speed things up. We need a clean exit. Someone has to take the fall for this."

"Alright then."

"Good," said Gretchen, then she turned to leave.

Each exited the way they'd entered. Less than three minutes had elapsed. The day was still young, blue, and full of possibilities.

The Old War: Chapter Two

Northern Syria, Middle East

A half-dozen insurgents skittered around the village outskirts, ducking behind stone walls older than most nations. They wore black headscarves and tactical vests pilfered from the Iraqi Army—the usual Islamic State outfit for murder and mayhem.

Captain Frank Sherman watched them fan out in front of the small village in the Badlands of northern Syria. Despite the defeat of the Islamic State's short lived caliphate, the jihadist threat remained. Sherman squinted into the spotting scope and marked down the time and location.

"What's the call, Cap?" asked Corporal Lopez, laying behind the .50 caliber rifle.

Sherman's team was on day six of a four-day mission and running low on supplies. Over the course of nearly a week, they'd clocked a dozen confirmed kills of the latest ISIS recruiting class. Bottom-of-the-barrel types, either desperate for money or horny for violence. Little remained of the caliphate's former manpower, but they still managed to recruit more fighters.

"Delta-Three-Six, this is Delta-Nine, do you have eyes on our new arrivals? Over," radioed Sherman.

Sergeant Raylan Gournsey's baritone voice replied, "Delta-Nine. We have eyes. Over."

"Is your angle good? Over."

"We are on the left flank. Over."

"Delta-Three-Six. Get ready for runners. Out."

Sherman turned back to his spotting scope and told Lopez, "Send it."

The heavy thumps of suppressed .50 caliber bullets rolled off the rocky hill. Sand sprayed out in wide plumes away from the muzzle.

Nine hundred yards and 2.8 seconds later, the chest of an Iraqi national who picked the wrong cause to join compressed and then popped like an overripe watermelon dropped on the supermarket floor.

Sherman saw him crack open in a modest puff of red vapor against the beige background. Before his compatriots could react, a second bullet struck the man next to him, followed by another puff of red.

Chaos and panic ensued. Men scrambled away from the dead with arms flung wildly about. Dire words that Sherman could not hear leapt from parched lips.

Lopez fired for the third time. The man was a machine. A cold-blooded, remorseless, ballistic calculator, and the best shooter Sherman had ever known, heard of, or seen.

A third jihadist splattered against the ancient stone wall, which caused the remaining three men to run full tilt away from the village. Flight or fight had turned to just flight. The men made it a dozen yards before Sergeant Gournsey and

Kurdish soldiers from the Syrian Defense Force cut them to shreds with rifle fire.

Less than twenty seconds had elapsed from Sherman's order to the death of six combatants, and he hadn't even fired his own weapon. Sherman felt no remorse for the dead. They sealed their own fate moments after they crossed into Syria.

"Delta-Nine. No sign of life down here. Over."

Sherman scanned the surrounding area, looking for anything out of the ordinary, but found nothing.

"Delta-Three-Six. Pack it up and circle back to us. We'll cover your exfil. How copy? Over."

"Good copy. Moving now. Out."

Sherman rolled to his side and called his commanding officer, Major Sanders, on a satellite phone. "This is Delta-Nine, requesting extraction at grid coordinate Whiskey-Alpha-Two-Three. How copy?"

"Good copy, Delta-Nine. ETA is thirty minutes."

"Heard, thirty minutes. Out," replied Sherman and ended the call.

"It'll take us forty to walk there," said Lopez, who was still glued to his scope.

"I guess we're running," said Sherman. "Do you want me to carry your rifle?"

Lopez chuckled. He would never let anyone else touch the gun, let alone carry the thirty-five-pound rifle.

"Good shooting," said Sherman.

"Could have been faster," said Lopez.

Sherman shrugged. Perfectionism was par for the course with Lopez.

"Maybe, but they couldn't be deader, so that's good shooting in my book."

The Blackhawk helicopter landed thirty-two minutes later, and Sherman's team jumped aboard, panting and soaked through with sweat. They stank from six days in the field, but no one on board said a thing. No one cared. The whole country stank of death and corruption and fifteen years of fighting.

A desiccated landscape of abandoned villages, burned fields, and charred cars slid by underneath as they flew back to the forward operating base—although, to call it a base overstated a few paltry prefab buildings surrounded by Hesco barriers filled with gravel and sand.

The Blackhawk landed in a swirl of pelting dirt but didn't take off again, as usual, which meant it was waiting for someone.

Guests, thought Sherman, and made for the command center to see what level of brass had visited and were waiting to return.

Major Sanders found Sherman just outside the fortified center of the base. His arrival was unexpected and unnecessary.

"Captain, welcome back," said Sanders. His wide frame and speckled gray hair reminded Sherman of a silverback gorilla stuffed into army fatigues.

"Sir, what brings you out here?"

"You assume I have an ulterior motive to visit my men."

"Major, no one flies out here for a visit," replied Sherman.

"How'd the hunting go?" asked Sanders, avoiding the question.

Avoidance made Sherman uneasy. "Seventeen in the dirt."

Sanders nodded. "Better here than Istanbul or Indianapolis."

Sherman agreed but said nothing. He was waiting for the next ask.

"I have something for you," said Sanders.

The singular tense of the major's pronouncement surprised Sherman. Normally, Sanders spoke in the plural regarding the team. Sherman stood at ease and nodded for him to continue.

Sanders looked over his shoulder and motioned toward a dead-end corner between two barriers.

"This is a sensitive matter," said the major.

Everything Sherman and his unit did was classified, so the major's unease piqued his interest.

"Your skill set is required for a few days," continued Sanders.

Sherman squinted at the major. The what and the where didn't matter. He had no choice in that, but he cared about his men.

"Are you rotating us all out?" he asked.

"No, this is only for you."

"That will raise questions," Sherman replied. "It sounds like this is the sort of thing allergic to questions."

"It is," said Sanders.

"Best to pull us all out at once."

Sanders chuckled to himself. "Okay. They get a week off, and you get a new mission."

"Can I tell them where?" asked Sherman.

"Germany," said Sanders. "Wheels up in ten."

Sherman nodded and walked off to find Lopez and Gournsey.

The two men were chugging liters of water and leaning back in plastic deck chairs when he approached. They gave skeptical looks when he did not sit down with them.

"Another mission," said Gournsey.

"We just got back," added Lopez.

"Pack your gear," said Sherman. "Wheels up in eight."

"Where are we headed?" asked Gournsey.

"Germany," answered Sherman, then walked away from incredulous looks.

By the time the Blackhawk landed at the nearest base in Turkey, a C-130 transport plane was already revving for take-off. Sherman and his men hustled toward the great steel belly of the cargo plane.

"Not there," shouted Sanders, and the men stopped. "That one."

The major held out a finger, pointing toward a commercial Gulfstream jet with its door open.

"This day is looking up," said Gournsey with a smile.

"Nothing comes for free," added Lopez.

"Don't worry," said Sherman. "I think I'm footing the bill. You guys get a free ride."

Lopez frowned and repeated, "Nothing comes for free."

Sherman couldn't have agreed more. The third law of motion dictated a reaction no matter how small the force. Nothing happened without a cost. His only question was how much he'd have to pay.

The two pilots shut the cockpit doors as soon as they boarded. They clearly had instructions to see or hear nothing.

"This is giving me black bag vibes," said Gournsey, and Lopez nodded in agreement.

But whatever their misgivings, the stocked bar did wonders to mitigate their doubts. As his men unwound from a week of intense combat and overwhelming boredom, Sherman took a seat next to Major Sanders in the first row.

"Are you going to brief me on whatever this is?" he asked.

"Soon," replied Sanders. "We have one more stop first."

Sherman nodded and leaned back in the plush leather chair. Minutes later, they were airborne, and the desert disappeared below. Yet, in the back of his mind, a warning bell tolled. They weren't headed northwest toward Germany, but east towards the unknown.

Grab your copy…
vinci-books.com/TheOldWar

About the Author

Joel Austin grew up in rural California under leafy oak trees and mountain views. He holds an M.A. in History and International Relations. Currently, he lives in Colorado with his wife and daughter.